Summer on Cape May

Summer on Cape May

Monica Garner

kensingtonbooks.com

Content Warning: parental death, terminal illness, infertility, suicide

Summer on Cape May

Chapter One

Lu

The sun had started to set over Cape May. Crickets chirped their medley in the distance, and waves from the ocean were much gentler now, not like earlier in the day when they'd crashed against the shore more aggressively. Clearly, there was a storm brewing. Weather in late spring on Cape May could be temperamental. Chill bumps danced up and down Lu's arm as the temperature began to drop and the night air drew in. Muni Long could be heard on the stereo in the house, crooning a familiar tune. Lu relaxed on the veranda, her favorite place to decompress after her day at the inn. She sipped on an oak-aged Pinot Noir, a favorite from her friend Natalia Oliveri's winery.

Lu noticed Natalia's husband, Nic, walking the stretch of beach toward her, shoulders slumped, the usual pep in his step nonexistent. She waved hello just as she did every single time when she saw him on his nightly walk. Usually they would exchange a *How's it going?* or *Beautiful night, isn't it?* that would lead into a more in-depth conversation about what was going on in their lives, but tonight was different.

As he got closer, Lu noticed the look on Nic's face was as

wrong as two left shoes. The wrinkle in his forehead, his pursed lips, his eyebrows raised—all alarming. He plopped down on the stairs of her veranda and rested his back against the railing as he did every night. Tonight, however, he was a mess— a real basket case. She asked if he wanted a cognac because that was what he drank when her fiancé, Zach, entertained him and the two of them hung out until all hours of the night, swapping stories and roaring with laughter.

Lu went inside and poured him that cognac and then returned to the veranda, handing it to him. He didn't take a sip. Instead, he finished it in a few gulps and then handed the glass back to her.

Nic took a deep breath and then let it all out for Lu to hear. "I don't know how to deal with Natalia and this desperation she has with wanting a baby. Every week there are doctors' appointments, treatments. Just tonight she told me that she wants to consider a surrogate, maybe pay someone to come and live with us. That's something that only happens in movies."

"I know. It's all she talks about." Lu was becoming equally concerned about her friend. "But I know that this is something she desperately wants."

"I want a child, too, just as much. But I want it to happen naturally. I don't want us to go through the pain of losing another child."

"Well, Nic, you must understand, *you* have a child already— with someone else. She doesn't. That makes all the difference. She wants her own child."

"I get it and I can respect that, but lately it seems to be more of an obsession than a desire."

"She just wants to make things right."

Had she really said those words aloud? She'd been thinking it, knew the reason for Natalia's obsession—but it wasn't her place to interfere in their marriage. *Yes*, she'd actually said it aloud.

"What do you mean, *make things right*?" Nic asked with eyes bulging and eyebrows raised.

She looked away, hoping he wouldn't press any further. She felt all the discomfort of knowing something that might help him understand her friend, but *again*, it wasn't her place to interfere.

"Lu, what are you saying?" he asked. "Or what is it that you're not saying?"

Lu sighed heavily. Her body tensed up and she trembled a bit. Betraying her friend's confidence was not okay. But if it was for Natalia's own good, could it really be considered a betrayal? A myriad of other questions began to tumble in and out of her brain. Questions about whether what she knew would help Nic understand his wife better. Whether or not telling him would be for the good of their marriage or cause its demise. By telling him, he would then understand Natalia's obsession, go home, hug his wife, and forgive her. Natalia was a good-hearted person. She needed his grace.

Lu's mind raced. "I don't know, Nic. Natalia overthinks things. You know that."

"I honestly don't know what to do. I don't know how much more I can take." His Sicilian accent was more pronounced, the wrinkle in his forehead deeper as he ran his fingers through his dark brown coils.

"I've said too much already. I've overstepped."

Lu's heart ached. She had the power to stop the hurt—to change it all for them. Obviously revealing Natalia's secret to Nic was risky. It occurred to her that she had the ability to save her friend's marriage. Natalia might be mad at first, but she would forgive her eventually.

Nic looked at Lu, tears brimming from his eyes. "You must tell me what's going on with her, Lu. Maybe she needs some space, some time to herself. Maybe she even needs to talk to someone—a therapist. Maybe we need to separate for a while—

try to figure things out—because I'm drowning in the uncertainty."

The words *maybe we need to separate for a while* struck a chord. Her hair coiled on the nape of her neck. She bit her nails, a habit she'd tried desperately to break. Those nails didn't stand a chance when she was deeply troubled about something. The last thing she wanted was for him to abandon her friend. She loved Natalia like a sister and felt the need to protect her from being hurt.

Natalia was pretty fragile. She wouldn't survive if Nic left. *She had to tell him.*

Her chest tightened before the words tumbled out of her mouth. "Her last miscarriage wasn't by chance."

"What? What are you talking about?" Nic stared at her as if she had uttered the most ridiculous thing he'd ever heard.

"She caused it." She looked away from him and watched as the waves rippled against the shore. The scent of the ocean crept gently across her nose.

"What are you saying, Lu?"

"Natalia had a terrible headache one night and found a bottle of prescription meds that the doctor had prescribed months earlier for pain—something she had in the medicine cabinet. I don't know exactly what it was that she took, or how much, but it was fatal to the baby. She wasn't thinking. She just wanted the pain to go away," she choked out. "That's what caused her to lose the baby."

Lu exhaled. She almost felt a sense of relief, having gotten it off her chest, but that feeling was short-lived after she glanced back at Nic. The look of disdain on his face made her instantly regret betraying her friend's trust. It was too late, though, to take the confession back. Her words floated through the night air, trickling as the ocean breeze had just done moments before. And now she'd have to deal with whatever came next.

He stood up, his stance defensive. "I remember that night very well. She called me in a panic because she was bleeding."

"I took her to the ER because you were traveling for work," Lu reminded him.

"She blamed me for not being there!" His voice raised quickly. "She blamed *me*."

Seeing the anguish in Nic's eyes, Lu wished she could take back her words, every single syllable.

He stepped off the porch, nearly stumbling. His imbalance didn't seem as if it was from the cognac but from anger. He was headed in the direction of their home, much sooner than Lu wanted. She was desperate now. She needed him to put his own feelings aside and consider hers. It might've been selfish, but it was what she needed. She nearly tumbled off the veranda to run after him. Sheer panic rushed through her body; it felt as if her legs might give out before she reached him. She desperately needed for him to hear her out. "You can't tell her that I told you. She will never forgive me. She will hate me for betraying her trust."

"She killed our baby with prescription drugs and you're talking to me about betrayal and trust," he spat out. The tears rolled down his face.

"It wasn't intentional. You know that Natalia would never hurt anyone intentionally."

"It's the reason for all this." His voice was still raised. "This . . . this obsession with conceiving again. To cover up what she did."

"She just wants a baby, Nic. She wants to be a mother."

"She's unfit to be a mother!" His words stung.

Lu understood his pain, but she had to make him comprehend *her* position. "Nic, she will come to hate me if she ever finds out that I told you." The pain in her chest was back, but more intense now. She could feel her heart speeding up, beating rapidly, could hear it in her head. She hurt for Natalia. She hurt for Nic. She hurt for herself. She hoped that Nic had heard her plea and would give her some empathy. She searched for a softening of his stance, a look that said her secret was safe.

Instead, he stormed off, walking briskly back up the stretch of the beach toward the home he shared with his wife. He was angry, and Lu feared what he might do.

"Nic Oliveri, do you hear me?" Lu called to him from the veranda.

He kept walking, his arms swinging back and forth with great intensity.

Lu walked back to the veranda, picked up her wineglass, and tossed the rest of the liquid to the back of her throat. Then she paced from one end to the other, her bare feet making a pitter-patter sound against the wood. Her heart pounded, feeling as if it might explode. Her mind raced as she contemplated calling Natalia, but decided against it. Her eyes veered toward the scarlet pimpernel flowers that grew in her flower bed next to the veranda. One of its petals blew with the wind and landed at her feet. She picked it up, smelled the hoppy, citrusy scent. She was reminded of the old tale named after the flower, *The Scarlet Pimpernel*, written by Baroness Orczy in the early twentieth century—a story she'd read in college. She kept a copy on a bookshelf in one of the rooms of her inn, Lu's Seaside Inn. She thought it ironic that the petal blew at her feet now, at this very moment, because at the center of the novel was loyalty—loyalty to one's country, one's spouse, and one's family. Lu examined her own loyalty toward Natalia and found that she'd been anything but. Instead, she had betrayed her friend. As the petal of the red flower, with its winged corners, blew away with the wind, she wondered if her friend would ever forgive her.

"What have I done?" she whispered to herself. She slid her behind back into the chair, pulled her knees into her chest, and wrapped her arms around her legs. Tears burned her cheekbones. She needed Zach there to hold her, to assure her that everything would be all right. He was good at that— rescuing her. She found solace in him. His consolation was exactly what she needed now because she knew with every fiber of her being that if Nic left Natalia over this, it would be her burden to bear. She trembled at the very thought.

Chapter Two

Lu

Three Weeks Later

Lu heard the voice on the other end of the phone, but she needed a minute to gather herself. To remember where she was, or better yet *who* she was. When he'd called a few minutes before, she'd hung up, figuring it was just a prank. She'd only answered in the first place because she thought it was someone calling to make a reservation at the inn. But here he was, calling again, disturbing her peace. This time she listened closely, especially because the voice was familiar. She'd heard it before, though she couldn't place when or where.

"Are you there?"

She stood on the veranda barefoot, facing the ocean, a ceramic mug in her hand filled with a rich brew of coffee, watching as the waves moved swiftly back and forth. Usually in the mornings the waves were gentle, moving with a nice peaceful rhythm. She would have her coffee while she planned her day and reveled in the calmness of the ocean. The calmness reminded her of why she lived on Cape May, why she'd traded the fast life for a more peaceful and tranquil existence. Today the waves were downright aggressive, as if they sensed the conflict around her. Not just the conflict from her conversation with Nic a few weeks before, but now this.

"Hello? Lualhati?"

No one called her by that name but her mother. To almost everyone else, she was simply Lu.

"Lualhati?"

"I'm here," she managed to say. "I'm still here."

"I know this is a lot for you to take in. And I'm sorry it had to be by phone instead of in person. But you see, I'm dying—"

She steadied herself by grabbing the arm of the wrought-iron chair she'd picked up at one of the antique shops on the island before cutting him off. "Wait a minute, let me get this straight. You called to tell me that you're my father and you're dying? What kind of game are you playing? My father is dead." She sat—*more like fell into the chair*—and rested her head against the seat back, shutting her eyes for a moment, trying to make sense of it all.

"I'm sure your mother had her reasons for not being truthful with you."

"How do I know that you're being truthful?" She breathed deeply from her diaphragm to manage the quiver in her voice before speaking again. She didn't even realize she was shaking.

"About being your father or about dying?"

Her father. Yana Abalos, her mother, had always been the only parent she'd ever known, yet here was this stranger who knew things—intimate things about her—and she wasn't quite ready for it. She was so confused. Her heart felt as if it was going to explode inside her chest. She needed to wrap her mind around all of this.

"About all of it." The word *dying* was the reason for that awful lump she was suddenly feeling in her throat.

"I don't know anyone who would lie about dying, especially if they had nothing to gain. As for being your father, well, you were born at Mercy General Hospital here in Sacramento. April 2, 1978, around six o'clock in the evening. You weighed six pounds, seven ounces, and you were the most beautiful girl I'd ever laid eyes on. You had big, bright eyes like your mother's." There was no denying he'd been infatuated with both Yana and the baby he spoke about, voice dripping with pride. "You had a minor respiratory issue when you were born. They kept you in the hospital for a few days for observation."

The fact that he knew about her respiratory issues sent her emotions into overdrive.

"I grew out of it."

"You didn't have any other problems, at least until the age of two."

By the time she was two, he'd vanished.

"Why did you vanish after I turned two?" she asked, almost in a whisper. Lu frowned and then sighed deeply. She was alternating between wanting to shout a few expletives and slam down the phone and wanting to ask more questions to find out the truth. Her patience was wearing thin.

"I didn't vanish. Your mother took you away. She left California and moved to New Jersey with you. She cut all ties. When I found out where she was living, I flew there, wanting to see you, but Yana wouldn't allow it."

She'd somewhat resolved that this man on the other end of her phone, this stranger who had interrupted her usually calm morning, this person who had suddenly turned her world upside down with a simple phone call, quite possibly might be who he claimed to be—*her father*.

"How did you find me this time?"

"I called your old law firm and got a hold of your former assistant. She told me about the inn."

"What prompted you to call my old law firm?"

"I've followed you over the years, Lualhati. I knew when you graduated high school, college, and law school. The *Press* of Atlantic City did a spotlight on your law firm. That's where I learned that you were one of their up-and-coming attorneys. You'd interned with them, came highly recommended. I was quite proud." He was silent for a moment. "Yana warned me to stay away. She didn't want me complicating your life, so I watched from a distance, until now. It was imperative that I find you now."

It was only seventy-two degrees on the veranda, but she could barely breathe from the heat that burned so deeply within her. At the age of forty-five, she was experiencing personal hot flashes more often than she could count. She exercised—did the treadmill every morning—watched her sugar intake, and tried to stay fit to minimize them, but they were persistent. *The things women endured.* She was grateful that neither she nor Zach wanted children because she didn't know if she'd survive a nine-month bout with pregnancy.

"I need some time to digest all of this."

"I understand, sweetheart."

"Don't call me that. You've not earned the right to call me anything endearing."

"I'm sorry. Take your time. It's a lot to take in all at once. I would like for you to fly out here to Sacramento. I'd like to see you, talk with you. But more importantly, I would like to discuss my will, and I would like for you to meet my children, your siblings—Milan, Jess, and John Jr. I'll take care of all your expenses. Just come. Please think about it and let me know."

It was happening too fast. Just a moment ago, he was dead to her. Then he was alive and knew details that only a parent would know. Now he was trying to interject himself into her life, and suddenly there were all these other moving pieces— death, a will, and siblings. *Siblings?*

"I will. I'll think about it." Because, clearly, *thinking* was not something she could do right now. She needed time to sort out this kaleidoscope of new emotions, time to stop her head from spinning, and her heart from feeling like it might explode. Time to get a grasp on reality. "That's all I can promise. It's not the best time, though. I'm getting married soon and I—"

"You're getting married? When?"

"In September."

"That's wonderful. Congratulations."

"Thank you." The awkwardness of the moment was so thick, and so present, she was sure he felt it, too. She felt she needed to say something, explain something. Fathers walked their daughters down the aisle at weddings. But her mother, Yana, would be escorting her in his stead. *Because he was dead, right?* And speaking of Yana—she needed to get her on the phone. Immediately! "I will let you know what I decide."

"I will be waiting patiently for your call, Lualhati. Bye for now."

And with that, John Samuels was gone, and she instantly felt his absence. She wanted to talk to him again. The thought that she might have a living, breathing father intrigued her. Having a father in her life would certainly add value. He'd be the piece that she'd always felt was missing. Hearing his voice on the other end of her phone felt surreal. She'd thought about him so often over the years.

All she'd had was a black-and-white photo of him taken with Yana in the Philippines, he in his military uniform and her with an orchid in her hair. He was tall and handsome, dark-skinned. He had a military crew cut and a thick mustache. He held on to Yana's small waist, and her mother looked happy.

Lu kept the photo tucked away in a small treasure chest where she kept all sorts of things that were important to her.

Yana had given her John Samuels's dog tags and an old military identification card. Also in her treasure chest was a letter that he'd written to Yana, promising her the world. There was no doubt he had loved her.

She dialed Yana's number, pacing back and forth. There was no answer, so she walked to the wraparound veranda. The porch had been what first attracted her to this property, that and the gorgeous chef's kitchen, and the view of the ocean from almost every room in the house. She loved Cape May and all its surrounding beauty.

She was caught up in her feelings, so anxious to get her mother on the phone that she hadn't even noticed Zach standing in the doorway, observing her.

"You okay?"

So much had happened during her conversation with John. She didn't know if she could even put it into words because there was still some doubt in her mind as to whether it was real or not. Zach's concern for her was the thing that made her love him so much, though. She loved him with everything in her, which was why she was marrying him in a few weeks. But this—she needed to absorb this for a while before she brought him into the fold. She needed to not only understand but accept what she had just been told. She needed to reach Yana. Most of all, she needed to compose herself, think fast, because Zach wasn't leaving until he knew she was okay.

"I'm fine. Some craziness surrounding Yana." She waved her hand in a sweeping motion, hoping that would deter any more of his questions.

"What has she done this time?"

"You know she's always up to something. That mother of mine is so extra." She forced a nervous laugh and then changed the subject. "Is everyone having breakfast in the dining room?"

Her staff had been inherited from the previous owners of the inn but came with a good sense of the business and invaluable expertise. She couldn't have asked for a better group of professionals. Marissa, her housekeeper, assisted with chores and the run of the house, while Max, her morning chef, prepared breakfast and lunch daily for her guests. Lorenzo was her evening chef, who, with his exotic dinners, offered her guests something more than just a regular meal. He took them on culinary adventures.

Her regular guests at the inn deserved to be pampered and she went out of her way to make sure they were. They were loyal to her and her business. Most enjoyed a short staycation or two throughout the year. Some spent the entire summer or holiday. All were equally important to Lu.

"Most are, except the Thompsons. I think they're sleeping in today."

"Good for them. That's what vacations are for."

"Can I replenish your coffee?" he asked, his fingers stroking the few little hairs on his chin.

A beautiful chocolate man with just a tad bit of gray in his hair, Zach stood at almost six feet tall. It was his perfect smile that had first attracted her to him. That is, once she woke up after fainting right in the middle of the Asian supermarket. He had revived her and then stayed with her until the paramedics arrived, even rode in the back of the ambulance to the hospital. An off-duty physician, he had been her angel in disguise that day. He was still her angel.

"No, I'll be in soon."

"What is it, sweetheart? What's going on?" He stepped out onto the porch. "I know when something is bothering you. You start being weird and your eyes get all shifty."

"My eyes aren't shifty." She laughed.

"Your eyes are shifty, babe." His smile was like the sunshine.

He knew there was something she wasn't saying. She was terrible at hiding things from him, especially something that had her emotions in a whirl, like the conversation she'd had with Nic a few weeks earlier about Natalia and the whole baby thing. She hadn't told him about that. It was something that she'd wanted to forget happened, hoping it would dissipate. She certainly didn't want to tell him about this John Samuels thing either, not yet at least. Not until she'd had time to make sense of it herself, and not until she'd had time to speak to Yana. But he wasn't going to leave until she gave him something. She hadn't wanted to spring it on him in passing, but he left her no choice.

"I just received the oddest phone call from a man claiming to be my father." She took a long, deep breath and shut her eyes for a moment.

"What?" A wrinkle formed in the middle of his forehead, the one he always got whenever he was thinking too hard. He tried to make sense of what she'd just said. "Was it a prank phone call?"

"I thought it was at first. But I'm not so sure now."

"But your father is dead. Remember? Yana told you so."

"I don't know that Yana has been truthful with me. I mean, he has these . . . details, *intimate* details about my life. He said things that only someone close would know; for instance, where I was born and all of it." Lu hadn't realized just how shaken she was until she began to describe her conversation with John Samuels.

"Wow," he said.

"I know! Exactly what I said. Now I just need to get Yana on the phone."

"After all this time, what does he want?"

"He's dying.

"What?" Genuine concern flooded his face.

"Yes. And he wants me to come to Sacramento to discuss his will, among other things. He also wants me to meet my siblings." She wasn't quite sure how she felt about the thought of siblings. She had been a badass attorney once upon a time, who had represented some unsavory characters. She could handle most anything and was able to go toe-to-toe with the best of them, but *this*—the thought of meeting John *and* siblings—spooked her.

"You have siblings? Wow. That's a good thing, right?" Zach smiled, trying to read her.

"I don't know how good it is. I need to validate his claims first. I've got to get a hold of Yana. She needs to give me some answers." She didn't want him to know her fears. He'd worry. And she didn't need him worrying about her.

"Well, you know, I'm here for you, right?" he asked. "For whatever you need."

"I know." His words calmed her a bit.

"We can talk more later."

"Yes, I know you have to go." It was for this reason she hadn't wanted to bring it up, didn't want to discuss it in passing. She needed him to help her figure things out, talk it through, make sense of it.

"And Lu, if you need me to go with you to California, I'm there. You won't have to do this alone."

His words made her heart soar, allowed her to completely release some of her fearfulness. He would be there, and that meant the world. Zach had a knack for calming everyone's anxiety, which was why he was such a great physician.

"I love you, sweet man." She placed the palm of her hand against his cheek.

He pulled her into an embrace, held her as if he knew she'd needed it. He'd read her mind. "We'll navigate this together, I promise."

"Thank you." She looked up at him, her chin resting against his chest.

His arms squeezed her a bit tighter. He said, "I'll make sure Marissa has started the laundry for the day and then I'm off to the hospital. But if you need me, call me. Even if it's just to talk things through."

"Okay," she said.

"I mean it, Lu."

He knew she was terrible at asking for help, careful to never impose. But she said, "I promise, I'll call you if I need you."

"Okay, babe. I love you." He pulled up her chin and gently kissed her lips. "Even with your shifty eyes."

"Oh my God." She shook her head and giggled. "Love you more."

He released her from his embrace and went back inside, leaving her to her roller-coaster ride of emotions. As she stood on the porch, she dialed Yana's number one more time. When she received her voicemail *again*, she decided that Yana was probably stuck in front of a penny slot machine at one of those Atlantic City casinos. Or perhaps she'd gone gallivanting about in New York City again with one of her gentleman callers. Men clamored for her attention. She wasn't quite the young Filipina girl in the photo with John Samuels, but she was still very beautiful even at sixty-seven years old. Yana was a ball of energy, too. She never met a stranger and was always quick to give everyone a piece of her mind.

"Hello, Ina," she said, calling her mother. "It's your favorite daughter. I need to speak with you before the sun sets over the Atlantic Ocean." That was their code phrase to let each other know the matter was urgent.

She hung up and held the phone against her chest. She had so many questions that she needed answers to and only her *ina* could provide them.

After placing vases of freshly picked pink and lavender petunias in each of the guest rooms, Lu pulled freshly washed towels from the dryer, folded them, and put them away. Then she headed to the chef's kitchen to pour herself a glass of Chardonnay. She played soft music on the Bluetooth speaker and stepped out onto the veranda before collapsing into one of the easy chairs. Her mind had raced all day long.

The sun had already begun to set by the time her phone rang. She answered on the first ring when she saw it was Yana. "Where are you, Ina?"

"Playing a game of bridge with Margaret, Ernestine, and Lorraine. We've been at it all day and I forgot to charge this silly little phone. So I didn't realize you were trying to call." Yana giggled; she sounded tipsy. "What's so urgent, sweetheart? And be careful what you say, you're on speaker phone."

The ladies all giggled and shouted hellos to Lu.

"Hello ladies." Lu loved her mother's friends, but she had other things on her mind today, so she couldn't entertain them like she usually did. "You should take me off speakerphone, and maybe step out for a minute. I need a word with you."

"Oh, this sounds important, ladies. My daughter needs a word with me," Yana chuckled. "I swear, sometimes she thinks she's the mother and I'm the daughter. I'll be right back."

"Don't be long, Yana. We need to finish this game," Margaret warned.

Impatience almost consumed her. Waiting for most of the day for Yana to return the call had been grueling.

"Okay, my darling. What's going on?"

Lu wasn't up for any song and dance. She started her inquisition once she confirmed Yana was alone. "I received a phone call today from a man claiming to be my father. It seems that John Samuels is very much alive."

The ensuing pause seemed like a lifetime. The woman who

had never been at a loss for words was completely quiet for a lot longer than Lu had anticipated.

"How is that possible?" Yana asked. "John Samuels died years ago."

Her lackadaisical tone didn't sound convincing. The lack of passion in her voice made Lu wish like hell she could scrutinize her mother's face, to see if there was something reflected there that would help her understand Yana's position. As much as she wanted to believe that her mother hadn't lied, the odds weren't in her favor *at all*.

"Are you sure about that?"

"Well, what did he say—this man who claimed to be your father?"

"What did he say? Seriously, Ina?"

"Lualhati, let me explain . . ."

"I'm listening." Her ear was glued to the phone.

She analyzed every single word, every pause, every single syllable that came out of her mother's mouth.

"John Samuels is not the man you think he is." Yana became defensive.

"Tell me, then, who I think he is. Better yet, tell me who *you* think he is. Because he had a hell of a lot to say about you." Lu stood up and began to pace back and forth along the stretch of the wraparound veranda.

"Like what? What could he possibly have to say about me?"

Lu could just imagine a hand on the hip of that four-foot-nine frame at that moment. Her mother's offhanded tone had suddenly become sassy.

"Like how you left California with his child, didn't look back or leave a forwarding address. He searched for you and once found you. But you wouldn't allow him to see me. Is that true?" She felt like an attorney in that moment, going after a witness to get to the truth.

Yana deflected from the question. "There's so much you don't understand."

"Fill me in on the details. I'm old enough to understand now. Why did you allow me to go all these years believing that my father was dead?" Lu pressed on relentlessly.

"It was better that way."

"Better for whom? For me or for you?" She had no intentions of letting Yana off the hook. She wanted real answers. She had hoped to hear something that would make her believe that Yana was being forthright.

"Better for you. I didn't want him complicating your life. You're *my* child. I was the one who worked two jobs to keep a roof over your head, raised you, fed you, took care of you. It was me who put you through college. He did nothing."

"I'm forever grateful for what you did for me. You were a wonderful mother, but that doesn't excuse the fact that you lied to me, kept him from me, denied me a relationship with him. Good, bad, or otherwise, he was still my parent, and you took that away. What do you have to say for yourself?"

"I say that I did what I had to do. And it sounds like you're taking his side."

Yana was notorious for playing the loyalty card. Always wanting Lu to choose a side, to prove that she loved her more than anything or anyone else.

"He's dying."

There was that long pause again, this time more uncomfortable than the first one.

"What did you say?" Yana's voice shook a bit, and for a split second there was real concern in her voice.

"I said that he's dying. And he wants me to come to California to see him. To meet his other children. I'm considering it," she said matter-of-factly.

"I think it's a mistake to go there. You would be opening up old wounds that are best left unopened. I'm sorry to hear that John is dying, but I think you should leave well enough alone."

"He's my father and I deserve to know him, just like you knew your father." Lu's voice became escalated. She could feel her heart beating fast, could hear it thumping. She was hurt by Yana's selfishness. "You knew your father all your life. You even flew to the Philippines to be with him when he was ill. You were able to say your goodbyes to him before he died. You had no right to keep my father from me, especially when you had yours."

"I had every right to protect you."

"You were protecting yourself. From what? I am not quite sure yet, but I'm going to find out. There's more to this story." Lu breathed in through her nose and then let out a long sigh. "I love you, Ina, but I'm angry with you right now. And I don't know if I can forgive you for this."

"Give an old woman some grace, my darling. It was for your own good. You know, I would never do anything to hurt you."

Lu could hear the women in the background, calling on Yana to finish their card game.

"You should go finish playing cards," Lu told her.

"I'll call you later tonight and we can talk more, huh?" Yana asked.

"It's Friday. You know I have dinner with the girls on Friday. I need some time to absorb all of this. For years you lied to me, and I need to understand why." She didn't like being upset with Yana, but she was.

"I'm sorry for lying. I pray that you'll forgive me," said Yana. She attempted to lighten the conversation. "Will you give Kenya and Natalia my love?"

"I'll tell them you said hello," Lu said. "I have to go now, Ina. Goodbye."

Lu hung up before her mother could respond and sat there for a moment with her back against the chair, stiff, unmoving. Tears threatened to fill her eyes, and she fought them back unsuccessfully. Her life had changed drastically in less than twenty-four hours and there wasn't a thing she could do about it. But she could allow herself a good cry.

Chapter Three

Kenya

This little hidden gem was so much better than the other overrated coffee chains; this cozy café, tucked away off the beaten path of Atlantic City's downtown area, was Kenya Lewis's favorite retreat. It was the best place to write a brief or get work done without all the distractions from her colleagues, who constantly wanted to run something by her, or the young ones who insisted upon standing in her office's doorway on a Friday afternoon to boast about their weekend plans, as if she cared to hear them.

She had to admit, though, those youngsters lived some exciting lives. She remembered the days when she, herself, had a life—a vibrant, exciting one. Now the most exciting part of her life was her daily commute between Cape May and her office in Atlantic City. If you counted the binge-watching of a host of series on Netflix with Ralph, her golden retriever, at her feet, a bowl of Ben & Jerry's Half Baked in her hand, then that was excitement, too. She went on an occasional date with a suitor here or there. However, her standing Friday night dinners with her girls, Lu and Natalia, topped her weekend excitement list, by far.

She sipped coffee from the café's ceramic mug, the scent of jasmine floating through the air and Sade's voice soothing her soul. She'd managed to snag the perfect spot near the window, where she could both work and people watch. Good thing, too, because the minute she glanced out the window, she saw Zach, her best friend's fiancé, crossing the busy street.

Had she been in a cozy little café on Cape May, the island that she called home, it would've been a perfectly normal thing to see Zach at a traffic light or at the grocery store. But to see him walking the streets of downtown Atlantic City on a busy Friday afternoon, well, that was anything but normal. The fact that he was walking and deeply enthralled in a conversation with Danielle Curry was even more extraordinary. Danielle, who was one of Atlantic City's big shot divorce attorneys, made her millions by getting women what they wanted in divorce proceedings with their wealthy husbands. A woman scorned; Danielle had taken her own ex-husband to the cleaners some years ago. Since then, she'd become quite the jezebel.

Seeing them together sent shock waves up and down Kenya's spine, made the little hairs on the back of her neck stand up. Surely Zach had better sense than to step out on her best friend, Lu. Kenya fidgeted with her phone while she contemplated whether she should call Lu at the inn and ask her if she knew where her fiancé was. She decided to text instead.

What are you up to on this beautiful sunny afternoon? Did Zach take the afternoon off, and are the two of you sitting on the veranda watching the waves like two old people? LOL, Kenya typed.

The reply was swift. **I'm in the kitchen. Laboring. LOL. Not really. Zach's at the hospital. He got called in for an emergency surgery.**

Emergency surgery?

Kenya glanced out the window again to see Zach and

Danielle enter the thirty-story, mirrored office building where Danielle operated her private law practice. With a huff, Kenya shut her laptop and crammed all her belongings into her bag. She wasn't a private detective—not even close—but she was about to do some investigative work. And she was about to confront Zach!

She rushed out the door of the café and pulled the jacket of her suit a little tighter before heading toward the crossing light. Though she hated to, she decided to jaywalk. She stepped inside the glass building and took the elevator to the fifteenth floor, to Danielle's office. Her stilettos sunk into the carpet. *Plush carpet.*

"How bourgeoisie," she whispered to no one in particular.

Millicent, Danielle's assistant, looked up from her computer screen, smiled, and asked, "Can I help you?"

"Uh, no, I'm waiting for someone, thanks. My friend . . . he's meeting with Danielle."

"Should I let him know that you're here?"

"No." Kenya smiled. "I'd really like to surprise him."

Millicent gave her an inquisitive glance, her eyes narrowed and her eyebrows raised. Her lips perched as if she wanted to say something more, but instead she went back to working. Kenya took the liberty of having a seat on the leather sofa, crossed her legs, picked up a recent copy of *Essence* magazine from the end table, and flipped through its pages.

A few minutes later, Danielle's door swung open and Zach walked out. His eyes widened, became big as saucers when he saw Kenya. His stride slowed. Kenya dropped the magazine onto her lap as the two of them locked eyes.

She threw her head back. "What are you doing here?"

"I could ask you the same," Zach declared.

"I followed you here," Kenya said in a low tone once he was closer and out of Millicent's earshot. "Now, back to my question: What are *you* doing here?"

"I'm busted, aren't I?" He blew wind from his mouth and gave a nervous laugh.

"I guess you are." Kenya stood and placed her hands on her hips. "Why on earth are you here in Danielle Curry's office . . . in Atlantic City, no less, when your fiancée thinks that you're at the hospital . . . *on Cape May*, performing an emergency surgery? Are you having an affair?"

"What? No."

"Are you certain about that? Because I just watched you strolling down the street, smiling, and cheesing with another woman."

"Have you been following me?"

"Don't even . . ." Kenya pointed a finger at Zach.

"Kenya, I'm not having an affair," he reiterated.

"You'd better not be," Kenya warned through clenched teeth, trying to keep her voice just above a whisper. "Why the hell are you seeing a divorce attorney?"

He was silent for a moment, then sighed heavily. "Because I need a divorce."

"You what?" Kenya blinked a few times and tried to make sense of his words. "You're going to have to explain this to me slowly, so that I can understand."

He had the nerve to say, "If I tell you, you can't tell Lu."

Was he serious?

"Excuse me, but my loyalty lies with Lu, not you." She wanted to grab him by the collar but thought it best not to as she stole a glance at Millicent, who was pretending not to eavesdrop. "Dude, I can't make promises like that."

"I just need a little time to work something out," he pleaded.

He needed to give her more than an I-need-a-little-more-time response. "What exactly do you need to work out, Zach? Because so far, you've given me nothing."

Zach rubbed his bald head. "You're not letting this go, huh?"

"What do you think?"

He closed his eyes for a moment. "Okay. Just hear me out . . ."

"I'm listening. And it better be good."

"Several years ago—and I mean *several* years ago—long before I met Lu, I was fresh out of med school, a kid even . . ." He paused, shifted his stance, and loosened his tie a bit.

"Keep going."

"I had a friend. She was Ethiopian. And . . . well . . . I married her so that she could gain her US citizenship. . . ."

"You're joking, right?" She laughed.

"I'm quite serious. And unfortunately, we never divorced."

"Zach!" Kenya shrieked.

"I know. It's bizarre."

"Did you forget that you were already married when you asked my friend to marry you?"

"I didn't forget, I thought it was something I could fix right away. That it would be a nonissue."

"Is this woman causing problems, like contesting the divorce? Will she show up at the wedding and act out? What's the delay with the divorce?" Kenya was in his face, her eyes blinking rapidly. She wanted answers.

"She won't show up at the wedding. She won't contest the divorce, either. That is, if I can find her."

Kenya's eyes widened and her mouth flew open. "What do you mean, *if you can find her*? You don't know where she is?"

"We lost contact over the years. I thought she was in New York City, but I don't have any information on her whereabouts. There was never any urgency for a divorce until now." Zach rubbed his hands together.

"Do I need to remind you that your wedding is in less than three months? And this wedding—this marriage means everything to Lu. She has literally poured everything into planning it." Kenya was becoming frantic. "She loves you!"

"And I love her."

Kenya offered him a cold stare.

"I *do* love her. Kenya, you know that better than anyone. And I want to marry her. I'm *going* to marry her. Which is why you can't tell her any of this. Not until I have a chance to fix it."

"I don't know if you can fix this."

"I can and I will."

"You'd better. This will kill Lu. And I know her. She won't hesitate to call off this wedding. You know that, right?"

"That is why you can't tell her. Not yet. Let me work it out," he pleaded.

"Why weren't you just honest with her in the first place?"

"Are you kidding me? She wouldn't have understood this."

"Give her a little bit of credit. She would've understood. But she won't now—now that you've waited so long. Were you in love with this woman?"

"It was never romantic. It was just me helping a friend. That's it."

"Helping a friend is loaning them fifty dollars or letting them borrow your car. Not marrying them." Kenya sighed heavily. "I can't keep this from her, Zach. Now that I know, I have to tell her. I'm sorry."

He placed his hands together as if saying a prayer. "Can you just give me a little bit of time? Please."

Kenya rolled her eyes. If she'd had the strength, she would've picked him up by his neck and flung him across the room. Why had he even gotten down on one knee in front of God and everyone and asked Lu to marry him if he wasn't ready? Why had he given her that enormous three-carat princess-cut diamond ring that she waved in the air every chance she got to show it off? Why had he asked Lu's mother, Yana, for her blessing, ordered that darn three-tiered cake, hired caters, booked their favorite band to perform at the reception, and sent out those fancy invitations to everyone who was anyone on Cape May before working out the skeletons in his freaking closet?

She breathed in, letting the air out slowly through her nose. She hated this position that Zach had put her in. This wasn't her problem, *it was his*. Yet she'd been thrust in the midst of his mess.

"You have exactly thirty days from today to find this woman and divorce her. After that, I spill."

"Kenya, I don't know if thirty days is enough time."

"You'd better make it enough time. Hire a private detective. You have the money." She closed in for a whisper. "And Danielle is very easy. She's one of the best divorce attorneys in the business, I give her that, but she's . . . well . . . a jezebel."

"That's why I hired her, but . . ."

Kenya raised an eyebrow and narrowed her glance at Zach.

". . . not because she's a jezebel, but because she's a great attorney. I was referred to her by one of the doctors on staff at the hospital."

Danielle walked out of her office, shut the door behind her, and said something to Millicent before approaching them.

"Oh, hello, Kenya."

"Danielle." Kenya gave her a nod to greet her.

"I didn't realize you two knew each other."

Kenya spoke up first. "Yes, Zach is my best friend's fiancé. They're getting married at the end of the summer. Didn't he tell you?"

"He didn't." She turned toward Zach and gently caressed his arm. "We'll be in touch, Zachary."

"We will. Thank you." His voice raised an octave.

Danielle walked away and Kenya gave him a side-eyed glance. "You have thirty days," she warned him.

As she walked away from him, she couldn't help but fear

that what was supposed to be the wedding of the summer, might be the breakup of the summer. Zach would be to blame for all of it if he didn't work out his dilemma—*and fast*. He had placed her in quite the predicament and caused her to be unsettled. He was asking her to keep a secret from her best friend—one that would destroy Lu. She would keep quiet for now because she wanted to see Lu happy. And she wanted the wedding to take place without any drama. Yes, she'd keep his secret, but not for long.

Chapter Four

Kenya

Kenya pulled her locks into a bun on top of her head. With her denim jeans rolled up at the ankles and her cropped plaid top tied at the waist, she walked the stretch of the beach from her home toward Lu's inn carrying a laptop computer in her hand. She closed her eyes briefly and yawned. The hour commute from her firm in Atlantic City to Cape May always left her feeling drained. One of the benefits of living near the ocean was that she could always retreat after a hard day and unwind. And it had certainly been a hard day dealing with Zach's shenanigans.

She removed her embellished sandals from her feet. The water felt good between her toes. Kenya stared at them. She didn't know how she'd allowed her nail tech to talk her into that hot pink color. Hot pink didn't go with everything, particularly when it was the beginning of the summer and most of her summer heels were open toe.

Those stilettos sure were cute, and though they made her feet ache like crazy, she wore them anyway. She thought of Glen. He used to tell her that she was crazy wearing those heels every day, that they were going to catch up with her one day, ruin her feet and leave her with bunions, corns, and calluses. He would laugh at his own jokes about it. She laughed now as she thought about it. Though he'd admonished her, he always gave the best foot massages on the planet—the most glorious in-between-the-toe action a girl could ask for.

Oh how she missed him.

Kenya and Glen met Brooklyn. They were high school sweethearts and he'd been equally as tough. Bigger than life, he stood at six feet tall at the age of seventeen and weighed about two hundred pounds. He'd played varsity football, though football was never his first love. No, he loved American history, calculus, and working at his father's corner store after school. And though he'd been offered both academic and athletic scholarships, he'd opted for the Coast Guard after high school.

"Wherever I end up being stationed, I'll send for you," he'd told Kenya.

"And I'll come to wherever you are, but only after I finish undergrad."

But Kenya had plans of her own, and her dreams were just as big as his. She'd attended NYU on a track scholarship, and by the time she'd graduated, Glen was stationed in Japan. He wanted her to join him there. Though she loved him and wanted to follow him around the world, their career paths were different. She wasn't willing to sacrifice hers for his, at least not at first.

"I brought the wine." Natalia startled her; shaking her out of her thoughts of Glen. Her long flowy white dress blew in the wind and her sun-kissed brown hair danced as she held a bottle of Pinot Noir in the air.

"Thank God. I need a glass so badly." Kenya locked arms with Natalia as they continued the stretch to Lu's place. "Today was exhausting, and then traffic from the city was even worse."

"I don't know how you do it every day."

"Now I understand why Lu quit the firm. I didn't understand it at the time, but I know now."

It was at Taylor, Taylor, and Fisch where Kenya first met Lu. It was six years since Lu traded the courtroom for a full-blown inn, but it seemed like decades ago. As associate attorneys at the prestigious Atlantic City law firm, at first they'd been competitors, clamoring for the coveted cases that would position them for partner. Both bright and ambitious, the competition was tough, but because they were the only two women of color at the firm, it forced them to form a bond—a bond that withstood the test of time.

They stepped onto the veranda to see Lu pacing before she plopped down at the table. She seemed a bit agitated and kept glancing at her watch. She peered at Kenya's laptop. "I know you did not bring work!"

The aroma from something delightful tickled Kenya's nose and made her stomach growl. Lu's chef had prepared dinner for them, as he did every Friday. She couldn't wait to see what it was.

"I won't be long, I promise." Kenya took a seat at the table next to Lu.

"Kenya! You know the rules. We leave work at the office. Our Friday nights are sacred . . . a time for us to unwind, catch up, let our hair down after a long week."

It was something they had done almost every week for the past five years. Even though Lu's inn was always fully booked, she made sure to carve some time and space for her friends. Natalia took a seat at the table, the crisp white tablecloth blowing in the wind as the waves whispered in the distance. A bouquet of red poppies was situated at the center of the table.

"I know, I just need to wrap up the notes from this deposition. I bolted from the office so quickly, I didn't have time to do it. I just need five minutes," said Kenya.

"Five minutes and not a minute longer," Lu warned.

"I promise."

"Pinkie swear." Lu held her pinkie in the air.

"Seriously?" Kenya gave Lu a crooked smile before opening her laptop and began pecking keys.

"Yes, seriously. We need to talk about the wedding. Plus, I have something I need to share with you both."

Lu's and Zach's wedding day was quickly approaching. The elegant affair would take place on the beach in front of her seaside inn, with a reception to follow. Kenya thought that September in Cape May was perfect for a wedding, with milder temperatures and less tourist traffic. But honestly, as happy as she was for Lu, all she could think of was Zach's secret, and how she'd been dragged in on it. Carrying it around made her physically ill.

"I have everything lined up for the rehearsal dinner." Natalia opened the red wine and immediately poured three glasses, handed one to Lu, and slid another in front of Kenya's laptop.

"You should be proud of me," Kenya said. "I finally scheduled some time with the seamstress. I'm meeting with her this weekend to have my dress altered." She peeked over the top of her laptop, sipped her wine, closed her eyes, and savored it. "This is good."

"I'm glad you finally scheduled with her. You were making me nervous," Lu said.

"I know. I procrastinated a little."

"Yes, ma'am, you did procrastinate. Had me worried to death." Lu giggled. "But you ladies are the best. I couldn't possibly pull off this wedding without you."

"We're here for you. Always." Kenya pecked a few keys on the keyboard. She stopped typing for a moment, almost got misty-eyed. Talk of Lu's wedding made her think of Glen again. Her eyes veered upward to the skies toward the dark clouds. It looked like rain.

In a short-sleeved chef's jacket, Lorenzo stood near the

door, awaiting Lu's signal that they were ready for dinner to be served. She motioned for him to bring their salads.

"Okay, now on to more interesting conversation, like how Kenya's date went last night. Particularly since she didn't call either of us afterward."

Kenya gave Lu the side-eye.

Lu giggled. "Judging from that look, I take it things didn't go well."

"Not at all. He wasn't really my type."

Her type was *Glen*. Her friends knew it and so did she. No one could compare to him. He was the reason she lived in Cape May to begin with. She was a city girl at heart, loved living in the city, the rat race, the energy of it all. He was the one who'd convinced her to sell her posh Alpine, New Jersey apartment and move to Cape May with him. *He* had asked for her hand in marriage and wed her in a quaint ceremony before a justice of the peace, and then, two years later, he'd abandoned her.

Every time she said that, Lu was straightforward with her. "He didn't abandon you, Kenya. He died."

Glen's car accident and untimely death two years after their courthouse wedding had left her volatile, questioning God, challenging everyone and everything. Lu and Natalia had helped her through it, forced her to get out of bed. To bathe. To eat. To breathe.

That was three years earlier, yet the loss still felt like yesterday. And though she told herself she was ready to move on, to date again, here was yet another date gone south.

"Was he at least a gentleman?" Natalia asked.

"He was the perfect gentleman."

"Then what was it?" Natalia leaned back in her chair and sipped her wine.

Lu's voice was gentle. "Glen would want you to be happy. He was one of the most unselfish people I've ever known."

"I know. But he wouldn't want me to settle."

"Settle? You won't let anyone in. If anyone gets close—" Lu began.

"You'll know when it's right, honey." Natalia placed her hand on top of Kenya's.

Kenya nodded, but she'd already decided she was never entrusting her heart to anyone again. She had no intentions of ever settling down or remarrying. She went back to pecking on her computer keys.

Natalia changed the subject and looked at Lu. "So, what is this *thing* you wanted to talk to us about? It sounded serious over the phone."

Lu started to explain the details of her call from John Samuels. "So today, I received this . . . crazy . . . phone call from a man claiming to be my father. After I finally tracked down Yana to demand an explanation, she says, *I thought it better that you thought he was dead. I didn't want you to go looking for him.* Can you believe it?"

"Oh Yana." Natalia smiled.

"I know she was wrong, but cut her some slack." Kenya laughed. She knew Lu's eccentric mother all too well, a woman who danced to her own beat.

"I'm furious with her right now."

"She was just protecting you."

"You two." Lu pointed at Kenya and then at Natalia. "Don't give her grace right now. She doesn't deserve it. She let me go my entire life without knowing my father. I don't know if I can forgive her for that."

Listening to Lu carry on about forgiveness for Yana, her own mother, made Zach's secret even more troublesome to Kenya. It would be difficult to hand her friend yet another platter of betrayal, though she knew at some point she'd have to tell her, and she knew it wouldn't be easy. In fact, she hoped it would be long after she'd said *I do* at the altar, and then it would all be water under the bridge. But for now, keeping Zach's secret seemed to be the best option, even though she hated it.

"Oh, you will forgive her. She's your mother." Kenya hoped that Lu would offer *her* the same forgiveness that she was advocating for Yana.

"Doesn't give her a right to lie."

"No, it doesn't, but think about it, Lu . . . you were her baby . . . *still are* her baby. She didn't want to share you with Papa John," said Kenya.

"Well, she doesn't have a choice now."

"So, does that mean you're going?" Natalia asked.

"Thinking about it. Zach thinks I should."

Natalia gave her friend a warm smile. "I think you should, too. I think it's wonderful that he reached out and wants to see you."

"But what took him so long? I mean, why now? Because he's dying?" Kenya never let anyone off the hook.

"He claims that Yana forced him to stay away."

"He should've fought harder. I'd have questions," said Kenya. "I'm just saying."

"Well, now is the time to get those questions answered. You should go," said Natalia.

"If I do . . . and I'm not saying that I will, but if I do, Zach will take some time off from his practice and we would both fly out there next week. Which is what I needed to talk to you two about."

Kenya shut her computer to give Lu her undivided attention. "What do you need from us? You know we're here for you."

"Natalia, I would need for you to finish handling the details of the rehearsal dinner without me. And maybe meet with the wedding planner to finalize the plans for the ceremony, and follow up with the vendors in my absence. Everything is all set; I would just need for you to be my eyes and ears while I'm gone."

"Consider it done."

She turned to Kenya. "Huge favor."

"What is it?" Kenya's eyes held deep concern as she watched Lu.

Lu clasped her hands. "I need you to run the inn, only because you've done it before and you know how things work. Not to mention you really look like you could use a break."

Running Lu's inn while she traveled to California would require that Kenya take a vacation from the firm. It had been years since she'd taken one. After Glen died, she'd taken a few days to make the arrangements at the funeral home and to attend the service. But just as quickly, she was right back at the firm. Vacations offered too much idle time to dwell on things that needed to be put to rest, in her opinion. She needed to stay busy. Work had been her coping mechanism back then, and Lu and Natalia believed it still was.

"Wow," Kenya exclaimed.

"I know how busy you are, and everything you have going on at the firm. I would totally understand if you can't. I can hire someone."

The timing couldn't have been worse for Kenya, considering she was in the middle of a high-profile murder case, and not just any case. Deacon Charles had been like an uncle to Kenya. She couldn't remember a time before he became a part of her life. He was always there—birthdays, Christmas, Sunday dinner. He'd even attended her graduation from law school. His wife, Eleanor, had done the alterations for Kenya's dress for the occasion. Deacon Charles was a long-time member of her father's church, someone she had known for most of her life, and he was being accused of murdering his business partner. She hadn't wanted to take the case, but her father urged her to since he and Deacon Charles were good friends, almost brothers. He was like an uncle to Kenya, so she obliged. The entire congregation of Cornerstone Baptist Church had eyes on the case, and *her*. She wanted to make sure their beloved deacon was handled with care. However, the trial wouldn't be for a couple of months. She had a couple of weeks to spare.

"No. I'll do it. You're right, I do need a break." She couldn't believe those words had come out of her mouth.

Natalia and Lu looked at each other, undoubtedly astonished by her words. They were always advocating for her to take time off.

"Really?" they said in unison.

"Of course. Why are you two so surprised?"

"You've literally never taken a real vacation," Natalia said.

"Well, this is important." And it was. This was her chance to be there for Lu, like she'd been there for her so many times.

"What will you do about your case?" Lu asked.

"I have time before he goes to trial. Much of the prep work I can do from here. It's not like you have a lot of traffic at the inn. It's a nonissue." She said it was a nonissue, but really Deacon Charles had already become a thorn in her side, talking to the press when she'd warned against it. And switching up his routine when she'd already explained the importance of sticking with his normal everyday functions. People were watching and he needed to maintain as much normalcy as possible. He did the opposite. Deacon Charles was working on her last nerve. She'd have dropped him as a client had it not been for her father.

Natalia turned to Lu. "So, I guess you're going to Sacramento, then."

Lu exhaled. It was obvious that she'd expected Kenya to say no, to let her off the hook. But Kenya knew that the seaside inn was Lu's baby. She wouldn't entrust its operations to just anyone. Though she threatened to hire a manager to run the inn, she wouldn't, and Kenya knew it.

"Well, then. I guess I am."

She was happy for Lu. She had her reservations about this whole John Samuels thing, but she would allow it to play out. Kenya had grown up in a two-parent household and had always known her father. Yes, Pastor Lewis had been an active figure in her life, all up in her social life, trying to re-arrange things since as far back as she could remember. She also had two dysfunctional siblings who drove her crazy on a regular basis. Lu didn't have any of these people in her life. It was time she experienced a real family, and all that came along with it.

Chapter Five

Natalia

The lyrics of Lady Gaga's "Always Remember Us This Way" played faintly from the speaker mounted above. The waves seemed to be dancing to the beat just a few feet away. It was such a beautiful night. Springtime on the Jersey Shore was warm enough for sunbathing or a little dip in the ocean.

Lu's flower beds around the veranda were fragrant. The daylilies and colorful perennials attracted butterflies and hummingbirds on the island. She reached over the wooden railing and plucked one of the daylilies, its scent like jasmine. She loved Lu's seaside inn. Heck, she loved Cape May and the life she'd built there with Nic.

"Earth to Natalia." Lu waved her hand in the air.

"You okay?" Kenya asked.

"Of course. Just a little tired. It's been a long day."

"He isn't back home." It was more of a statement, not a question from Kenya.

Natalia put a smile on her face. Not a real one, but it was all she could muster without tears. "Not quite."

Lu frowned. "What? I thought for sure he'd stop being an ass and come back home by now."

After their last huge argument about her obsessing over having a child, Nic had moved out of their home in Cape May. It was almost as if he'd started the argument to justify his leaving. He'd claimed that they needed some space. *A temporary arrangement*, he'd said. It didn't matter that she thought time apart was the last thing they needed, he moved anyway. That was three weeks ago.

"Is he at least talking to you again?" Kenya asked.

"We haven't spoken in a few days." She hated saying it aloud because that made it real, and by speaking it, she'd have to face it. She wasn't sure she was ready to admit that her marriage was on the decline, let alone deal with it.

Lu gripped Natalia's hands in hers. "Things will work out." Kenya placed her hands on top of Lu's.

Natalia fought back tears. Her voice cracked. "Hope so."

She hadn't told them everything. They would judge Nic, and she didn't need that right now. They would worry about her, and she didn't need that either. The truth was, she hadn't had a full night's sleep since Nic left for Sicily. She wasn't even aware that he'd left the country. He'd been staying at one of his firm's corporate apartments in the city and hadn't slept in their home. He claimed it was easier to commute back and forth to the office if he stayed in Atlantic City. Then he casually mentioned his location when they spoke a few days ago.

"Well, I have something that will cheer you up, sister," said Lu. She motioned for Lorenzo.

"Are we ready?" he asked.

"We are indeed."

A few minutes later, Lorenzo emerged from the kitchen with three desserts. He placed one in front of each of them.

"Oh my God. Is this what I think it is?" Natalia asked.

"Pastéis de nata!" Lorenzo said in his strong accent, handing Natalia a spoon.

"This is so amazing. You are so amazing." She smiled at Lorenzo. The dessert reminded Natalia of her childhood, reminded her of home. It also reminded her of her grandmother, Leonor—God rest her soul—with whom she'd always been close. Gram Leonor had made pastéis de nata often when she was growing up in Portugal, and especially during times when Natalia was feeling down. Grandmothers were special that way. They always knew just the thing that would make everything better.

Lorenzo's eyes danced at the compliment. His smile, with perfect white teeth, was the brightest ray of sunshine. The touch of gray in his beard and on his temples made him look distinguished, but Natalia always thought he acted younger than he looked. She was always careful, though, not to stare, for fear of him getting the wrong idea. But he was certainly handsome, in her opinion. Though he was Argentinean, he'd spent some years cooking in Portugal. They'd talked about that before.

"I will grab the wine," he said and disappeared into the kitchen.

"He's such a cutie." Kenya was the first to dip her spoon into the tart, tasted it. "So yummy."

"Him or the dessert?" Lu asked with a giggle.

"Both."

The ladies laughed.

"This is certainly a surprise." Natalia smiled at Lu. "Thank you."

"You are welcome, my friend. I asked Lorenzo to make you something special. I remember you telling me how your grandmother's dessert always cheered you up when you were feeling down. I know that you're having a hard time right now. But believe me when I tell you, this too shall pass."

"Yes, it will," Kenya chimed in. "Look at me. I'm a perfectly functioning adult after all I've been through."

"Barely." Lu laughed.

"Yes, barely functioning, but you get it."

"You just need a little sex in your life," Lu teased. "Clean out those cobwebs."

"I have sex in my life, thank you very much. I have a little friend. He runs by battery."

"Oh my God!" Natalia blushed and then shushed her friends before Lorenzo returned with the wine.

The trio giggled as he poured sweet sherry into each of their glasses.

Natalia changed the subject. "So, how soon will you leave for Sacramento?"

"I'm thinking next week."

"That's soon," Kenya said, "but I'm good. I'll put the time in tomorrow."

"I'm really happy that you're going." Natalia savored her dessert and then took a sip of her sherry.

"Me too," Lu admitted.

"Yesterday, you just had Yana. Now you have an entire family," said Kenya.

"Imagine that," Lu said sarcastically.

They all giggled.

After dinner, Natalia made her way back up the stretch of the beach with Kenya. She bid her friend a good night and watched as she stepped inside and turned on the light. She walked the rest of the way to her two-story beachfront home. She and Kenya had been intentional about finding homes near Lu's Seaside Inn. As luck would have it, they'd both found oceanfront properties, not just close but within walking distance of the inn and each other.

She dropped her sandals in the mudroom and flipped on a hallway light. Her bare feet pitter-pattered against the mahogany hardwood as she made her way upstairs to the master bedroom. She pulled up her hair, undressed, and then wrapped her body in Nic's thick white robe. Natalia turned on the television and found some soothing music on the Pandora app.

She stuck her hands into the pockets of the robe and was surprised to find a package of Marlboro cigarettes. Though he'd claimed to have quit, she was constantly finding little telltale signs that Nic was still smoking. There were signs he was doing a lot of things that he shouldn't have been. She'd always warned him that smoking caused cancer, just like it had for Kenya's late husband, Glen. Unbeknownst to his wife, Glen was diagnosed with stage four lung cancer. It was a secret he'd shared with Nic before Glen's fatal car accident and had sworn him to secrecy. All would've been well and good in the universe, but Natalia had the misfortune of overhearing Glen's secret, thus placing her in the most dreadful position of her life.

She'd heard them talking one night right outside her patio window. She'd opened the window to catch a breeze and what she'd heard changed her life, giving her the burden that she'd been bearing for the past three years.

"I have cancer. Stage four lung cancer. I haven't told Kenya. In fact, I haven't told anyone—*but you.*"

"Stage four is pretty serious, man," she heard Nic say. "Don't you think it's serious enough to tell your wife?"

"I'll tell her in my own time," Glen said. "The doctors think that I should do chemo. I'm not interested in any of it. Those drugs are nothing but poison, give a false sense of hope."

"I've known people who have added years to their lives with chemotherapy and radiation therapy. Wouldn't it be worth it to have a few extra years with Kenya?"

"It puts such a strain on your body, and a strain on the lives of your loved ones. I'd have a few extra years, but what type of quality of life would I have? Cancer's bad enough, but the hardship that those treatments place on your family. I won't put her through it. I'd rather die in peace, knowing that I protected her from it."

"Wow, man. I had no idea."

"Yeah. I'm just getting my affairs in order. I want to make sure my wife is taken care of. You know?"

"I hear you."

There was a long pause between the men—they were both silent. Natalia covered her mouth as she took it all in. Hearing Glen's words had caused her to cry and feel a piercing in her heart. It took everything in her not to pick up the phone and call Kenya right then and tell her all that she'd heard. She wanted to warn her friend, prepare her for what lay ahead. Perhaps she could urge Kenya to plead with her husband to seek treatment. In fact, she wanted to rush outside on that deck and urge Glen herself—to fight for his life—if not for him, for her friend. But to do that, she would've had to admit that she'd been eavesdropping in the first place. What gave her the right to stick her nose in their lives unwarranted anyway?

She'd been edgy and fidgety and unable to focus the entire next day at the winery. What type of friend would she be if she kept this from Kenya? A million questions just like this one had clouded her brain all day. She finally resolved that Kenya needed to know, had a right to know, in fact. After meditating about it, Natalia decided that Kenya should have a say in her husband's future—*her future*. She deserved at least that. Natalia's drive from the winery back home seemed to be the longest one of her life, as she'd contemplated the words that she would use to tell her friend—what might possibly be—the worst news of her life. She rehearsed what she would say. As she replayed Glen's heartbreaking words in her head, *I'd rather die in peace knowing that I protected her from this,* tears filled her eyes again, just as they had the night before. Didn't she have an obligation to tell her friend what she knew?

She had contemplated calling Kenya at her law office but decided that wasn't the type of news to be revealed over the phone. No, this was something that needed to be shared in person, and it needed to be sooner rather than later. She stood in her kitchen staring at the ocean just outside the window for a moment. Her mind raced as she dressed a piece of salmon with cloves of garlic, herbs, and lemon juice, placing the fish in a saucepan and then into the oven. She glanced at the television, which was mounted in the corner of the wall. The newscaster was reporting at the scene of a horrific car accident. The visual of several paramedics and a mangled sports car on the interstate was what caught her attention. She grabbed the remote control and turned up the volume on the television. She listened as the newscaster described the events of the fatal crash.

Her phone rang and she struggled to peel her eyes from the television. She grabbed her phone from the kitchen counter and saw Nic's face on the screen of her phone. She answered right away.

"Turn on the news!" He was frantic. "Glen was in a car accident. It's all over the news."

"I'm watching. I thought that car looked familiar. Is he okay?"

"I don't know, but you need to get Kenya on the phone right away. Let her know."

"Okay, I will." She hung up. Her heart began to beat fast. Her hands shook uncontrollably as she searched for Kenya's phone number—a number that she dialed nearly every single day of her life. She breathed in through her nose and then breathed out through her mouth as she tried to calm herself. Natalia closed her eyes and then opened them. She continued to search for Kenya's number again.

As she searched, she heard the news reporter say, ". . . and the man driving the newer model Mercedes has been identified as forty-five-year-old Glen Allen of Cape May, who died at the scene . . ."

Those words seemed to trail in her head—*died at the scene*. The screen of the iPhone shattered as it hit the floor. Natalia shrieked as her body slid down the side of her white cabinets and onto the floor. She covered her mouth with both hands, tears streaming down her face. She heard the reporter's words again in her head and tried to wish them away. She tried to convince herself that they had it all wrong—that Glen was still very much alive. It felt like she was stuck in a nightmare as she continued to listen to the newscaster's words.

". . . the driver of the eighteen-wheeler, who we're told survived the fatal collision, has been taken to Cape Regional Hospital. Authorities are trying to make sense of how the Mercedes ended up in the lane of oncoming traffic to begin with . . ."

Natalia closed her eyes tightly. She couldn't help but wonder if Glen's death had truly been an accident. There was no reasonable explanation for how his car had veered over into the wrong lane. The thought of it troubled her. She managed to pick up the iPhone from the floor and finally dialed Kenya's number. There was no answer. Instead, she received her voicemail.

Her voice shook as she managed the words. "Kenya, I need for you to call me right away. It's an emergency. It's about Glen."

After Glen's death, Kenya had been in such a dark place. There never seemed to be a right time for Natalia to reveal the news about his cancer. It would've only intensified her grief. Kenya had her hands full just dealing with Glen's death, and she wasn't navigating that very well. Natalia argued—*with herself*—that if Kenya knew, she'd have tortured herself over it. And besides, now it was a moot issue. Natalia thought there was no value in her knowing, as there was nothing that Kenya could've done to change it. It was better left unsaid, so Natalia had buried that secret right along with Glen. Three years later, that secret was still buried.

She stepped out onto the deck just off the master bedroom that overlooked the ocean, slid a Marlboro out of its package, lit it, and took a long drag from the cigarette. Natalia didn't smoke. She'd only tried it a few times in college, but it had never been her vice. She needed it now, though. Her emotions were all over the place, and she'd hoped to reel them in a bit. She needed her husband back home where he belonged. In Cape May, with her, but she knew that wasn't happening, at least not anytime soon.

In her heart of hearts, she knew that he was with Angelina quite possibly at that very moment. The thought of it tore her apart and there was nothing she could do about it. She felt helpless. Her eyes watered. She thought about the conversation she'd had with Nic days before. The one that had left her feeling hopeless.

He'd said, *"I needed to come home. Needed to be with my family."*

"What about me? I'm your family. We need to work through this, and we can't if you're there and not here."

"I can't deal with this right now. I'm tired of all the fertility treatments, all the doctors, all your craziness about it. You're obsessed with this whole baby thing, and I can't deal with it."

"*You know how badly I want to be a mother. How badly I want a child of my own to love—for us to love. And I resent that she was able to give you a child and I'm not.*"

"*This has nothing to do with Angelina.*"

"*It has everything to do with her. Why can't you see that?*"

"*That's the problem, Natalia. You're focused on the wrong things.*"

She took a deep breath, calmed herself. "*Have you seen your daughter?*"

"*Yes, I've seen her.*"

"*So, I guess that means that you've seen Angelina as well.*"

"*Of course I've seen her. She's Bella's mother.*"

Bella was two when Natalia met Nic. They both happened to be on holiday in Duoro Valley, Portugal—Natalia's home. He'd visited her family's vineyard, and she'd been the one to show him around. He'd been fascinated by the vineyard and her. They fell in love instantly.

Natalia's family had been in the winemaking business for centuries. Her great-grandparents had worked the vineyard and then ultimately passed it down to her grandfather. When her parents arrived in the United States in the late seventies, they continued the family's winemaking tradition by starting another vineyard in Cape May. It was where Natalia and her sister learned the business, and when their parents were no longer able to operate the vineyard, Natalia and her sister took over operations.

"*When are you coming home? Not just home to the US but to our home, here, in Cape May?*"

"*I don't know.*"

That was all he'd said before hanging up.

She blew the last puff of smoke into the air, put the cigarette out, stepped back into the house, and started the shower. She gazed at her reflection in the mirror until the steam began to block her view. She stuck her hand into the opposite pocket of the robe. She could feel something in there and pulled it out to see what it was. It was a small silver key. She wondered what on earth it unlocked. In fact, she wouldn't get a good night's sleep until she figured it out. She went back into the bedroom, opened Nic's bedside dresser drawer. There were a few personal things—allergy medicines, a nail clipper, a book. But nothing that a key would unlock.

She sat on the bed to think for a moment before making her way to their walk-in closet, to his side, and started sorting through his things, moving items about. She'd never been the type to invade his privacy, but she felt the need to now.

An old saying came to mind: *If you go looking for things, you're sure to find them.*

She didn't care. She was looking, and with great intent. She tore up the closet in search of something—*anything*. She needed to know what this key unlocked. When she finally stumbled upon the gray steel box, her hands shook as she tried the key. It turned with ease. Opening it, she could see several letters addressed to Nic at his architectural firm. The return address was Angelina's.

Sitting in the middle of the floor of her closet, she placed the letters in chronological order. Some of them dated as far back as when she and Nic first got married, and some of them had been written as recently as the past couple of months.

The scent of sweet perfume oozed from each page, with a white, pink, or red oleander tucked inside of every single envelope.

Natalia pulled out one of the letters and read a few lines. This wasn't a note from a woman interested in coparenting their small child. No, this was much more intimate.

Her hands trembled as she began to read them one by one. Letters filled with lots of passion, some heartache and pain, and a few ultimatums. She cried with each handwritten letter. When she'd finally read the last one, Natalia was certain that Angelina wanted nothing more than to have him back in Sicily, *with her.*

She thought of her phone call with Nic. His words stuck with her. *"Natalia, this is why we can't move forward. I fear that this whole obsession with having a child is about Angelina. You're so insecure."*

He was wrong. Her obsession was that she desperately wanted a child of her own. However, she'd have agreed with him and thought herself to be insecure had she not read the letters. In every one of them—all twenty-two of them—Angelina expressed not only her undying love for Nic but her dislike for Natalia. *You were supposed to have married me, but instead you went away and fell for a woman who can't even give you a child. What good is a barren woman, Nicolai? What good is she? And she's not even Sicilian.* Her words cut deep.

It was true, Natalia wasn't Sicilian. She was Portuguese. She was Catholic, at least, which was something his parents took comfort in, knowing before they'd exchanged vows at the little Roman Catholic chapel in his hometown of Catania.

"I'm not insecure," she had whispered to him through tears.

She wasn't insecure. No, she was equipped now. She was certain that Nic had no intention of her ever opening his little gray box. He knew she wasn't the type to pry, which was probably why he hadn't been more careful. But now that she *had* pried, she needed to figure out what she would do with the information that she'd found. Still on the floor, she attempted to regain her composure, wiped away the tears, but she was still numb.

She reflected on her dinner with Lu and Kenya, and how she'd wanted to tell them exactly what was going on in her miserable world. But she couldn't. Wouldn't. They both had their own stuff and she refused to bring them down because she was. One of these days she'd tell them just how bad things really were, but until then, she'd just be happy that John Samuels had come back into Lu's life. This way, she could continue to live her own lie.

Chapter Six

Lu

Even at sixty-seven, Yana was still quite the beauty that she was at forty-seven. With a long dark mane, high cheekbones, and a fit body, she could pass for a much younger woman. She'd had a boob job four years ago, against Lu's wishes. She'd threatened to have her butt lifted, too, but Lu warned that she'd gone too far and she wouldn't stand for it.

"I'm the mother, dear heart," Yana had reminded her.

"And I'm the daughter who's saying that enough is enough, old woman!"

Yana sucked her teeth. She threw her hand in the air to blow off what Lu was saying. She was known for doing exactly what she wanted to do. As much as she had her own mind, she listened to Lu. Respected her. Loved her. Bragged to her friends about her brilliant daughter, who was a badass attorney-turned-innkeeper. She was proud of her only child.

After thinking things over all night, with barely a wink of sleep, Lu decided that she needed to see Yana in person. Their conversation the evening before had left her an emotional wreck. After she hung up the phone, she wasn't certain when she'd ever talk to her mother again. But after dinner with her friends, who insisted that she give Yana some grace, she summoned her mother to the inn first thing Saturday morning. She needed more answers about her father, and Yana was going to give them to her, whether she wanted to or not.

She told Yana, "Get in that Toyota of yours and make your way here as soon as possible, Ina. I need to speak with you, and not by phone. In person."

Though she wasn't an early riser, Yana was on Cape May by seven o'clock. Just in time to smell the fresh morning ocean air and hear the birds chirping their morning medley. Early enough for coffee on the veranda, she plopped down in the wicker chair with a floppy beach hat perched upon her head and a big colorful, embroidered hobo bag that held God only knew what draped over her shoulder. It landed on the porch near her feet. Lu handed her mother a ceramic mug. The one she'd picked up in Cabo a few summers ago when she and Zach had traveled there for vacation.

"Did you use sugar or that crap in the pink packages?"

Lu raised an eyebrow at her mother. She almost laughed but had to remember that she was still mad at Yana. "I used that crap in the pink packages. You know you need to watch your sugar."

"Good news. I don't have diabetes anymore. I've even managed to ween myself off that horrible medication."

"Dear Lord, Yana! You can't ween yourself off medication without your doctor's consent."

"I had my doctor's consent. Dr. Nubee said . . ."

"Dr. Nubee is not a medical doctor."

"He's just as capable as any of those doctors with degrees on their walls. Half of them don't know what they're doing anyway."

Dr. Nubee was the holistic doctor who prescribed Yana medical marijuana for her ailments. According to her, he was the smartest man alive.

Zach poked his head out the door. "Morning, Yana."

"Good morning, my handsome son-in-law-to-be."

He walked out onto the veranda and kissed Yana's cheek. "You look beautiful this morning, as always."

"Thank you, my sweetheart. You sure know how to make a woman feel good." She blushed. "Can you do me a little favor?"

"Anything."

"Take this cup of coffee back into the kitchen, pour it down the drain, and bring me another cup with two *real* sugars in it? And just a splash of cream, darling."

Zach took the mug from Yana and gave his fiancée a curious glance, as if to ask permission.

"Go ahead," Lu told him. "If she doesn't care about her health, why should I?"

"I care."

"I can't tell." Lu shook her head.

Helping her mother navigate her health issues was an uphill battle, particularly since Yana didn't believe she had any, or she believed that she'd been magically cured of them all. Either scenario was dangerous, in Lu's opinion. The door slammed as Zach went inside.

"So, why am I on Cape May at the crack of dawn anyway? I thought we cleared up everything yesterday, *mahal ko?*" Yana called Lu her love.

"We didn't clear up everything and you know it. You lied, and I want to know why. And not just what you want me to hear. I want real answers."

Yana breathed in deeply. Her eyes shifted from one side to the other. She always did that when she was thinking of the perfect response to get herself out of hot water. "I'm sorry I lied to you, but I had my reasons."

"Yes, you told me that, but I don't like your reasons. I had a right to know about him. To meet him. Do you know what it's like to feel like a part of you is missing?"

"You weren't missing anything. You had me. I gave you everything you needed."

"I needed to feel whole. And you took that from me."

Zach returned with Yana's coffee and handed it to her.

"Thank you." She smiled at him.

Yana loved Zach and had always told him so. She'd always openly told him that she loved how he loved Lu. How he spoiled her, catered to her. Told him that her daughter deserved someone who would show her such care. She'd always been an advocate for their love, and Lu appreciated that. Yana had never been able to find such a man. She always talked about how she was too impatient as a young woman, and now she was too set in her ways to ever settle down. Lu knew that her mother could be downright difficult at times.

Zach disappeared, giving Lu and Yana their space.

"I was protecting you."

"From what?" Those same feelings from yesterday had returned. She gave her mother a sideways glance, breathed in deeply, and then exhaled. Then she massaged her temples for a bit.

"He abandoned us once. I didn't want him abandoning you again. Truth is, I told you he was dead because I didn't want you to go looking for him."

"Yana, that was my choice. Not yours." She attempted to keep her voice from raising, wanting to remain calm.

"You are my child. So, I made that choice for you."

"Well, I'm not a child anymore. And now that he wants to see me, I'm anxious to go meet him—to go meet my siblings."

Yana shook her head. Exhaled. "Is this something that you really want to do? I don't want you going down that rabbit hole."

"It's too late. I'm booked on a flight next Wednesday. I'm going." She said it casually.

"The past sometimes . . . well, sometimes it's painful. And there's a lot of things you don't understand—*wouldn't* understand."

"Like what, Ina? Here's your chance to lay it all out for me. *Make me* understand."

One of Lu's guests interrupted, stepping out onto the veranda. "Mornin'," he said.

"Good morning, Paul. And how did you sleep?" Lu asked the older gentleman.

"Like a baby. I always sleep soundly when I'm here. It's why I come here, to get away from it all." He sipped coffee from a mug.

"That's good to hear," said Lu. "You've met my mother, Yana."

"Indeed, I have. Good morning beautiful lady. So nice to see you again."

"And a good morning to you," said Yana, batting her lashes. "The pleasure is all mine."

"Okay, we're going for a walk. We'll talk later, Paul." Lu grabbed Yana's hand and pulled her up from the chair. She whispered, "Walk with me."

Yana stood, grabbed her bag, and bid Paul a farewell. "Have a wonderful day."

"You as well."

They stepped off the veranda and onto the sand, walked toward the ocean, stood side by side. and watched as the waves gently swept against the shore. The tide wasn't high just yet. The waters were calm.

"You're such a flirt," Lu told her mother once they were alone. She couldn't contain her giggle. She wanted to still be mad at Yana, make her suffer a bit, but it was hard. The two had been like peas in a pod Lu's entire life. They took care of each other.

"What?"

"Tell me about you and John Samuels, that's what. Did you love him?"

"Once upon a time. Yes." Lu noticed that her mother's eyes danced when she said it.

"Why didn't you marry him?"

"Things were complicated, Lualhati. Life was complicated back then." Yana brushed Lu's windblown hair out of her face. "My beautiful girl. You look like him. You have his eyes and his smile, and that round face of his. And you're strong like him."

"He's strong?" Lu asked. This was her first real *something* of him, besides that black-and-white photo. She needed for Yana to make him real for her. Yearned for anything she could offer.

"He was a cocky son of a bitch." That's what she offered.

Yana laughed. Lu did, too.

"Where did you meet him?"

"I worked as a laundry woman during the day and waitress at night. He was coming off a six-week deployment when he came into the bar where I worked. He was handsome. Oh, so handsome." She closed her eyes, as if she was savoring the thought of him. "Very nice to me. He wasn't like the other sailors, the ones stationed there permanently. He was a gentleman."

"He asked you on a date?"

"More or less," said Yana. "If dating him meant that he came into the bar where I worked to see me every single day, then yes, I suppose we were dating. It was weeks before we were intimate, though. He was patient. Cautious. Didn't want to rush things. We would go for long walks and talk. We talked about everything."

"And . . ."

"And then, one day, he kissed me. And I felt like the most beautiful woman in the world. He made me feel that way."

"That's sweet. And then?"

"And then we had a whirlwind love affair, like the ones you used to read about in those romance novels that you kept under your mattress when you were a teen." Yana was in her own world at that moment. Lost in her thoughts. "Then I became pregnant with you, and at the same time, he was due to be deployed back to the US, to California, and my entire world turned upside down. You see, he was an officer who had been deployed to the Philippines only for a short time. His life was in the States, not Manila, honey. I knew that he would be leaving one day, but it didn't make it any easier when the time came."

"Did he ask you to go with him to the States?"

Yana nodded a yes. "But my home was in the Philippines. My family, everything I ever knew, was there. I knew nothing about the United States."

"But he insisted?"

"My father, your grandfather, wasn't having it any other way."

"So, Lolo was involved? I'm just trying to get an understanding."

"You must understand, we lived in great poverty. Even though I held down two jobs, it was just enough to get by. It was hard enough to make a living for myself, but now I had a baby on the way. Lolo insisted that John own up to his responsibilities, that he be honorable."

"Oh, Lolo." Lu placed her hands over her chest as she remembered her grandfather. She remembered picking up the frail little Filipino man from LaGuardia airport when he flew into New York for her college graduation. He was like a

SUMMER ON CAPE MAY   61

child, observing the sights as she drove him through Manhattan in her Volkswagen.

Yana looked at her, then handed Lu her coffee mug. "I would love to keep going down memory lane with you, my darling, but I have to go."

"Casino?" Lu asked.

"No. Bridge club again. And let me tell you, these ladies don't have a clue. I took their money yesterday, and now they want to try to win it back."

Lu shook her head. "What am I going to do with you, Ina?"

"I don't know, my darling. I know I can be a handful. I do know that." Yana kissed her daughter's cheek. "I hope that you abandon this whole idea of going to California. Nothing good will come of it. I have to go."

"You're opening old, painful wounds. Some things are better left alone. I don't like that he contacted you. What gives him the right?"

"He's my father. He has a right."

"He hasn't been there for any part of your life. He had his family, his children, his life," said Yana. "If you go, you go without my blessing."

"I really want your blessing, Ina, but if I don't have it, you need to know that I'm going anyway."

"You should honor your mother's wishes," Yana urged. "You're choosing sides."

"That's a ridiculous statement, Ina. And you know it. I'm not choosing his side. Not to mention, he's dying."

Yana was quiet for a moment. She blinked, and then her eyes saddened. Shoulders slumped, she placed her hands against her chest. "I didn't know, my darling. I'm sorry to hear that."

"Yes, they've given him a short time to live. I'm not sure that I'll have this opportunity again, to meet him. To speak with him. So, I'm going." Lu and Yana circled around to the front of the inn, to where Yana was parked. With arms locked, they walked to her car. Lu pulled the driver's door open. "I'll call you later. Drive safe."

"I love you more than life itself," Yana said as she climbed into her car.

"I love you more than that."

She loved her mother. Admired her. Having grown up in a single parent household, she watched Yana work multiple jobs just to make ends meet—for them. She remembered that sometimes their lights were shut off or they had to go to the neighbors to fill bottles with water just to bathe. Life had been tough for them, which was why Lu had worked so hard to position herself for a positive future. She attended Columbia University on a full scholarship, and later Vanderbilt to study law. But she was a Jersey girl at heart and had been eager to return home after graduation. She vowed to take care of Yana. Her mother had done so much for her, but she couldn't honor her wishes this time. She needed to honor her own wishes, even if it meant driving a wedge between them. It was necessary.

She watched as Yana pulled the old model Toyota out of the parking lot. Lu had already gone to the dealership and shopped for a newer version of the same car for her mother—a candy-apple red one with a convertible top. She'd planned to surprise Yana for Christmas. She already knew that Yana wouldn't want a new car. She was perfectly fine driving her old Toyota and wouldn't want Lu making a fuss over her. But Lu needed to know that her mother was safe when driving back and forth between Atlantic City and Cape May, and God only knew where else she went on a regular basis. She rarely sat still for long. Lu had made many attempts to get her to abandon the city and move to Cape May.

"You're getting older," Lu had explained. "You need to simplify your lifestyle."

"Who's old?" She'd completely missed the point.

"I didn't say you were old. I said you're getting older."

"Well, I'm not dead yet. And as long as I'm on this earth, I'll live in the city."

She watched as her mother pulled away from the inn, hoping their love would survive John Samuels.

Chapter Seven

Kenya

Kenya sat in the car and allowed the song to continue playing for a few minutes longer. She closed her eyes and got lost in the lyrics of "The Way" as Jill Scott's vocals soothed her. It was one of her favorites. One of those songs that made her stop whatever she was doing—no matter how important—to move her neck from side to side and sing the chorus right along with Jill. She remembered that time she and Glen had made the almost-three-hour drive to Newark for her concert. He loved Jilly from Philly just as much as she did. They had camped out on his buddy's couch before heading back the next morning, stopping for breakfast along the way.

As she sat in her parents' driveway, engine running, windows rolled up, she needed a moment to herself before going inside. Sunday morning service at her father's church could be exhausting, but she made it there at least twice a month. Today had been the church's anniversary service, so she certainly couldn't miss that. She thoroughly enjoyed Sunday dinners, particularly since she wasn't the best cook. Most days she grabbed something on her route home or or-

SUMMER ON CAPE MAY   65

dered takeout, so having her mother's cooking every now and then was a treat.

She was in her zone, had already worked her way into the ad-libs when a tap on her window startled her. She opened her eyes and then glanced over at the set of bright brown eyes that only two people in the universe shared—her father and her younger brother, Xander. Xander was eyeballing her and motioning for her to lower her window. Reluctantly, she did.

"Do you mind?" she asked him.

"How long are you going to sit out here?"

"I was having a moment to myself before I have to go inside and deal with your family."

Xander laughed. "I don't blame you, Sis. They can be a handful."

"Tell me about it," she said. "Why weren't you at church?"

"Work." He pointed to the name badge pinned to his shirt. "Got a gig."

Xander, who was two years younger than her, was great at getting a gig, but keeping it had always been his weakness. Kenya wished her brother would find a gig that aligned with his engineering degree, but for some reason he wasn't interested in pursuing those types of jobs. Instead, he worked lower-paying jobs that barely required a high school education and quit after only a few months. The hours were always wrong, the pay wasn't enough, or someone had it in for him. She also wished he was better at coparenting with his ex-girlfriend. Their five-year-old daughter needed him, but he couldn't seem to manage that either. He loved Emma more than life itself, that much was true, and if love were enough, he'd be father of the year. Though she was the healthiest, happiest little girl on the planet, she needed more than her father's love.

"Good for you! You gonna keep this one?"

"Yeah, Sis. The benefits are great: medical, dental, life insurance. Even has a good pension." He pulled a Newport cigarette out of its package, lit it, and tugged his jacket a little tighter. "Now I can finally get my own place. Move out of our parents' house. Pull my weight with Emma."

She'd lost count of how many times she'd heard this same song and dance. She also couldn't count the number of times Yvonne had called and asked her, *"Kenya, can you please talk to your brother? I don't want to file for child support, I just want him to be a responsible adult."* Even when they were a couple, Kenya had always been their referee, their sounding board, had always offered an objective ear. It was who she was with her entire family—the perfect balance.

"That's good, Xander. Yvonne needs your help."

"I know." He took one last draw and threw the butt of the cigarette on the ground.

Kenya rolled up the window, turned off her car engine, reached for her purse, and stepped out of the car. She and Xander went inside. He disappeared upstairs. The smell of fried chicken and the subtle smell of collard greens reminded her of growing up in her family's two-story, three-bedroom house in Brooklyn. After her father's retirement, her parents moved from Brooklyn to Chelsea Heights, a suburb in New Jersey. It was where he'd built his church.

Inside, her father was perched in his recliner in the corner of the room. He'd changed out of his Sunday suit in which he'd preached his sermon earlier. Now he wore a pair of sweatpants and a Morgan State University T-shirt. Walter Lewis was proud of his alma mater, had wanted Kenya to attend there, but she'd chosen NYU instead. It was Xander who had followed in their father's footsteps and attended the historically black college, excelling in their engineering program.

Walter was engaged in a loud conversation about absolutely nothing with his longtime friend, Henry Adams, who was always at her parents' house on Sunday afternoons. Kenya often wondered if he ever went home to be with his wife on the Sabbath, wondered if the poor woman even knew how to cook a Sunday meal.

"Sweetheart, you're just in time to settle a debate for us." Walter leaned up in his recliner when Kenya walked in. "I'm trying to tell Henry here that Marvin Gaye was the best entertainer who ever lived."

"And I'm trying to tell your daddy that Ray Charles was the real legend. His music catalog was far greater than Marvin's. He won all sorts of awards and Grammys." Henry looked her father in the eye. "He was inducted into the Rock and Roll Hall of Fame, the Country Music Hall of Fame, and some black music something or other."

"I think he might have you on that, Daddy."

"So, you're taking his side?"

"It's not about sides. What Hall of Fame was Marvin Gaye inducted into?"

"You're missing the point. You both are missing the point."

She was grateful to hear her mother's voice cry out from the kitchen, "Kenya, is that you, honey? I need your help in here."

Kenya welcomed the escape and entered the kitchen. She kissed her mother's cheek. "Thank you."

"I figured I'd give you a hand." Melba Lewis's entire face lit up when she smiled. "But I do need you to whip up a pan of corn bread."

"Of course." Kenya washed her hands in the sink, dried them, and then grabbed a mixing bowl from the cabinet.

"How are Lu's wedding plans coming along?"

"Wedding plans are good. I finally got fitted for my dress and I'm almost finished with the song that I've written for her."

"That's wonderful, baby. I know how close you two are. I love your friendship; it's strong and genuine. I would love to hear the song you wrote for her wedding."

"Now?"

"As good a time as any." Melba gave Kenya a smile.

Kenya unlocked her phone, searched for the lyrics that she'd written and kept in her notes. She began to sing the words that expressed her love and happiness for Lu. Though a cappella, she hit all the notes perfectly.

Her mother smiled and clasped her hands together. "Baby, it's beautiful."

"Thank you. I'll sing it after the nuptials. It will make her cry and mess up her makeup," Kenya said with a laugh.

Melba shook her head. "Your dad is excited to officiate. He feels honored that she asked him."

"Of course. She loves you both."

"And we love her. And are so very happy for her and Zach." Melba went back to her cooking.

Zach. The mention of his name made Kenya cringe. She wasn't happy with him at all.

"Lu had an emergency arise and she'll be leaving for California soon. I'll be taking over the inn for a few weeks."

"How will you do that?"

"Taking a much-needed vacation."

"Wow, really?" Melba asked. "What about the firm, your cases? What about Deacon Charles's case?"

"We still have time before he goes to trial. I'm on top of it."

"I hope so, honey." Melba placed her hand against her daughter's cheek. "Everyone is counting on you. Your father, the congregation, the deacon. Everyone."

"No pressure, right?" Kenya asked sarcastically.

"I'm just saying. We all have so much confidence in you. He's lucky to have you as his attorney. You're the best there is. And for the church to pull together to pay his legal fees that says a lot about what they think of him *and you.*"

When Deacon Charles was arrested for the murder of his business partner the previous month, it was the church that had posted his six-figure bail. Kenya was hesitant about taking the case, had all but insisted that her cocounsel, Mitch Murphy, take the case. After all, Deacon Charles was her father's friend and had been a deacon at their church for years. But no matter how hard she tried to pass him off, Deacon Charles insisted that Kenya represent him. He didn't trust his life in anyone else's hands.

She had no doubt that she could win the case. She was confident—borderline cocky. It was because she'd only lost three cases in her entire career. She was a barracuda in the courtroom—relentless and respected. She knew the law and she was an expert at commanding the room when cross-examining. She left no stone unturned. Her team was the best in the state. Deacon Charles was in good hands.

"Well, if it isn't the golden child." Patricia stepped into the kitchen from the back door, the palm of her hand massaging her protruding belly.

Kenya was particularly fond of the little person who followed her sister into the house, her nephew, Malik. She stopped what she was doing, grabbed him, and lifted him into the air, then kissed his plump cheek. "How's Auntie's baby?"

"Fine," he said, wrapping his arms tightly around her neck.

"Fine? Oh, you're fine?" She tickled him and he giggled right out of her arms.

"Where's Pop Pop?" he asked.

"You know where he is." Kenya watched as he rushed into the living room in search of his grandfather.

"No running, little boy," Patricia warned her son.

"Hello to you, Tricia," said Kenya.

"Are you having supper with us today?" Patricia asked. "I'm just asking because usually after church you bolt right out the door headed back to Cape May to your *friends*."

"Don't start," Melba warned her oldest daughter as she stirred a pot of greens while giving her an evil eye.

"Yes, I'm staying for supper. In fact, I'm whipping up a nice pan of corn bread right now." Kenya returned to her mixing bowl, dumped the box of corn bread mix into it, and then reached into the refrigerator and pulled out the carton of eggs and milk.

"It's not like you can cook much else."

"Oh, that's cold," said Kenya.

"It's the truth," Patricia said. "Are you here because you're working on that case of yours with the deacon?"

"I'm here to spend time with my family."

"Well, that's a first," Patricia mumbled.

"That's enough, Patricia Ann!" Melba said. "Now take off your coat, grab some plates from the shelf and set the table. Please."

With a huff, Patricia removed her coat and headed to the living room to hang it up. She returned to the kitchen and reached for the plates from the shelf. Then she took them into the dining room.

"What's her problem?" Kenya whispered.

Melba shrugged. "You know your sister."

She did know her sister, at least she thought she did. They'd grown up in the same home in Brooklyn, slept in the same room, swapped clothes, attended the same schools. Tricia had been her first best friend, her confident. That is, until Kenya went away to college. Though she was only a few miles away at NYU, Kenya had a new life and made new friends, only returning home during the holidays and school breaks. Tricia had opted to join the workforce rather than attend college as her parents had desired. She'd been at the same government agency since then, so she'd certainly built a career over the years, fighting her way through the ranks. It hadn't been an easy climb. Nor had her love life, as she'd endured her share of bad relationships over the years. Her high school sweetheart, whom she'd hoped to marry, actually ran off and married another woman, leaving her an emotional wreck. Her most recent relationship had been with a married man, Malik's father—a huge disappointment to their father, particularly since Devin Jackson *and his wife* had been longtime members of their church. Their family was still recovering from the scandal.

Kenya popped the corn bread into the oven. "Corn bread's in the oven, Mother dear. Is there anything else you need from me?"

"No, baby, thank you. We'll be eating soon."

"Okay."

Kenya retreated to the den, seeking peace and quiet for a moment. That peace didn't last long, though, because the moment she collapsed onto the sofa she heard her father's voice.

"Kenya, come quickly!" he called.

She rushed into the living room, where everyone was gathered around the television set.

The redheaded newscaster, dressed in a plaid blazer, stood in front of Deacon Charles's home in Ventnor City, New Jersey. "Prominent businessman Donovan Charles, who was formally charged with *murder* just a few weeks ago by the Atlantic County prosecutor's office, was seen on video leaving the scene of the crime on the night of the murder. The owner of the bodega across the street from the victim's condo released the footage to the press this afternoon. ACTV5 was the first to report on this new information in the case and now we'll show you the video footage."

In the video, a man who appeared to be Deacon Charles walked briskly into the breezeway of the condominium subdivision where his business partner lived. The man wore a wool peacoat pulled tightly, a scarf wrapped around his neck, and a skullcap on his head. He briefly turned his head toward the camera. Kenya couldn't tell beyond a shadow of a doubt whether it was him, but it certainly appeared to be the deacon. She covered her mouth with her hands as she watched.

The newscaster continued, ". . . before this video was released, Mr. Charles had maintained that he was innocent and had an alibi. He also stated that he had not been near the scene of the crime that night. However, the video shows otherwise. . . ."

Kenya dialed Deacon Charles's phone number.

"Kenya, this is crazy! I don't know what to do. . . ." Deacon Charles's voice sounded panicky.

"Calm down," she told him.

"They're in front of my house. Reporters are everywhere!" he exclaimed.

"Stay put. I'm on my way," she told him and then hung up.

"Oh my goodness," Melba said.

"Baby, did you know about this video footage?" her father asked.

"What are you going to do about it?" her mother asked before she could reply to her father.

"Do you need me to go with you?" Her father walked over to the hall closet and grabbed his hat and coat.

"No, Dad, I don't need you to come. You stay put. I'll handle this."

Their questions were coming all at once. Kenya's head was spinning. She needed to get Mitch on the phone. She dialed his number.

"I'm already on it," he said before she could say anything. "The owner of the bodega originally claimed that their cameras were inoperable that night, but then out of nowhere, boom . . . video footage is leaked to the press."

"Why wasn't I made aware of this? How does this stuff get leaked to the news media before I'm made aware of it?"

"Your phone has been going to voicemail all afternoon."

Kenya shook her head and sighed. "I turned the ringer off during church and forgot to turn it back on."

"I'm headed to Charles's place now. I'll meet you there."

"Thanks, Mitch," Kenya said. "If that's really him in that video, we need to know why he lied to the police, or better yet, why he lied to us."

"Agreed."

"I'll see you there." She hung up.

"What does all of this mean, baby?" Walter Lewis's eyes were filled with concern for his friend.

"I don't know, Daddy. I'll keep you posted." Kenya grabbed her coat and slipped it on. "I'll be back for that fried chicken in a bit."

She rushed out the door.

Mitch pulled up at the same time. The two of them fought their way through the mob of reporters, declining to answer any of their questions as they made their way to the front door of the home. Kenya rang the bell, and Deacon Charles answered. He swung the door open so they could come inside.

The three of them stood in the foyer with its marble floors and grand staircase. Expensive art hung on the walls.

Kenya cut right to the chase. "Deacon, I have one question for you and I need for you to be completely honest with me."

"Of course."

"Did you visit Julian Miller's condo the night of the murder? And before you answer, I need you to know that the camera footage resembles you a lot."

Deacon Charles was completely silent. He wrung his hands together. His wife, Eleanor, came from the kitchen and stood next to him. Kenya nodded a hello to her.

"If you lie to me, I can't represent you! You must tell me everything or you're going to find yourself rotting in a jail cell. Is that what you want?"

"No, that's not what I want." He hung his head.

"You have my father and the entire church congregation on your side. *I'm on your side.* But if you lie to me, I'm dropping this case. Today."

"I admit it. I went to his condo that night. I needed to get his signature on some documents. That's all. I was only there ten, maybe fifteen minutes. I assure you, he was very much alive when I left."

"Why didn't you tell me this? I could've gotten in front of it."

"I thought it would make me look guilty."

"Well, you look guilty now."

"I didn't do this." His voice was soft, his eyes pleading.

As damning as the video was, Kenya believed him. Now she had to prove that someone else had visited Julian that night, someone who wanted him dead *and* killed him.

"Do you know of anyone who might've wanted Julian dead? Business deal gone bad? Love interest?"

"He *was* seeing a woman. Some . . . mystery woman."

Kenya's eyebrows raised. "So, you don't know her name?"

"All I know is that she's married."

"Why didn't you tell me this? This is important information." Kenya turned to Mitch. "We find this mystery woman and maybe we have motive."

"Maybe," Mitch said.

"In the meantime, do not talk to the press," Kenya told Deacon Charles. "Keep a low profile. Go about life as usual."

"I will," he assured her, grabbing her hand. "Thank you so much, Kenya. You're a godsend."

"You have an army of people on your side, praying for you, Deacon. We're going to fight this."

"I know," he whispered.

Sunday dinner with her family was usually just that—Sunday dinner. However, this Sunday had been anything but. She couldn't wait to return to Cape May, her peace, her bubble. Her home.

Chapter Eight

Natalia

She'd completely slept Saturday and most of Sunday away. However, she had managed to peel herself out of bed on Sunday morning and brewed herself a cup of coffee. After that she returned to her bed and covered herself in the light blue cotton sheets. She'd seen Lu's two calls but sent a text that she'd call her back. She also received Kenya's text that she'd had a good time at church and was spending the evening at her parents' house.

Should I bring you a plate? Mom fried chicken. I had to leave unexpectedly, but I'm still in the city. I can run back by there and grab you something, Kenya texted with all sorts of happy faces and other emojis.

No thank you. I'm going to cook something, Natalia lied. She had no intention of cooking anything. In fact, it had taken every ounce of energy she had just to brew a cup of coffee that morning.

On a normal day, Natalia would have devoured Kenya's mother's fried chicken—no doubt the woman could cook. But she hadn't had an appetite for food. She only responded to the text in order to deter Kenya from popping up on her once she returned to Cape May from her parents' home. Luckily, she'd pulled her car into the garage on Friday. If Kenya returned and saw her car in the driveway, she might stop by. She didn't want any visitors. Didn't want her friends to see her this way: vulnerable, weak, wounded. She didn't want to talk. All she wanted to do was hide beneath the covers and never emerge.

In the quietness of the house, all that could be heard were waves from the ocean crashing against the shore. It had been one of the selling points of the house, the fact that the ocean was just outside their bedroom's balcony. There were countless nights that she and Nic spent on that balcony, sipping glasses of Cabernet from her vineyard, discussing their future. They would spend most of the night out there making plans and then retire to the bedroom for passionate lovemaking. That was before talk of a baby had ever come up, before the fertility treatments and doctors. Before their communication started to crumble. Before he stopped loving her. Before Angelina had completely stolen her life.

The doorbell sounded louder than usual and seemed to have an echo. She pressed her face into the pillow and groaned.

"No," she whispered.

Her phone rang almost simultaneously with the second doorbell ring. It was Lu. It was a ritual that she spoke with Lu and Kenya daily, sometimes several times per day, so it was unusual for her not to see Lu or hear her voice for almost two days. She knew she wasn't going away. She'd ring that doorbell until she got an answer.

Natalia pulled herself from the bed, wrapped herself in Nic's robe, and made her way down the wooden stairs and to the front door. She peeped through the lace curtains. Both Lu and Kenya stood on her front porch, Lu with her hands on the hips of her small frame.

She opened the door. Lu stepped inside without an invitation. "Neither of us have heard a peep from you in two days. What's going on? Are you okay?"

"Of course. Come on in." Natalia opened the door wider for Kenya and she stepped inside, too.

Lu was already headed for the kitchen, turning on lights in the hallway as she went along. "Why is it so dark in here? So quiet?"

"I was resting." Natalia followed behind Lu, the walnut-colored hardwood cool against her bare feet.

She and Nic had stained the unfinished hardwoods after they'd moved in. It was a project that they'd tackled together, the flooring as well as painting the walls throughout the house in beach-inspired hues like moss green, light yellow, and baby blue. They'd spent hours at the local hardware store picking just the right paint colors.

"Are you sick?" Lu opened the stainless-steel refrigerator and grabbed a bottle of water.

"No . . ."

"I called you yesterday." Kenya entered the kitchen, her eyes busy observing the space, looking for anything that might be out of place. "I wanted to go antique shopping."

"Oh yes, I got your message too late," Natalia lied. "Did you find anything?"

"I found an old chest. I've already started sanding it, prepping it for the mahogany stain. It's going to be beautiful when I finish." There was always a bit of excitement in Kenya's voice when she talked antiques. She loved antique shopping just as much as she loved refinishing old pieces. It was her thing. Then, observing the empty stove, she said, "I thought you cooked."

"I haven't gotten around to it yet."

"Well, honey, it's almost eight. What time do you plan on eating?" Lu asked.

"I . . ."

'What's going on, Natalia? Something isn't right." Lu cut right to the chase, as she always did.

"Is it Nic? Has he told you when he's coming home?" Kenya asked. She was a straight shooter also, but with a bit more compassion.

Natalia stood there in the middle of her kitchen filled with white cabinets that brightened the room, black marble counters, and, just outside of the floor-to-ceiling windows, she could see that the sun was setting over the ocean. She began to busy herself by placing Fridays' dishes into the dishwasher. She grabbed the empty bottle from the wine that she'd finished off on Friday and tossed it into the trash. She wiped down the counters, though they weren't dirty at all. Midstream, her emotions got the better of her, and before she could prevent them, the tears had overtaken her face.

Lu rushed over and hugged her tightly. "Sweetheart, what is going on?"

Natalia exhaled. She'd been lying to them and now she was exhausted. It was time she stopped making excuses, telling them half-truths. They were her friends, after all, who had been there for her and she for them. Her pride had gotten the better of her, but she needed them now. She needed to make sense of what was happening in her life. She collapsed into Lu's arms and glanced over at Kenya, who had a look of concern on her face. Natalia recognized that look because it was the same one she'd given Kenya when Glen died. She knew that Kenya hadn't been okay even when she kept saying that she was. She imagined that her friend had fallen apart, just as Natalia was doing now. Back then, she'd even had the nerve to chastise Kenya for not being honest and forthright with them about her feelings and emotions. And here she was, doing the same thing.

"We're your friends. We're here for you. Don't shut us out," is what she'd told Kenya when Glen died.

Though Kenya hadn't said those words to her, the look on her face was conviction enough.

"I don't think he's coming back," Natalia managed to say through the lump in her throat. The tears were uncontrollable now.

"What? What do you mean?" Kenya grabbed Natalia's hand and held it tightly.

Natalia exhaled, then sighed deeply. She wiped her tears away with the back of her hand. "Follow me."

Lu and Kenya looked at each other, puzzled.

Natalia led the way out of the kitchen and up the wooden stairs. They followed. They stood in the bedroom while she went into the walk-in closet and pulled out the gray box that had changed her life. She came back into the bedroom, stuck her hand into the pocket of the robe, and pulled out the key. She unlocked the box and pulled out the stack of envelopes.

"I ran across these letters. They're from Angelina to Nic."

"Angelina, his child's mother, right?"

"Yes." She pulled the very first letter that Angelina had written from the stack, handed it to Kenya. "Here. Read it."

Kenya read the letter aloud, stopping midway to look at Natalia and then Lu. "Are you kidding me?"

"Keep reading."

Kenya did as Natalia asked and read to the end.

"This is a bunch of crap!" Lu exclaimed.

"There are twenty-two of them in all."

"You've got to be kidding me! Twenty-two letters? About what?" Kenya asked.

"About how much she loves him and wants him. And about how he made a mistake in marrying me. I read every one of them and I crumbled."

"Why didn't you tell us? You should've called us the moment you found them. We should've been here with you reading every single word *with you*."

"You both have your own stuff."

"Excuse me, ma'am," Kenya started on her tangent. "Remember when I lost Glen and you all but cursed me out because I was trying to deal with it alone?"

"I remember." She already knew it was coming.

" 'You can't do this alone,' you said. 'You have friends to help you through it. We're sisters.' "

"I remember. And you're right." Natalia sighed. "I was just in so much pain after reading the letters, I didn't even know what I was feeling or how to express it to you."

"I can only imagine how you felt, honey," Lu said. "Had to be pretty devastating."

"I really want to get my hands on Angelina." Kenya locked her fingers together and made a strangling motion. "Home wrecker!"

"She never stopped loving him. The letters are dated back as far as when we first got married. Makes me question everything. Like if he ever loved me at all."

"Of course he loved you—*loves you.*" Kenya folded the letter and stuffed it back into the envelope.

"Maybe I should just stay here instead of going to California," said Lu. "You need me here."

"Oh no, no, no. Absolutely not! You have to go to California," Natalia said.

"I don't mind staying here to help you through this," Lu said matter-of-factly. "I can always go later."

"I'll be fine. Plus, Kenya will be here."

"Yes, Lu, you have to go. Meeting your father and your siblings, that's important," Kenya chimed in.

"You don't know how much time your father has, and if you don't go, you'll regret it," Natalia said.

"But I'm so worried about *you* right now."

"I know, and I'm sorry for making you worry—making you *both* worry. I should've been honest at dinner the other night. I should've just told you the truth, that Nic has no intention of coming home anytime soon."

"Sisterhood is about transparency, and about being honest with one another. We can't be here for you if we don't know what's going on. You never have to go this alone, Nat Pack." Kenya called her by the nickname she'd given her after they'd first become friends. She plopped down onto Natalia's bed. "Not when you have us."

Kenya's words caused her to feel the guilt of keeping Glen's illness a secret; caused her knees to buckle as she plopped down on the bed to break the fall. "I know."

"So, what's next? What are you going to do?" Lu asked.

"I don't know what *to do*."

"I think you should tell him that you've read the letters. Give him an opportunity to explain himself," Kenya said.

"I agree. He's over there with that woman, knowing full well that she's still in love with him. I want to just choke him." Lu clasped her hands together this time.

"You need to know what his intentions are." Kenya was always the levelheaded one. When the world was falling apart, she always managed to bring things back into focus.

"That's the part that scares me. What if his intentions are to stay there—to be with her? What do we do about the marriage—this house . . . our finances?"

"Whoa, whoa, whoa! Did he tell you that he's not coming back?" Kenya asked.

"No, but . . ."

"Then let's not get ahead of ourselves. Start with a conversation. Tell him that you found the letters and give him a chance to explain," said Kenya.

"You're right."

"One step at a time, honey." Lu smiled at Natalia.

"I love you both." Natalia pulled them both in for a group hug. "I felt like I was going to die earlier today. But I feel better already."

"We love you," Lu said.

"I love you, but don't you ever suffer alone, ever again," said Kenya. "Promise us."

"I promise."

"When one of us hurts, we all hurt," Lu chimed in.

"Exactly."

"Now, let's go down to the kitchen and see what we can whip up, because I know you haven't eaten," Kenya said.

"Maybe we can just head over to the inn and I'll have Lorenzo cook you something before he leaves for the night."

"That sounds wonderful," Natalia said.

"Get dressed. We'll be downstairs," Lu told her.

When Lu and Kenya left the room, Natalia exhaled. She plopped down on the edge of the bed for a moment. Less than an hour before, her world had been turned upside down. It was still a bit topsy-turvy, but at least she had her girls there to keep it steady.

Chapter Nine

Lu

Her morning started early with a cup of coffee and her showing Kenya the ropes. Her housekeeper, Marissa, was running late and hadn't prepped one of the rooms for a guest who was arriving, so Lu pulled sheets out of the dryer. She grabbed one end of the fitted sheet and Kenya the other one, and together they pulled it onto the mattress.

"Marissa normally does this, but she's running a bit late today and this room needs to be ready for the next guest who's arriving this afternoon. Phoebe Cashay . . . she's a writer and prefers this room because of the view. She comes every year at this time. She'll stay locked in here for hours while writing her next breakout novel. She might come down for a meal or two, but not often."

Kenya looked around. "It's a beautiful room."

"Yes, it is. It's the one that everyone wants, but it's always booked," Lu explained.

"I can see why."

The room, with its vintage Hollywood décor, boasted a huge black-and-white portrait of Ginger Rogers wearing a long, flowy white dress, with her porcelain skin and bright red lipstick. The black antique furniture in the room had been refinished by Lu and Kenya themselves—a project that took them most of last summer. The sheer white curtains blew with the breeze from the morning wind. The faint, fresh scent of the ocean made its way in through the window that was slightly cracked.

"Breakfast runs from six thirty to nine." Lu gave Kenya a refresher on the run of the house. Although she'd run Lu's Seaside Inn before, it had been a while. She said, "It smells like Max has arrived and already started cooking."

"Oh yes, I smell it. Nothing like Applewood smoked bacon to get your morning started."

"And his world-famous French toast. Let's not forget that. It's all they rave about in the reviews." Lu laughed. "You'd think they would rave about the accommodations, all the work we've put into this inn, but no, the French toast."

After making the bed, Lu led the way downstairs. "I'll show you the computer system. I know you've done this before, so I'll just give you a quick refresher."

"It shouldn't be too difficult."

"I don't know if I told you how much I appreciate this, Kenya, but I really do."

"It goes without saying. I'm just glad I can help."

"You're a godsend. A true friend."

"I want this, for you to meet your father and your siblings. To find that missing part of you." Kenya smiled. "And I can't count the number of times you've been there for me. It's my honor to do this, really."

"I love you, sister." Lu gave Kenya a tight squeeze and fanned away the tears that threatened to fill her eyes. She'd been on an emotional roller coaster ever since John Samuels's phone call. Nowadays it seemed as though everything made her cry.

"I love you more."

"Okay, no time for crying today! I have stuff to do. I have a flight to catch soon. Zach did my packing for me, but I have to go behind him and make sure he didn't miss anything." Lu laughed. "He's so good to me. I don't know where I would be without him."

"He's going to make a great husband," said Kenya.

"Zach is a wonderful man. He reminds me of Glen. He was a wonderful man, too. And you know what, you're going to find someone else just like him—I just know it. Someone just as wonderful."

"Not that I'm looking. But anyway, show me this computer system." Kenya avoided any talk of meeting anyone who might replace Glen.

"Let me just say this; I know you're on these dating sites. . . ."

Kenya interrupted, "Looking for companionship only, someone to take in a movie with, maybe go to dinner. Maybe a little woo-ha . . ."

Lu looked Kenya square in the eye. "Woo-ha?" She giggled.

"Yes, woo-ha." Kenya laughed, too. "Nothing more than that. Nothing permanent."

"Don't close your heart to love, Kenya."

"Love hurts, and it's disappointing. I'm never going down that road again."

"Never say never." Lu unlocked her laptop computer and logged into her property management system.

"Well, I'm saying never."

Lu gave her friend a nod and a raised eyebrow and simply said, "Okay."

She had been praying that Kenya would find someone just like Glen, and so she simply left it alone. For now, she was going to leave the details for God to work out. She continued to show Kenya how to navigate the system. She walked her through several processes, and when she was confident that Kenya was well refreshed, she snuck away to the terrace and dialed Natalia's number.

"Good morning!" Natalia answered and was like a burst of sunshine. "Today is your big day."

"Yes, it is."

"Are you ready to meet your father and siblings?"

"I'm a little nervous, but I'm ready," Lu said. "And how are you? Any better today?"

"I'm better. I'm at the winery already. Work will be a great distraction."

"I agree," Lu told her. "Please don't hesitate to call either me or Kenya if you need us. We love you and we're never too busy."

"I know. And I love you guys, too!"

"Well, I must go finish packing and preparing. My flight is in a few hours."

"Safe travels and please let us know you made it safely."

"Will do, honey. Talk soon."

Lu felt good that everything on Cape May was in order.

It wasn't until she arrived at the airport that she felt anything that resembled anxiety. She was nervous. She bit her nails and her knee bounced up and down as she sat there, a copy of the *Cape May County Herald* folded in her lap. She held on to a cup of Starbucks Pumpkin Spice latte. Zach placed his hand on her knee and stopped it from bouncing. He grabbed her hand and held it tightly. "Relax, babe. Everything's going to be just fine."

"You promise?" she asked with a half-smile.

"I promise."

She'd been fine until her arrival at the airport. She'd been fine after she called John Samuels a week ago to let him know that she'd made her decision to honor his wishes and fly to Sacramento. She heard the joy in his voice—he was happy. He'd insisted on covering all her travel costs and accommodations. His secretary had made all the arrangements for her and Zach. All she had to do was show up. She'd been fine after calling Yana to let her know that she was indeed going to meet her father. Even after Yana all but had a fit about it, her mind was made up. She'd even been fine after leaving the inn in Kenya's hands this morning, and after making sure that Natalia was in a somewhat good place emotionally.

She thought about the family on the other side of the country who awaited her arrival—John Samuels and his children. She wondered what they were all like, if they would embrace her. John had been excited and welcoming, grateful that she'd accepted his invitation. She, too, was excited to meet him. She had so many questions that she needed answers to. Answers that Yana hadn't given her. She didn't know if all of them would be answered over the course of this trip, but she was certainly going to ask as many as she could.

She pulled her jacket back on, zipped it up.

"I don't think I've ever seen you like this. Nervous. Anxious." Zach gave her a smile. "You're always in control."

"Yes, I know. It's tripping me out, too." Lu giggled nervously. "This is new for me."

"What are you worried about?"

"Just wondering what I'm going to be faced with when I get there. What if they hate me?"

"What if they love you?" Zach countered.

Lu sighed. Zach was always her ray of sunshine, her positive energy.

"I have so many questions. I should've written them down, so I don't miss anything."

"You can always call him if you forget something."

"What if I don't have time? He's a very sick man."

"I think you're worrying too much. You should just let things occur as they should—freely. Stop trying to control everything."

"You're right." She closed her eyes.

She needed something a little stronger than coffee and knew she'd order something just as soon as they boarded the flight.

Chapter Ten

Kenya

Though Lu had left detailed instructions, Kenya had filled in at the inn on many occasions on the weekends or some evenings when she had time. The property was secluded and only drew a particular type of vacationer—not the touristy ones, so there wouldn't be many people walking in off the street. Most were vacationers who had standing annual commitments at the property or referrals from her regulars.

She recognized the award-winning author the minute she walked through the inn doors. Phoebe Cashay was dressed in a pair of old jeans and a T-shirt. A pink baseball cap on her head and a pair of sunglasses on her face. If she was trying to be inconspicuous, she was certainly accomplishing just that, but Kenya recognized her the moment she removed the shades from her face.

"Good afternoon. I'm looking for Lu," she said.

"I'm sorry, she's not here now. I'm Kenya. How can I help you?"

"I have a reservation for the week. Phoebe Cashay."

Kenya smiled, starstruck. "I know who you are. I'm a huge fan."

"Wonderful." She stood there waiting for Kenya to get past her moment and check her in.

"I'm sorry. I'll just need to see your identification and credit card, please."

"Really? You need my ID?" Phoebe teased and smiled.

"I do. I mean, I trust you are who you are, but I just need to take a picture of it."

"Of course." Phoebe slid her driver's license and credit card from their compartments, handed them to Kenya.

She took a picture of Phoebe's driver's license and then slid the credit card into its compartment of the computer.

"Lu has you in the Vintage Hollywood suite. She said it's the one you prefer."

"I always stay in the same room." Phoebe leaned in for a whisper, "It's my favorite."

Kenya whispered back, "Truth be told, it's everyone's favorite."

Both women giggled.

"I can see why."

"Great! Then you know where it is. Here's your key." Kenya handed her a gold key. "You're all set. Dinner is served in the dining room at four. That is, if you'd like to join us. And I'll have someone bring up your luggage."

"Fantastic, Kenya," Phoebe said. "I won't be eating in the dining room, but when Lorenzo gets here, if you could have him bring up a bottle of Chianti, that would be great."

"Will do. When he arrives, I will."

"Fabulous." Phoebe grabbed her computer bag and made her way upstairs to her room.

Kenya opened her own computer and began typing. Though she was on vacation, she took every moment possible to get in some work. She needed to build her defense for Deacon

Charles. After that video footage fiasco and the discrepancy in his timeline, she needed a new strategy for his defense.

When she heard the door to the inn chime, she looked up from her computer. Lu's place was a rare hidden gem, so when the tall, dark, handsome stranger walked into the lobby wearing a tailored navy business suit, Kenya knew he hadn't walked in off the street. He had the most beautiful set of eyes she'd ever seen, a perfectly trimmed beard, and a smile that lit up the entire room when he used it.

"Hello." He smiled.

"Good afternoon. May I help you?" she asked.

"I'm looking for Lu or Zach."

"I'm sorry, neither of them is here right now. Can I assist you?"

"I spoke with Lu over the phone last week about a room. I'm a good friend of Zach's."

"And your name please?"

"Gideon Harper."

Kenya checked the reservations list. "Ah yes, here you are. Looks like she has you in the Cherry Blossom suite. For two weeks?"

Why was he staying for two weeks?

"Yes."

"Great. I just need your ID and a credit card, please." Kenya took his American Express and identification, checked him in. "You've missed lunch, but I can have Max, our chef, make you a sandwich if you'd like."

"No, thanks. I grabbed something at the airport."

"Very well, then dinner is at six. You can eat in the dining area with the other guests or on the veranda, if you prefer some alone time."

"The veranda sounds nice, but I wouldn't want to eat alone. Will you be joining me?" he flirted.

"I'm sorry, but no." She did her best to avoid eye contact

as she handed him his identification, credit card, and the key to his room.

His presence unsettled her. It made her nervous and giddy all at the same time, and she wondered how she would ever survive until Lu's return. No man since Glen had made her blush, but here she was, blushing. Though she pretended to mask her attraction to him, this stranger, this friend of Zach's, began to awaken things—in just that short encounter—that had been dormant for a long time.

He gave her a quick glance and the smile again before grabbing his bag and heading to his room. She stood there for a moment after he was gone, attempting to regain her composure. What was happening to her?

"Girl, get yourself together." She thought she'd whispered it in her head but literally heard the words come out of her mouth.

She breathed in deeply and then went back to what she was doing before Gideon Harper had clearly interrupted her entire afternoon.

She didn't realize just how long she'd buried herself in the prep work of Deacon Charles's trial until the smell of something delightful tickled her nose. Max was gone and Lorenzo had arrived and started cooking dinner. She had forgotten to have him deliver a bottle of Chianti to Phoebe's suite and made her way to the kitchen to tell him. She heard the loud and boisterous conversation before she even made it down the hall, and the laughter that bounced against the walls. Lorenzo was fully engaged in a conversation with Gideon— the two men behaving like old friends, swapping stories and laughing uncontrollably.

Gideon was the first to catch her eye when she appeared in the doorway of the kitchen. His face lit up and he gave her a smile.

She looked past him. "Good evening, Lorenzo. Something smells awfully good in here."

"It's my carbonada criolla. It's a beef stew of sorts, but with an Argentinian twist. It's made with sweet dried fruits, sweet potatoes, and winter squash. It's perfect for a chilly evening like this one."

"Sounds scrumptious." Her eyes just happened to veer toward Gideon after she'd mouthed the word *scrumptious*.

He raised his eyebrows and gave her a wicked smile.

"It will be ready soon." Lorenzo wiped his hand on his white chef's coat, leaving traces of red sauce behind.

"Phoebe Cashay is in the Vintage Hollywood suite. She'd like you to bring her a bottle of Chianti."

"Absolutely." Lorenzo stepped over to the wine cooler and grabbed a bottle from it. "It's perfectly chilled. I'm going to run it up to her now."

"I can run it up there if you'd like," Kenya offered.

"Oh no, no, no. I'll take it." Lorenzo grabbed a long-stemmed wineglass from the shelf, then held it in the air to observe it. He walked out of the kitchen, leaving Kenya alone with Gideon.

She could've walked away, gone back to working on her case, but she stood there.

"Is your room okay?" she asked to break the awkwardness of the silence.

"It's perfect." He'd changed out of his tailored suit and now wore a pair of sweatpants and a long-sleeved Howard University T-shirt.

"Is Howard your alma mater?" She pointed at his shirt.

"Yes. I was born and raised in the DMV. Maryland mostly. What about you?"

"I attended NYU, both undergrad and law school."

"Ahh, you're a lawyer. Civil law, I presume?" Gideon said.

"And why would you presume that?" Kenya asked, "because I'm a woman? Because I look like I might be fragile?"

She was used to men being surprised that she was in criminal law, as if women didn't have the ability to practice good criminal law.

"I . . . um . . ." he stumbled over his words.

"I'm actually a criminal attorney, for your information. And a damn good one!"

"My apologies. I didn't mean to offend you."

"You didn't." Kenya walked over to the commercial refrigerator and grabbed a bottle of water.

"Let's start over. I'm Gideon . . ."

"I know that. I saw your driver's license."

"And you're . . ."

Kenya exhaled deeply. The truth was, he *had* offended her, and she was turned off by his arrogant disposition. "I'm Kenya."

"Kenya, it's a pleasure meeting you. Would you please do me a favor? Let me make up for my rudeness. Do me the honor of having dinner with me on the veranda this evening?"

Not this again.

Lorenzo walked back into the kitchen. He had heard Gideon's proposition. "I think that's a wonderful idea. If you want, you can both go out there now and I will bring a bottle of wine. I think an Argentinian Malbec would pair nicely with the carbonada criolla."

"I don't know. I have a lot to do this evening. . . ."

"I don't see an overflow of guests waiting to check in," Gideon said.

Kenya had plans of spending the evening working on her case. "I have other work to do."

"But I've made such a huge pot of criolla." Lorenzo smiled.

"We certainly can't let good food go to waste . . . there are children starving in the world . . ." Gideon interrupted.

"Oh my God, not the starving children line."

Both men laughed heartily. Kenya giggled, too.

"Well, what do you say?" Gideon asked. "You have to eat, don't you?"

Kenya groaned, then exhaled. "Why not?"

He stood near the door of the kitchen and stretched out his arm, giving her that award-winning smile. "Ladies first."

She breathed deeply, gathered herself, and then walked past him. "Just dinner."

She wondered if he was watching her walk, observing her rear end. She'd chosen an old pair of jeans that day, not the cute ones that made her butt look good. She wore a yellow fitted T-shirt, the one she loved, with the word MELANIN plastered across the front. Had she known she'd be bumping into Gideon Harper today, she'd have worn those cute jeans, though. Not that she cared anyway.

Kenya chose one of the tables on the veranda, the one that offered the least wind on a somewhat chilly evening. She took a seat and watched as Gideon pulled out his chair. He had to be much more than six feet tall, she thought as he plopped down into the chair across from her, stretching his long limbs across the wooden porch.

"It's so beautiful out here."

"Yes, it is."

Though Lu's inn had so many little nooks and crannies, the veranda by far had always been Kenya's favorite. The flowers were always fragrant in the spring and summer, and it provided one of the best views of the ocean that she'd ever seen. Even with partly overcast skies, it was still quite a beautiful afternoon on Cape May.

"So, you're an attorney—a *criminal attorney*—but today you're an innkeeper?"

"I'm filling in for Lu. She had to leave town for a while to handle some personal business."

"I know. I spoke with Zach earlier. After I got here and they weren't here, I called him. He'd forgotten that I was coming in today."

"Bummer," Kenya said sarcastically. "Two weeks is a long time."

"I'm on vacation."

"And what is it that you do back there in . . . Maryland . . . to be on vacation from?"

"I'm a physician. Orthopedic surgeon."

"Okay, like Zach."

"Yes. We've been friends since medical school. Did our residency together." Gideon leaned back in his chair and said proudly, "I'm his best man."

"I see." Kenya placed her elbows on the table and her hands beneath her chin. How did she not know that Gideon was Zach's best man? "Well, I'm Lu's maid of honor."

"Maid of honor, not matron of honor, meaning you're single." He said it emphatically.

Kenya held both hands in the air. "No rings."

"That's good to know." He smiled.

"And why is that?"

"Well, I wouldn't want to be having dinner with someone's wife."

"There's no harm in dinner."

"I wouldn't want to be having dinner with someone's wife and having the thoughts that I'm thinking about her."

Kenya blushed. She could literally feel her cheeks turning red. *Why was she blushing?*

"Why is someone so beautiful, single?" he asked.

"Widowed."

"I'm sorry."

Kenya shook her head. "It's okay. No need to be sorry; life happens. Besides, it's been three years."

Not that the time since Glen's death mattered; it still felt like yesterday. She'd only recently stopped feeling numb when she heard a song or saw a photograph. She was happy to see Lorenzo approach with a bottle of red wine and two long-stemmed wineglasses. He placed one in front of each of them and poured a bit of wine into Gideon's glass. Gideon picked up the glass, swirled the wine around, and gave it a sniff. Then he tasted it.

"It's perfect," he told Lorenzo.

Lorenzo smiled and filled Gideon's glass the rest of the way, then hers. "I'll be right out with dinner."

"So, you live in the city or here on Cape May?"

"I live just up the stretch of the beach from here."

"And where's your law firm? Or . . . are you in private practice? I certainly don't want to make assumptions and offend you again."

"I work for a firm, in the city."

"I bet that commute is pure torture."

"It has its disadvantages. It can really weigh on you after a while—the traffic, the rat race—but I deal with it. Truthfully, I love the city, but I also love living on Cape May, so it's worth the sacrifice."

"I can see why you love it here," Gideon said. "It's a beautiful place. I see why Zach loves it. I see why he loves Lu. He's found his soulmate."

"And what about you? Have you found your soulmate?"

"I thought I had. A couple of times."

"You're divorced?"

"Two years. We have two children. Mia is twelve and Ethan is eight. They spend most of the year with their mother and most of the summer with me. I also have the weekend after Thanksgiving and spring break. It works out fine for all of us," he said. "What about you? Do you have children?"

"No children. I have a golden retriever who is my child."

"Really? What's his or her name?"

"Ralph. And he's spoiled rotten."

Lorenzo appeared with two bowls of beef stew and placed a bowl in front of each of them. "Bon appétit," he said.

They both thanked him and savored the meal together. They finished off the bottle of Malbec and Lorenzo brought another one. The ambience and wine had gone straight to Kenya's head. Every time the wind blew, she took in Gideon's scent. It was intoxicating. She was enjoying the evening with this man, this stranger, this friend of Zach's of whom she'd never heard. Why hadn't she ever seen him on Cape May before, at the inn? She'd have remembered him.

Gideon was easy to talk to. She could've spent the entire night just shooting the breeze with him. He felt like an old friend—like they'd known each other their entire lives. The ease of conversation reminded her of Glen, and that scared her. Actually, it unnerved her. She loved the way he touched her hand when he talked, when he really wanted to drive home a point. His laughter made her smile. She could've sat there and stared into his eyes for the rest of the night. He was handsome, charming, and everything warm and fuzzy, but she knew better. As nice as dinner was, she would never let Gideon Harper into her bubble—her sacred space—no matter how hard he tried.

Chapter Eleven

Lu

Lu had no idea what she would encounter upon her arrival, but she braced for it. She relaxed her back against the leather back seat of the black Yukon, peered out the tinted window, a pair of Tory Burch shades on her face as she squinted from the sun. She found herself counting the tall, majestic palm trees with their arching blades—one by one, she counted. Zach grabbed her hand and gave it a squeeze. She looked over at him and he offered a gentle smile, although her stomach was in deep turmoil and her head spun from thoughts of what to expect when she arrived.

"Whatever happens today, I got you." He gave her a reassuring smile.

She smiled back at him, relieved that he was there with her for emotional support.

They'd already checked into their Hyatt Regency hotel suite and dropped their bags. Now they were headed to Mercy General Hospital to meet John Samuels, where he'd been a patient for the past few weeks, and possibly meet his family. She'd anticipated this day, had played it repeatedly in her head. She had even rehearsed what she would say to him, what she'd say to her siblings when she met them. She wondered what they looked like, if they shared her skin tone, her hair, her eyes. Would they have her smile, her demeanor? Would they accept her or give her the cold shoulder? Would they like her? Would she even like them?

She knew that many of her questions would be answered in a matter of minutes as she and Zach hopped out of their Uber and he held the door for her. They made their way through the automatic doors and down the long hospital corridor with its colorful shiny floors. After passing the nurses' station, she started looking for the room number, and with each passing number she took a deep breath. There was no turning back now. She was there, standing in front of the door, which was slightly ajar. The conversations and laughter on the other side of the door contributed to her nervousness. She inhaled and then exhaled, gathered herself, calmed her nerves, arched her back, stood tall.

"You ready?" Zach squeezed her shoulders from behind.

"I'm ready."

He slowly pushed open the heavy door and stepped aside so that Lu could walk in first. Four sets of eyes all landed on her as she entered the room. The nervousness that she was sure she had left in the hallway had followed her inside. It overtook her as she first made eye contact with the man who stood near the window, wearing khakis and a navy-colored blazer—a bald head and a perfectly trimmed goatee. His hands stuffed into the pockets of his pants, he stared, though his face was friendly. He gave her a smile, and she felt the warmth of it. The tension in her shoulders relaxed a bit. Standing next to him was a beautiful woman with a golden-brown face and long black tresses that lightly brushed her shoulders. She stared but offered no smile.

The man in the hospital bed, on the other hand, gave her the widest welcoming grin. His face lit up at the sight of her.

It was the face in the photo that she kept tucked away in her chest—John Samuels, her father. Though much older than he had been in that photo, his face was still the same. He still wore his hair in a military crew cut and a thick mustache danced upon his face.

"Lualhati," he said and held his hand out to her.

She walked over to his bedside and took his hand. It was warm to the touch as he covered her hand with both of his.

"Hello." Her voice cracked. She wished she was more self-assured, but this was what she had to offer. Fragility. Diffidence. Her entire body stiffened.

"You've grown to be so beautiful."

She smiled at the compliment. She hadn't been this nervous since taking the bar exam. "Thank you."

Everyone stared. Observed. Lu wished she hadn't been the center of attention. She'd argued cases in front of an entire courtroom of people, given speeches to full auditoriums, but this was different.

"This is my son, John Jr." He motioned toward the young man standing near the window—the one who had offered her warmth.

"Pleased to meet you." John Jr. gave her a nod, one that urged her to relax.

"And that's Jess over there. She's the baby of the family."

Jess smiled this time and politely said, "Hello. It's nice to meet you."

"Glad to meet you, too," Lu said.

"My wife . . ." John motioned toward the woman seated in a dark corner of the room, who was leaned back in the chair, legs crossed. Guarded. Shielded. "That's Lillian."

She peered at Lu. Though it seemed to pain her, she managed a "Hello."

"Hi, nice to meet you." Lu gave Lillian a smile even though one wasn't reciprocated.

Just when she thought she'd survived all the introductions, she heard a woman's voice behind her. ". . . but Dad, you know it's true that only a handful of college ball players go on to play professional football anyway. I mean . . ." A young woman had emerged from the bathroom, drying her hands with a paper towel. She stopped in midsentence when she saw Lu.

Lu couldn't help staring at the woman, like a deer caught in the headlights. It was as if she was glaring into a mirror, only the reflection was living, breathing, moving, even though Lu was stiff as a board. The woman could've been her identical twin—same build, eyes, nose. This woman had her entire face, and it felt eerie.

"Milan, this is Lualhati," John told her. "Lualhati, Milan."

"Hello." Lu smiled after being completely dumbfounded for a moment.

"You didn't tell me that she was coming *today.*" Milan peered at her father, disregarding the introduction and Lu's greeting.

"I asked her to come. I wanted her to meet you . . . *all* of you. This is my daughter, your sister. And I felt that she needed to be here sooner rather than later."

"I only have one sister, and that's Jess." Milan refused to even look in Lu's direction.

"Milan!" John Jr. admonished her. "Stop being a brat."

"I'm not being a brat! It would've been nice to know that Dad had invited her here. You should be upset, too. He never asked what *we* wanted . . . if *we* wanted her here. He just made the decision for us." Milan groaned.

"It wouldn't hurt you to be polite," Lillian said.

The anxiety that Lu had felt after John's phone call that first day, and the fear she experienced when arriving at the airport and the jitters in the Uber ride over to the hospital— all felt justified now. She wanted to run away, retreat to her simplified life in New Jersey. Her life had been just fine before John had interrupted it. She didn't need this complication. She tried to will her feet to move, to turn and walk away—no, run away—but she was stuck.

"I'd like a moment with Lualhati. *Alone.* Would you all mind stepping out for a bit?"

"Of course, Dad." John Jr. grabbed Jess's arm and playfully ushered her toward the door.

Lillian gave her husband an inquisitive look, reluctantly stood. "You want *me* to leave?"

"Yes, darling, if you wouldn't mind. Just for a bit."

Lillian grabbed her Louis Vuitton purse, tossed its strap over her shoulder, and moved toward the door. "Come, Milan."

"I'm not going anywhere, Mom, and you shouldn't either." Milan folded her arms over her chest. "Dad, we have every right to be here."

"Sweetheart, I just need a minute," John pleaded.

"Let's go grab some lunch, honey," Lillian suggested. She stood there and waited for her daughter to join her.

With a huff, Milan grabbed her embellished clutch purse from the chair next to John's bed, gave Lu a scornful look, and then followed her mother out the door.

Lu raised an eyebrow and shook her head. The room had felt so small, so cluttered. It felt as if the walls had been caving in with all of them in the room. But with them gone, she could literally feel the wind leaving her body. She could breathe again.

"I'm sorry about all of that. This is very difficult for them, as you can see. Particularly Milan." John struggled to sit more upright in the bed.

Lu helped him. "Is that good?" she asked.

"Yes, thank you." He smiled at her.

"This is my fiancé, Zach," Lu finally said.

"A pleasure meeting you, Zach." John gave him a nod.

"You as well, sir." Zach had been standing in the shadows of the room like a bodyguard, keeping his distance but ready to rush in at a moment's notice. But he walked over to John's bed, shook his hand, and then told Lu, "I'm going down to the cafeteria to grab some coffee. Do you want anything?"

"No, thank you," Lu said.

"Do you need me to stay?" He attempted to whisper, but not very well.

"No. I'm fine," she said.

"Call if you change your mind," Zach said before heading toward the door.

Lu watched as he walked toward the door. He looked back at her, and she gave him a look of assurance that she was okay.

John started talking right away. "They've only recently learned about you."

"You mean you never told them that I existed?"

"Only my wife knew."

"No wonder everyone is angry at me. I feel like I just walked into a hornet's nest."

"They're not mad at you. It's me they're angry with. It's my fault for keeping you from them. I was just protecting them; at least I thought I was. They just need time. You all . . . just need time. Have a seat." John motioned toward the chair next to his bed, where Milan had obviously been seated before Lu had interrupted her entire world.

She gently slid into the chair.

"I'm going to be frank with you, Lualhati. I don't have much time to live. I'm very ill. I've done the chemotherapy, the radiation, and all the other treatments and therapies. I've exhausted all my options at this point, and now they're just keeping me comfortable. Make no mistake, I've lived a full life, but now, I've simply reached the end of my road." He turned from her, stared out the window. His eyes suddenly filled with tears. "The doctors have given me just a few months to live. Milan, John Jr., Jess . . . they don't know."

"They don't know the severity," she determined.

"They know that I've been battling this horrible disease for three years now. But they don't know that the doctors have done all they can do, that they've given me this short time frame."

"Wow. I'm so sorry." Tears threatened to fill her eyes, but she willed them away. Her heart pitter-pattered. She handed John a tissue from the box on his nightstand.

He dabbed his eyes. "That's why it was imperative that I reach out to you now; time is of the essence. I've included you in my will. I wanted you to know that. My attorneys have handled all of it."

"I don't want anything."

"How did I know you would say that?" John chuckled lightly. "You remind me so much of your mother. I know you don't want anything, but as a man and as your father, I should've been allowed to carry my weight, to do my part, but I wasn't. I'm not pointing the finger at or blaming anyone. Your mother has a lot of pride."

There was an awkward silence when he mentioned Yana. She knew that her mother hadn't done the right thing when it came to John. Lu gazed at the television, which was muted. CNN correspondents were discussing the latest political news story.

"She's stubborn," Lu admitted.

"Indeed she is," John agreed. "I know you have many questions. And while you're here, I'll do my best to answer as many of them as I can."

She decided to begin her inquisition right away. Why wait, since time was not on their side? "How did you meet my mother?"

John explained, "Many years ago, when I was a young officer in the navy, as I'm sure you know, I did a tour of duty in the Philippines. In Manila. There, I met this . . . beautiful Filipino woman who I fell deeply in love with—your mother. I wanted to be with her, but times were complicated. *My life* was complicated. Before I was set to deploy back to the United States, I learned that Yana was pregnant, and I knew I couldn't leave her there. Because she was living in poverty and such deplorable living conditions, I thought that bringing her to the US would at least offer her and the child, *my child*, a better life."

"If you were so in love with her, why didn't you marry her? Why did you take her away from her home only to abandon her?" Lu asked.

"I couldn't marry her." He looked away, stroked his goatee, and then dropped his head, "because I was already married, *and* with a toddler child."

It all made sense to Lu at that moment—the reason Milan had so defiantly refused to leave the room. The reason the woman—Lillian—had been so unfriendly. Lu was a walking, living, breathing reminder to them of John's betrayal. Hearing John admit that he had been married when he met her mother caused Lu great pain. Her chest hurt. She held on to it, hoping that the pain would stop, but it was persistent. She wanted to storm out of the room and never return, but she hadn't come all this way for nothing. She came for answers, and she wanted them.

"Did my mother know that you were married?"

"Yes." He said it emphatically.

It was that response that caused Lu the most pain. Yana had known, yet she still pursued a relationship with him, and moreover had followed him to the States anyway.

"She was able to get a work visa and followed me to California. I rented her an apartment, provided financial support for her. But the arrangement became too difficult for her."

"The arrangement?"

"I'm not proud of it. My wife knew about Yana and you."

"Why did it become difficult?"

"Because Yana wanted more. Much more than I was able to offer. And Lillian gave me an ultimatum. She was going to leave me, and I had no intentions of losing my family. So, when Yana told me that she had a relative in New Jersey and preferred to live there, I had to let her go. I gave her the money that she needed to get there, to start her new life."

"So, just like that, you sent her away—sent *us* away?"

"I didn't send her or *you* away. She insisted upon leaving. She didn't want to be in the same city, knowing that my family was here, in California. We kept in touch for the first two years of your life. When I indicated that I wanted to fly to New Jersey to see you, she thought it best that I didn't. She said it would only confuse you. I supported her financially for a few more years, and then I lost contact with her altogether."

"And so you just went on with your life?"

"I've made mistakes, Lualhati, no doubt about it. I'm not proud of them and I can't change the past, but I'd like to try to create a future for you and your brother and sisters. I don't have much time, but all of you still do . . . you have time to build relationships and get to know one another. To not let my past mistakes determine your futures. You are siblings, whether you like it or not. Even if you don't build relationships with one another, I wanted to make the introductions. I wanted you to know the truth."

Lu could no longer contain the tears as they streamed down her face and she stood up. She needed some air, needed to breathe, to digest all that she'd learned in just a few hours of arriving in Sacramento. Even though she had so many more questions, she'd had enough for one day.

"I'm leaving."

"Are you leaving California?"

"I don't know yet. I just need to absorb all of this."

"I know it's a lot to take in, but please don't leave the city just yet. Please come back tomorrow, so that we can talk again. I just want you in my presence. It feels good having you here."

She nodded a yes, gathered herself, and headed out the door with not so much as a goodbye. She didn't know if she would return the next day, didn't know if she could. Her instincts were to hightail it to the airport and get on the first plane leaving for New Jersey in the morning, but at the same time it also felt good to her, too, being in John's presence, though she didn't want to admit it even to herself.

She needed to find Zach. She was grateful that he had accompanied her on the trip because she would need his support more than she thought. There was so much to digest. Her usually uncomplicated life had suddenly become so complicated, and she didn't like it one bit.

Chapter Twelve

Natalia

Natalia had left at least five voice messages and texted numerous times. She paced the floor. She was going out of her mind because he wasn't answering, and worse, not replying. She managed to pull herself out of bed and made it to the winery. Though physically Natalia was there, mentally and emotionally speaking, she really wasn't there at all. Her mind was thousands of miles away, in Sicily. The day was longer than usual, but she was grateful to be home—in her safe space now.

She opened the bottle of Australian Pinot Grigio that she had brought home from the winery and poured herself a glass. She pulled a filet of salmon from the freezer and dropped it into a bowl of hot water to thaw. Next, she turned on Nic's expensive stereo system and found some music. Alina Baraz's "Maybe" rang out from the speakers. It was a song that reminded her of what she was going through with Nic. She'd worn that entire album out when they first met.

She pulled up her hair into a ponytail on her head and then headed upstairs, the glass of wine in her hand. She placed the glass on her nightstand and began undressing as she walked into the bathroom to start the shower. She lit each of the jasmine candles that surrounded her garden tub and then stepped into the shower. Emotionally, she was drained, and hoped the water would wash away all the hurt, pain, and fear that she was feeling. Natalia wanted to cry, but forced herself not to. She was tired of crying—exhausted even.

Her phone rang and she quickly opened the glass shower door. She reached for it. Nic's face flashed across the screen, a wide grin on his face. She'd taken that photo of him at Lu's holiday party two years before. He'd worn a midnight blue tuxedo with a black bow tie to match its peak lapel. He'd been growing a beard for a few weeks before that. She recalled just how distinguished it looked, with just the right amount of gray in it.

She answered, "Hello."

"You've been calling?" he asked.

It felt good to hear his voice. It had been days since they last spoke.

"Yes."

"I was in the mountains today—Parco delle Madonie. I had trouble with my phone, making calls and receiving them. Is everything okay?"

"Yes, I just needed to talk to you."

"Well, talk, I'm listening."

She cut to the chase. No need beating around the bush, because there were no guarantees that she would reach him again. "I found your box. Your letters."

"What box? What letters?"

"The steel gray box in our closet, the one with the twenty-two letters handwritten by your little girlfriend, Angelina. That's what box."

She'd promised herself that she wouldn't become emotional when she spoke with him about the letters. She wanted him to take her seriously. She didn't want to be accusatory either, but her anger had gotten the better of her.

"What, are you rummaging through my things now?"

"I wasn't rummaging through your things." Her voice raised an octave. She was slowly losing her cool. "I found the key in the pocket of your robe and wanted to know what it unlocked."

"Well, obviously you found what you were looking for."

"So, what do you have to say for yourself? Do you share her sentiments? All those things she talked about in her letters. Do you love her like she so obviously loves you?"

"I'm not having this conversation right now."

"Well, I want to have this conversation right now, Nicolai!"

"Not now. My daughter is here with me now."

"Is Angelina also with you right now?"

"I'm not doing this," his voice raised.

"I want answers! Do you love her like she loves you?"

"I'm hanging up the phone."

"Don't you hang up on me."

"I'm hanging up, Natalia. I'm not doing this with you right now."

"Don't you hang . . ."

The phone went dead. He was gone. With no explanation, he was gone. She collapsed on the shower floor. Her soaking-wet bottom hit the marble; it was cold against her skin. As much as she'd wanted to hold it together, she couldn't any longer. The tears flowed.

Chapter Thirteen

Kenya

They both stumbled up the wooden stairs as Gideon held tightly onto Kenya's waist, and she was grateful because she needed him to hold her up. Climbing the stairs seemed like a massive undertaking and seemed to take forever, but they finally made it to the top. He began singing a song out of nowhere, one that she'd never heard before—off-key. She giggled and shushed him when they walked past Phoebe's room. The last thing she wanted to do was interrupt her writing or awaken her if she'd been asleep. Gideon delivered Kenya to the door of her room. She stuck the gold key in the lock, opened the door, and turned to face him.

"Good night," she said.

"You wouldn't want me to come tuck you in . . . would you?" he whispered with a slur.

She grinned like a schoolgirl. "Not a chance." Though her mouth was saying no, she was secretly wishing he would press the issue.

He leaned in, his nose almost touching hers. She could feel his breath on her face. She thought he might kiss her, and she wasn't sure about how she would react if he did. Would she turn away or would she welcome it, kiss back? Was a kiss too soon? After all, she'd only known the man a few hours. He'd only waltzed into Lu's Seaside Inn and into her life just after two o'clock in the afternoon. No matter how much she reasoned, she had to admit she wanted him to kiss her, even if it was just a peck on the lips.

"Good night, beautiful woman," he whispered into her ear.

She simply smiled and watched as he stumbled his way to the Cherry Blossom suite just down the hall. He stood in front of the door, searched for his key in the pocket of his sweats and, once found, he held it in the air so she could see. It took him a few minutes to get the key to work inside the lock, but once he did, he gave her a wink before going inside. She giggled, shook her head, and retreated inside her room.

She'd chosen the Harlem room, the one that proudly displayed paintings of a few Harlem Renaissance musicians— Billie Holliday, Louis Armstrong, and Duke Ellington. A portrait of Langston Hughes hung above the antique bed frame. The room had a jazzy feel with its bright colors. An old jukebox played music when you dropped coins into it. Kenya dropped a coin into it and selected Duke Ellington's and John Coltrane's "In a Sentimental Mood." She turned the volume down low, so as not to disturb anyone, wrapped her arms around her own waist and danced around the room, and reminisced about her evening with *the* Gideon Harper. She hadn't expected to enjoy herself so much. With him, she was able to just be herself, let her hair down, and she took note of how good that felt. With the men she chitchatted with on those dreadful dating sites, she had to put on a persona. But not with Gideon. She hadn't even worn her best clothing that day, hadn't made up her face, but he didn't care.

She stayed on the veranda with him much longer than she'd

intended and drank too much. Every time she had tried to tear herself away, they would start a new conversation and laugh about something else. He was certainly charming. She could've stayed out there for the entire night, but after they'd finished off the third bottle of wine and two shots of whiskey— *each*—she knew she needed to call it a night.

She shut the blind on the window that overlooked Lu's flower garden and began to undress. Her phone rang. It was Lu. Kenya contemplated whether she should answer. The last thing she wanted was for Lu to know that she had been drinking—*a lot*—and, worse, drinking with a guest. After all, she had entrusted her to run the inn, not be drunk out of her mind. She decided to let the call roll into her voicemail. She would return Lu's call in the morning.

After a few moments, Kenya listened to Lu's voicemail, placed it on speakerphone as she started the shower.

"Hi honey. I tried calling you earlier, but you didn't an-swer. Lorenzo told me that you were having dinner on the ve-randa with Gideon. I'm so glad you two got to meet. After all, he is Zach's best man and you're my maid of honor. I think it's important for you to get to know each other, up close and personal. He's a nice guy, huh?" Lu rambled on. "You won't believe the kind of day I had. I met John Samuels *and* his daughter from hell. She was so rude and just a total . . . never mind. Enough about her. Anyway, I had a nice conversa-tion with John about my mother, and let's just say I need to have a long chat with Yana the next time I see her. . . ."

Kenya stepped into the shower as Lu continued to ramble on about John Samuels and her visit. Soon, she closed her eyes as the water cascaded over her. Her mind drifted to Gideon. She thought about his smile, his voice, the way his eyes danced when he talked about the things he loved. She re-played their conversation in her head, laughed about the things that they'd laughed about earlier. After she'd washed all her intimate parts and stepped out of the shower, she dried off and put on a pair of silk pajamas. She collapsed onto the queen-sized bed, slid beneath the silk sheets as her head sunk into the softness of the pillow. She began to drift off—*slowly.*

As the sunshine crept across her nose in the morning, she opened her eyes and woke up in a panic. Kenya sat straight up in bed and reached for her phone to check the time. It was already eight o'clock. She'd wanted to be up by six thirty by the time the birds began chirping and Max had started breakfast. As the smell of Applewood smoked bacon drifted through the air, she knew she'd already missed that deadline. Plus, she wanted to return Lu's call before she'd called a second time. She'd overslept. After she pulled herself out of bed and rushed into the bathroom to wash her face, she dialed Lu's number.

"Good morning." Lu's voice was raspy, like her sleep had been interrupte

"Good morning yourself. Sorry to wake you," Kenya said, remembering that there was a three-hour time difference between the east and west coast.

"No worries. I'm still on east coast time anyway."

"Are you feeling better?" Kenya asked.

"Somewhat," Lu said. "You must have turned in early last night. How are things at the inn?"

"All is well. Both Phoebe and Gideon checked in yesterday."

"I know. And I heard you had dinner with Gideon. How was that?"

"It was . . . okay. He's nice."

"He's handsome, too, huh? *Huh?*"

"He's . . . attractive, yes."

"Zach and I both had forgotten that he was coming. So, I'm glad you took care of him."

"Of course."

"I'm really happy that you had dinner with him, too, made him feel welcome since we're not there."

"I did." Kenya changed the subject and plopped down on the bed. "So . . . you met the offspring yesterday."

"The offspring." Lu laughed at Kenya. "Two of them were nice. The oldest one, Milan—not so much. She was horrible. She's completely a daddy's girl and my presence really bothered her."

"Typical daddy's girl. Afraid that you might take her place."

"She doesn't have anything to worry about. I could never take her place. I don't even know John that well. John Jr. was the only friendly one."

"I'm sorry the introductions didn't go as well as expected, honey."

"I had no expectations, but I was certainly prepared. I guess I just wanted them to like me, accept me. I did get to speak with John alone, though. I got the chance to ask my questions. Some of them, anyway. I got some answers."

"Well, you should get them *all* answered. That's why you went there, right?"

"Yes. It's why I'm here."

"I know this is tough for you, to not be in control this time, Lu. This situation is making you feel very vulnerable and that's not a comfortable place for you. And on top of it, you can't be here at the inn to handle things. Your normal world has been disrupted," Kenya said. "But I assure you, everything is fine here. You have no worries. Your focus should be on why you're there, to connect with your father and find your answers."

"I must admit you're right, my friend. I'm out of my comfort zone. Though I'm not worried about the inn at all. I knew you would handle things. But I don't know how much longer I can take being here."

"You'll be fine. I'm sure of it. You should stay and get your questions answered. You might not get another chance if John is as sick as you say he is."

"They've given him a few months to live."

"Wow." The news saddened Kenya.

"You're right about everything. And thank you."

"Put your big girl panties on and get back over to that hospital. You have every right to be there." Kenya wished she could be there with Lu, to hold her hand and walk her through this process. But she knew that her friend was strong and capable. Plus, Zach was there with her. She'd be fine.

"I have my big girl panties on."

"Well, good. I have to go. I think Marissa just arrived. Plus, I want to check out Max's award-winning French toast."

"Ha, ha! Go eat the French toast and write a review about it while you're at it," Lu quipped. "Have a wonderful day, my friend, and we'll talk soon."

She was gone, and Kenya sat there on her comfortable bed for another moment. Reluctantly, she got up and quickly dressed.

Max was preparing breakfast as he did every morning. He smiled when Kenya stepped into the kitchen.

"Good morning." He held a glass pitcher of orange juice in his hand. "Would you like some breakfast?"

"Um, sure," Kenya said. "I don't know that the other guests will be down, though."

"I took Miss Taylor some coffee and toast up this morning."

"Maybe we should wake the other guest, Mr. Harper. See if he wants breakfast."

Max grabbed a crystal glass from the shelf, poured orange juice into it, and handed it to Kenya. "Mr. Harper has already eaten and now he's gone for a run."

"Oh, I see."

"So, where will you be dining this morning?"

"Um. I guess I'll eat in the dining room. It looks a bit chilly outside."

"Great. Have a seat and I'll make you a plate."

"Thanks, Max."

After enjoying Max's French toast, bacon, and scrambled eggs in the dining room, Kenya stepped outside. She needed to head home for a bit, let Ralph out and feed him. She made her way up the stretch of the beach to her home and opened the front door. Ralph met her at the door, panting. It smelled stuffy inside since she hadn't been there to open the windows as she did every morning to allow a breeze to flow through her space.

"Hey, Mama's sweet boy, did you miss me?" She massaged Ralph's head, something he thoroughly enjoyed, and let him out the front door.

While he was outside handling his business, she went into the kitchen and grabbed a bottle of water from her stainless-steel refrigerator. She pulled open the kitchen curtains and admired her view of the ocean. She opened a can of dog food with the electric can opener, replenished the food in one of Ralph's pans, and poured water into the other one. When she went back to the front door to check on him, it seemed he'd found a new friend. Gideon leaned down and stroked his golden mane. Kenya watched them both for a moment.

"I see you've met my baby," she said.

Gideon looked up and saw her standing there, "Who Ralph? Yeah, we're old friends now."

She couldn't help thinking how quickly Gideon had gotten under her skin.

"Well, your old friend needs to come inside and eat his breakfast," Kenya said. She called to Ralph, "Come on, boy."

Ralph was obedient and rushed toward her. He stopped just long enough for her to rub his head and then he went inside. Kenya stepped outside, shutting the front door behind her.

"You were up early this morning."

"I run every morning. At least two miles," he explained. "Maybe you can join me sometime."

"Maybe."

"How about tomorrow morning at seven?"

"Ooh, that's early."

"It's the best time for a run, really. You in?"

"You drive a hard bargain," Kenya was a runner in her younger days. She'd become lazy over the years, though, claiming that she was going to get back to a regular exercise regimen, though she never had time.

"It's exhilarating, really."

Running *was* exhilarating. And she was good at it. "Okay, why not?"

Gideon started to lightly jog, to finish his run. "Dinner again. This time on the beach."

It wasn't a question; it was a statement. Who did he think he was, anyway, making plans for her all willy-nilly? However, a repeat of last night's dinner sounded delightful to Kenya. She didn't want to seem too eager, though.

"I don't know, I . . ."

"We had too much fun last night. You can't say no."

"I can't?"

"No, you can't. You know that Lorenzo is probably cooking something fabulous again. Can't let good food go to waste. Remember the children . . ."

"Oh right, the starving ones. Yeah, we can't let that happen." Kenya giggled. "Yes, I will join you for dinner on the beach."

"Save the children," he yelled before his light jog turned into a brisk run back toward Lu's inn.

She watched as he disappeared into the morning sunshine. She was suddenly giddy with anticipation. Could hardly wait to see what the evening's dinner would bring.

Chapter Fourteen

Lu

Lu peeked inside of John Samuels's door, a Starbucks cup in one hand and a copy of the *Sacramento Bee* in the other. She tapped lightly, quietly walked in and tiptoed across the buffed tile floors. He was sleeping, so she took a seat in the corner of the room next to the window. She didn't want to wake him. She opened the newspaper and tried to read the latest local news, but ominous thoughts were busy swarming in the back of her mind. Her palms were sweaty. She had a thousand questions dancing in her head—the same ones that had danced all night and kept her from sleeping. She breathed in through her nose and out through her mouth a few times.

"Good morning." He startled her, giving her a smile when he awakened.

"Good morning," she said.

"You're up bright and early," he asserted.

"I'm sorry, I didn't mean to wake you."

"You didn't. Who can sleep when the nurses are in here ever hour on the hour poking and prodding? Taking my vitals." He maneuvered his body in the bed and raised himself up a bit. "What are you drinking?"

"Starbucks."

"I know it's from Starbucks, but what is it?"

"It's an almond milk honey flat white."

"Wow. That must be some of this new age stuff. Whatever happened to a simple caramel macchiato? That was always my favorite. Now I'm drinking these." He chuckled and held a bottle of Ensure protein drink in the air.

She held her cup in the air. "Cheers."

"Cheers," he said. "Where's Zach this morning?"

"He stayed back at the hotel. He wanted to take advantage of their state-of-the-art weight room. He's a gym rat."

"I see." John grabbed the remote control from the side of his bed, changed the channel to the morning news, but left the television muted. "Are you a gym rat, too?"

"I try to stay fit, do cardio, and a little yoga here and there, but it's nothing compared to his routine. He runs three miles every morning, hits the weights, eats a healthy nonmeat diet. He's fit."

"That's impressive. I was fit in my younger days, too, long after the military. It was nothing to run several miles a day. But then I just got old."

"You're not *that* old." Her body felt less tense. She was more at ease than she was the day before. Her shoulders were relaxed and her chest didn't hurt quite as much.

"Thanks, but I'm not as young as I used to be." John chuckled and then was silent for a few moments before saying, "You have more questions, I presume."

"Lots more."

"Lots more," he repeated. "Well, let's get to it. What is it that you want to know?"

"My mother told me that she met you at the nightclub where she worked."

"Yes. I would go there every single day, just to see her. We were all stationed in Manila. Some of the guys were only there for a short time. I spent several months there." He looked at the television and then back at Lu. "I know that people don't really believe in love at first sight, but I loved her the moment I first saw her. She was beautiful. Feisty, too."

"She is *feisty*."

"She doesn't take anything off anyone. That's what I loved about her. The sailors would come . . . would pay her to entertain them. She would give them fits."

"She was a waitress, right?"

"Of sorts."

"What do you mean, *of sorts?*" Lu was on the edge of her seat now. Wanted to know what it was he was saying but not saying.

"You don't know, do you?" he asked.

"Know what?"

John became silent. He glanced at the television again.

"Oh, don't get quiet on me now." Lu stood, walked to the center of the room. "What do you mean, she was a waitress *of sorts?*

"It was no secret . . . and not uncommon for . . ." He was silent again.

"For what?" Lu was panicky now, wringing her hands together. She was afraid of what it was he was trying to say but needed to hear it.

"Sailors would pay Yana for her services. There was an upstairs at the nightclub, and Yana would take sailors up there and . . . you know . . ."

"Are you saying that my mother was a whore?"

"I would never call her that. I prefer to say she was a lady of the night. Life was tough in Manila, Lualhati. You must understand, there was a lot of poverty there. People were destitute." He shrugged, as if what he was saying was normal. "Many Filipino women engaged in prostitution to earn a higher wage. Higher than they would performing some of the other domestic services. They had to do what they had to do."

"She never told me that." Lu's eyebrows raised; her posture stiffened. She paced.

John's revelation took her by surprise, hit her like a freight train and made her head spin. She was grateful that Zach hadn't been there to hear it because she needed to process it on her own before revealing it to anyone else. She was disgusted by what she'd just heard and suddenly felt ill.

"You shouldn't judge her too harshly. It was something that she had to do to survive," John said. "After I fell in love with Yana, I told her that she didn't need to do it any longer. I promised to take care of her, to take her away from all of it."

"But you were married." Trying to make sense of this love triangle between John Samuels, his wife, and her mother was exhausting.

"I was indeed married. Not proud of being unfaithful to my wife. Things were complicated back then. It's not pretty, but it's the truth. Isn't that what you wanted—*the truth*?"

"Yes." She said it almost in a whisper. She cleared her throat, lowered her head, and then raised it to look at him. "Why didn't you ever come for me?"

In that moment she was two again, a child.

"I reached out to Yana over the years, wrote letters. Yana wasn't having any of it."

"So, you just went on with your life as if I didn't exist."

"No, that's not true. There hasn't been a day in my life that I haven't thought of you. I wanted to be a part of your life as a child and after you grew up, but she was determined not to let me in. And when you went to college, I even attempted to pay your tuition once, which your mother returned. She warned me to never reach out again, said she didn't need me complicating your life."

Lu plopped back down into the chair and peered out the window. She was ready to be back in New Jersey. She needed to see Yana, to confront her about all that she'd learned from John. If the things that he claimed were true, then her entire life was a lie.

"Good morning, Daddy dear." Milan walked into the room, wearing a pastel blue pantsuit and heels. "I brought Krispy Kreme doughnuts. Shhh! Don't tell the nurses."

The last thing Lu needed was to see Milan. The sound of her voice was annoying enough. She needed to finish her conversation with John and didn't need another temper tantrum from his spoiled daughter.

"Good morning, sweetheart," John greeted his eldest daughter with a smile.

Milan was startled when she realized that Lu was in the corner of the room. "I didn't know you had company."

Lu rose to her feet. "I was just leaving."

"Good," Milan mumbled under her breath. "This city really isn't big enough for the both of us."

"Milan!" John exclaimed.

"Daddy, I'm so over this whole bastard child thing."

"Who are you calling a bastard child?" Lu asked.

She crossed her arms over her chest and gave Lu a wicked grin. "Well, if the shoe fits."

"Milan, that's enough!"

Milan raised her hands as if to surrender.

"I'm leaving. I'm going back to Jersey today," said Lu.

"Lualhati, I wish you wouldn't. I wish you would stay," John pleaded. "Milan, can you give us a minute please."

"Seriously, Daddy? You're asking me to leave *again*?"

"Just for a few moments, please."

"You're choosing her over me . . . and . . ."

"I'm not choosing anyone. You're both my daughters."

In a huff, Milan slammed down the box of doughnuts onto her father's tray and stormed out of the room.

"She's a daddy's girl. I'm afraid I'm responsible for her behavior. I've spoiled her."

"Shameful." Lu no longer cared about being polite. Her emotions were all over the place and she couldn't seem to get them under control.

"I'm grateful that you accepted my invitation. And I'm glad I got to meet you in person."

"I must say, the visit *was* productive. I learned a lot more than I expected. Now I need to process it all—go have a chat with my mother." Lu tossed her empty Starbucks cup into the trash can and placed the newspaper underneath her arm. "She has some explaining to do."

"I pray that I see you again, Lualhati. But if I don't, please take care of yourself."

"I'm praying for you as well." Lu walked toward the door. She looked back at John Samuels. "Take care of yourself. Goodbye."

Once in the hallway, she was grateful that there was no sign of Milan. She might've given her a piece of her mind, but she was nowhere in sight. Instead, John Jr. was making long strides in her direction. She wasn't in the mood for him either.

He smiled. "Good morning. *Lualhati,* is it?"

"It's just Lu."

"Where are you off to in such a hurry?" he asked.

"Jersey. I'm going home."

"Today?"

"Yes."

"Why so soon? I thought you were staying a few more days."

Lu shrugged. "Changed my mind."

"Don't let my sister run you away. I know she can be a handful," John Jr. said. "I was really hoping to spend some time with you. Maybe have dinner later . . . with you and your fiancé."

Lu exhaled. Her emotions were high, and suddenly she had her guard up. She wasn't in the mood for any shenanigans. "I don't know."

John Jr. reached into the inside pocket of his blazer. "Well, think about it. I really hope you change your mind. Here's my card in case you do. I'd love to just sit and talk and get to know you."

Lu reached for his business card, took a glance at it. He owned a software company.

"*If* I change my mind, I'll give you a call."

"There's a quaint little restaurant not far from your hotel. It's beautiful, nice ambience, great Italian food. They have a decent patio, live music. I'll be there at six today. No pressure if you can't make it. I'm going there for drinks anyway."

"Okay." Lu gave him a half-smile.

"Hope to see you later."

Lu let her guard down a bit and stuffed the card into the back pocket of her jeans. Then she headed toward the elevators.

Outside, she hopped into an Uber for the short ride to their downtown hotel. She took the elevator up to their suite and found Zach relaxing on the bed.

"Done working out already?" she asked.

"Yes, and had breakfast, too. I figured you'd be there for a while."

Lu exhaled, then removed her jacket.

What's wrong, sweetheart?" Zach asked.

"This trip is nothing like I expected. The things that I'm uncovering about Yana . . . just incredible."

Lu lay across the bed on her stomach alongside Zach. He massaged her shoulders.

"Whatever happened between the two of them, it was a long time ago, babe."

"Still very shocking. I don't know who Yana is anymore," Lu exclaimed.

"Come on, it can't be that bad. She's your mother."

"She's done some things that make me ashamed." Lu replayed John's words in her head: *I prefer to call her a lady of the night.*

"Really?" Zach stopped massaging for a moment, then was right back at it.

"Yes, *really.*"

"Well, honey, I think before you pass judgment, you should just talk to her."

"Oh, I will." She flipped over onto her back. "And that Milan person is just . . . dreadful."

"She was there?" Zach sighed.

"Called me a bastard!"

Zach laughed. "What? You're kidding, right?"

"It's not funny, and yes, she did." Lu couldn't help but laugh, too, at Milan's antics, "What is she, a kindergartener?"

"She's definitely immature, or crazy."

"Or both." Lu looked up at Zach, who was resting on his elbow and looking down at her. "There was one silver lining this morning. John Jr. invited us—me and you—to dinner tonight. That is, if I'm still within the city limits. I left there thinking I might catch the next flight back to New Jersey today."

"That was thoughtful of him, to invite us to dinner."

"It was."

"We should go." Zach leaned down and kissed Lu's lips, then her nose and her forehead.

"You think?"

"I do. I think it's nice that he extended the invitation. Looks like he's trying, at least."

"Yes, I agree." Lu breathed in deeply. "Okay, we should go."

"Good."

"What the hell is going on in my life?" she asked rhetorically.

"You're growing up, kid."

Lu closed her eyes for a moment. She didn't know who the heck she was anymore, nor did she know who Yana was either.

She chose a red backless after-five dress, the one that Zach had brought her from his medical conference in Honduras. She slipped a pair of leather strappy, sexy heels onto her feet. She couldn't remember the last time she'd worn heels so high; she'd traded them for flip-flops long ago, when she moved to Cape May. She pulled her curly hair up and off her shoulders and colored her lips with a candy-apple red lipstick.

"Whoa! You look amazing." Zack fastened the clasp on the white gold necklace on her neck.

"Thank you. And you look very handsome yourself, Doctor."

He wore a pair of tan slacks, a white crewneck shirt, and a navy blazer.

"I spoke with Gideon this morning. It seems he and Kenya are having dinner together again tonight," he told her.

"Interesting." Lu thought for a moment. "She didn't mention it when we talked this morning. You don't think . . ."

"They're becoming awfully cozy."

"She's not interested in becoming cozy with anyone right

now. She just wants . . ." Lu thought about Kenya's *woo-ha* comment and chuckled.

"Wait a minute, what's that laugh? She just wants what?"

"Nothing." Lu grabbed her clutch purse from the night-stand. "You ready?"

"I am. Let's go."

John Jr. was right. The restaurant *was* quite beautiful, with a nice ambience, and the patio was open and breezy. He had snagged a table with one of the best views. A live band sere-naded patrons with their horns, drums, and vocals. She spot-ted his raised hand.

"I'm glad you came." John Jr. stood to greet them.

"This place is just as you described it. Very beautiful." Lu looked around, taking it all in.

"I like it. I hang out here quite a bit. The owner is a good friend." John Jr. had their father's face, eyes, smile. "What are you drinking?"

"I'll have a Chardonnay."

"Chardonnay? Oh, come on. This is a special occasion."

"What is it that you're drinking?" Lu pointed at his glass.

"Vodka tonic."

"Well, I'll have one, too," Lu decided. She'd never been a heavy drinker. Wine had always been her drink of choice, ex-cept on rare occasions. But she was on vacation and John Jr. insisted, so she took a chance.

He motioned to the server, and the young woman made her way over to the table.

"What can I get for you?"

"She's having a vodka tonic. And make it really special, like you did this one." He gave her a wink. "And what about you, Zach?"

"I'll have a cognac on the rocks," Zach told the server.

"And Sandy, we'll start with some bruschetta for the table, and maybe some green olives."

"Great. I'll get that ordered for you, John."

"Thanks," he said and then turned to Lu. "I'm glad to see that you didn't run away. You're still here."

"I bet Milan won't be happy about that."

"Who cares what Milan thinks? I love my sister, but she's a self-absorbed brat. Always has been. You can thank my dad for that. I'm actually very happy that you're here."

"Thank you for saying that."

Lu wondered which details of his parents' relationship John Jr. knew about. Did he know that her mother had been John's mistress, that she'd been a prostitute, that his father had fallen in love with her? Did he know that her mother, Yana, was a home-wrecker?

"I don't care what went on between our parents years ago. Doesn't have a thing to do with us. And it doesn't change that you're our sister. You didn't ask to be here."

His words touched her heart. She'd never been called anyone's sister before, except maybe Kenya and Natalia. They called each other *sisters* from time to time. But she'd never been anyone's real, blood sister before now. It felt good.

Sandy returned with their drinks.

"Let's have a toast." John Jr. held his glass in the air. "To my sister, the badass attorney-turned-innkeeper. My dad told me that you traded your law career to run an inn."

"I did."

"I think that's so cool. Cheers."

"Hear, hear." Lu giggled. She liked him.

She spent the evening learning about John Jr.'s life. He'd almost gotten married a few years ago but got cold feet and called the wedding off. He had no children *that he knew of.* She told him about her life, her friends, the inn, and about her and Zach's impending wedding of the summer.

"You think it would be cool if I came to visit you in New Jersey? Maybe for the wedding, if you have room for another guest," he asked.

She inhaled deeply. A lump formed in her throat, but she managed to say, "I'd like that."

John Jr. nodded a yes and smiled. "Good."

And just like that, she had a brother.

Chapter Fifteen

Kenya

Kenya watched as the flames from the bonfire danced in the wind. The fire crackled against the wood, the waves on the ocean rippled, and the sun played peekaboo in the sky before finally descending upon the water. With every shift of the wind, she caught a whiff of the woodsy, lemony scent of Gideon's cologne. His long-sleeved linen shirt was unbuttoned just enough to give Kenya a subtle view of his sculpted chest. No hair, just smooth mountains of chocolate skin.

"Thank you for agreeing to have dinner with me." His smile was like sunshine.

On any given evening she'd have felt exhausted from her commute and would want nothing more than to relax on her reupholstered sofa, with the back door opened to allow a cool breeze to float through, Ralph at her feet, the remote control in her hand. Containers filled with takeout from one of her favorite restaurants strewn about on the coffee table. She'd be well into one of her strange dreams before the moon appeared in the sky.

Today she didn't feel exhausted at all. She felt exhilarated. Partly because she was on vacation and didn't have to make that commute. The other reason being that she was anxious to have dinner with Gideon *again*. She noticed how he'd disappeared from the inn early in the morning and hadn't returned until late that evening.

"This is very nice, this whole set up you got going on here." Though she tried to hide it, Kenya's heart was full as she observed the meticulous details of Gideon's romantic dinner—candles burning as the crisp white tablecloth blew in the wind, a bouquet of freshly plucked purple irises in a vase at the center of the table. The portable speaker was lodged into the sand, with contemporary jazz playing softly. A bottle of aged Chianti rested in an ice bucket on the table.

Gideon grabbed a glass and poured wine into it, then handed it to Kenya. He smiled. She took it, sipped while watching him, trying to figure out why he was smiling. He poured himself a glass.

"So, you're impressed." It wasn't a question. More of an acknowledgment.

"I must admit, I am." She wouldn't tell him just how impressed she was, holding back just a little bit.

The tail of her canary-yellow sundress blew as she pulled her denim jacket a little tighter. It was chilly in the wake of the sunset, but she didn't notice the chill much. She only noticed the warmth in Gideon's eyes and the heat in his smile. That smile did things to her heart, made it beat a little faster than usual, which caused her a bit of anxiety. What was happening to her?

"I'll take nice. You're having trouble giving me my props, but it's okay." He chuckled, motioning toward her glass. "Drink up."

"We're not getting drunk again, that's for sure." She stuck her finger into the air.

"You didn't enjoy getting drunk with me last night?" His eyes flirted when he talked. *That could be troublesome*, she thought, a coy grin on his face.

"I didn't enjoy being out of control. I like to be always completely aware."

"That's the attorney in you. Always needing to be in control."

"I didn't say I needed to be in control, I said *aware*."

"I read between the lines."

"And what is it that *you* need to be, Doctor?" she asked.

"I don't need anything; I'm just enjoying this beautiful moonlit night and the beautiful woman sitting across from me, wearing the hell out of that yellow dress. You look amazing tonight."

"Don't do that," Kenya warned.

"Don't do what?"

"That whole *beautiful woman* thing."

"It's the truth."

Kenya huffed while sipping her wine. "Okay."

"Tell me you're not one of those bitter women who've been hurt by someone and now you can't even accept a compliment." Gideon peered at her. "Who hurt you?"

"No one hurt me."

"Did he cheat on you? Break your heart?"

"He didn't cheat or break my heart. He died."

Gideon sighed, hung his head for a moment. "You've not been in a relationship since your husband's death. I'm sorry."

"No. I've been happily single ever since." Kenya raised her glass in the air. "And relax. I'm okay. I've gone through my grief process. I'm over it."

"I've heard that grief doesn't really go away; it just evolves into other things. But I don't know. I've never lost anyone close."

"Be thankful."

"I am." He sipped his wine. "But if you ever need to talk or vent about it, I'm here."

"I'm okay, but thank you."

"I mean it. I'm a great listener."

"Good to know." She wished he would let it be already.

"I've not lost anyone to death, but I've lost people in other ways. My wife. My family. Divorce is just as painful as death."

"I imagine so."

"Do you think that you could ever love again?"

"Doubtful."

"We'll see." He mumbled it, but she heard him.

"What?"

"Nothing."

Lorenzo approached with dinner—two thick pieces of grilled mahi-mahi resting atop a bed of wild rice and roasted asparagus.

"Here we are," Lorenzo said. "If you need anything else, let me know. Otherwise, I'll just disappear and give you two some privacy."

"Thanks bro." Gideon gave Lorenzo a fist bump.

"Enjoy." Lorenzo smiled and then headed back toward the inn.

"So, I see this was a team effort?"

"He cooked. I did the rest."

"I see." Kenya looked around at *all the rest*. Some effort had certainly gone into making an impression.

Kenya allowed the music to tease her senses, while sipping wine, eating fresh fish, and having a conversation with a handsome man.

"What's your all-time favorite song from the eighties?" he asked out of the blue.

"The eighties?"

"Yeah, that's our era."

"Yeah, I guess so." Kenya thought for a moment, then smiled. "Don't laugh, but I liked rap."

"Okay. Like whom?"

"Eric B and Rakim's 'Microphone Fiend.' " She said it with a little oomph in her voice.

Gideon pressed some keys on his tablet. "You mean this?" The familiar tune floated through the air.

"Ohhh! That's it." Kenya moved her body from side to side as the rap song teased her senses.

Gideon stopped the song midway. ". . . and what about this one?" He grinned as Kurtis Blow's 'The Breaks' played on the speaker, filled the atmosphere.

"Wait a minute! Wait a minute! I got one. What about LL Cool J's 'Rock the Bells'?"

Gideon played the song, and together they rapped all the lyrics.

"You might know a little something about old school rap," he said after the song ended.

"I'm from Brooklyn. Those are New York artists."

"Indeed they are." He smiled at her, placed his hands underneath his chin, and observed her for a moment.

"What?" she asked. He was making her nervous. She was shivering, and not necessarily from the chill.

"Nothing." Gideon slowed the music down and a familiar tune swept across the sky. "What about this?"

Gideon stood and held his hand out for Kenya to stand also. Donell Jones sang "U Know What's Up" as the candle on the table seemed to dance to the melody. She stood and took his hand. He grabbed her waist and pulled her close, then moved back and showed his moves. Together they swayed to the music as Donell sang about digging someone.

Kenya couldn't help wondering if Gideon was digging her as her heart began to beat faster than usual. She tried to match Gideon's moves.

As the moon and stars danced in the sky, they laughed and swapped stories about their lives. She took in all of him and could barely peel her eyes away, and her heart pitter-pattered against her sundress whenever he talked. She would never give him any indication that she was feeling things that she couldn't quite make sense of.

The night was no longer young; the moon seemed to be re-laxed in the sky and the ocean was calm. Dinner was long over, and two wine bottles were empty. Kenya and Gideon gathered empty dishes and the soiled tablecloth and made their way into the kitchen. Once inside, Kenya removed her denim jacket and hung it on the back of a kitchen chair. She started dishwater in the sink and added detergent. She began washing and rinsing dishes, handed them to Gideon to dry and put away. After washing the last wineglass and handing it to Gideon, she dried her hands and let the water out of the sink.

"We make a great team," he said.

"Maybe." Kenya shook her head. "Thank you for tonight. It was nice."

"I did good, huh?"

"You did good." She finally gave him the compliment that he'd been fishing for all night—his props.

As Gideon moved in, he closed the space between them. Kenya's heartbeat became faster.

"There's more where that came from." Gideon kissed Kenya's cheek and then walked toward the door of the kitchen. "We're running in the morning, right?"

After her heart recovered from him being in such close proximity to her, she responded, "Yes."

"Good. Seven o'clock."

He was gone, and Kenya immediately felt his absence. She dried the sink and wiped the counters, all while humming the tune to Donell Jones's "U Know What's Up." She was certainly *digging* Gideon right about now, and she didn't know what the heck to do with that feeling.

Chapter Sixteen

Lu

The Uber driver pulled into the circular drive. Lu gazed at the minimansion, perched atop a lush hillside. Tall palm trees stood on each side of the house, and in the immediate distance were mountainous cliffs. The beautiful view had to be the property's greatest selling point.

Zach gave her hand a tight squeeze. She looked at him for reassurance, and he gave it to her. "Let's do this."

She raised an eyebrow, gave him a grateful smile, and inhaled. "I'm ready."

She opened her door and stepped out of the back seat of the sedan. She led the way to the front door, rang the bell. She was greeted with a cheerful smile.

"Hey," John Jr. exclaimed. "You made it."

"Yes."

"Well, come on in." He stepped aside to allow Lu and Zach to enter. "Dad is in his favorite place, the back patio."

"Okay."

"Can I get you something to drink: water, soda, beer? Whiskey?" He chuckled.

"Water would be nice." Lu chuckled, too.

"I'll take a beer," said Zach.

"Y'all might need that whiskey in a little bit, so I'll just keep it on chill." John Jr. handed Lu a bottle of water and Zach a Budweiser.

Lu looked around at the massive living room in her father's home, with its thoughtful art on the walls and pieces of antique furniture that would cause Kenya and Natalia to swoon. It seemed John Samuels's wife was quite the decorator. Lillian Samuels was conservative, easygoing, refined—everything her mother, Yana, was not. Lu found the stark differences between the two women quite fascinating. It further drove home Lu's point that John wanted the best of both worlds, and unapologetically.

Her final day in Sacramento hadn't come too soon. She had accomplished what she'd come there for—*answers*. Though not the most favorable ones, they were answers nonetheless. She'd almost abandoned the mission a few times but stayed the course. Now she needed to tackle all she'd learned and confront her mother. But first, she needed to say goodbye to John Samuels—a man she'd just become acquainted with, a father that she wasn't sure how long she'd have in her life—who'd been sent home from the hospital because they'd done all they could for him. Home was where he wanted to live out the remainder of his days, for as long as that would be. And home was where Lu needed to return to—her own life. She needed to return to Lu's Seaside Inn.

She found John on the back patio of the home, relaxing in a lounger with a clear view of the cliffs. He beamed at the sight of her. Up until that moment she'd only heard about fathers looking at their daughters that way. She'd heard that a woman's early relationship with her father shaped how she viewed the world, and the way he looked at her, and the gentleness of how he spoke and treated her was surprising, even foreign to her. He seemed to genuinely love her, although he didn't know her at all.

"I see that you found your way here. Welcome to my home."

"Thank you. It's a beautiful home."

"I'm sorry I can't take the credit for its beauty. Lillian is quite the homemaker. She deserves all the credit." John went into a coughing spell and then regained his composure. "Have a seat."

"Hello, sir." Zach offered John a respectful nod before plopping down into the cushioned lawn chair.

"I need to find the restroom," Lu told them.

"It's just inside the doorway and to your left." John slowly lifted his frail hand and pointed in the direction of the door.

Lu stepped inside the house and made her way down the hallway to the restroom. Framed photos hung in the hallway on the light gray wall, and she stopped to observe them. She immediately focused on the photo of a young John Samuels in his Navy uniform—only this time it wasn't her mother whose waist he held on to—it was his wife, Lillian's. The photo to the left was a family photo—John, Lillian, and their three young children—a family that didn't include her. She stared for a moment.

"I had to be like five in that photo," the voice behind her startled her.

She turned and locked eyes with Milan.

"Relax. I'm not going to bite." She was much less acrimonious this time. "I realize I behaved badly the other day. It's my father I'm angry with, not you."

"He was so young. They were all young." Lu found herself attempting to protect their father, and her mother.

"Your mother knew what she was getting into. She knew that he had a family in the States, yet she persisted."

"She was a very . . . young woman. And she was poor."

"So, she saw my father as a meal ticket, a way out?"

"What would you have done?" Lu looked upon Milan, struck a defensive stance, hands on her hips.

"I never would have found myself in that situation."

"Never say never." Lu removed her hands from her hips and turned back to look at the photos.

"I'm saying *never*. I don't think I can ever forgive my father. My entire life has been a lie. All this time I looked up to him, held him in high regard. And now I can't even look at him. I haven't spoken to him since I left the hospital that day."

"Didn't you know before now? About me?" Lu faced Milan again.

"Of course I knew you existed, but I thought you were older than me. Thought you were born before my parents were married. I didn't realize that *I* am the oldest."

"He's the same man that you've always known. You've had him all your life. It's me who hasn't had my father. It's me who should be angry. He chose you—his family." Lu restrained the tears. The lump in her throat nearly choked her as she made her way to the bathroom, stood in the doorway, and looked back at Milan. "I've forgiven him for being absent. I don't like that he wasn't there, but I've forgiven him. I think if you search your heart, you'll find a way to forgive him, too . . . before it's too late."

Milan opened her mouth to say something, but Lu didn't give her the opportunity. She shut the bathroom door, stood on the other side, and breathed in deeply. Her hands shook, her heart beat rapidly. Before that moment, she hadn't realized that she had, in fact, forgiven him, but she had. Now she wondered if she could forgive Yana.

She returned to the patio and Zach telling John and John Jr. about what he did for a living, about the hospital where he saved lives every single day. She sat in a patio chair across from her father, stole glances at him—his face, his hair, even observed his hands. Somehow, she wanted to remember this time, as she was sure it would be something that she'd reflect on. She wanted to take in her last moments with John before returning to New Jersey. She sipped her bottled water, a half-smile in the corner of her mouth. She was happy she'd made the journey. Her trip had not been in vain.

As the Boeing airplane soared through the clouds, Lu rested her back against the leather seat. Earbuds in her ears, she leaned her head against Zach's shoulder. She watched as the flight attendant handed other passengers their pretzels and took drinks orders. She didn't want anything, just wanted to be left alone with her thoughts. She wanted to compartmentalize everything that had taken place over the past several days—place everything into their respective buckets of information. Lu also wanted to revisit all the conversations she'd had. She needed to fully understand all that she'd learned, as well as sort through her emotions. She didn't know if she would ever see John Samuels again. She hoped she would. In fact, the thought of him dying before she would get the chance shook her to her very core.

She closed her eyes tightly and wished the thought of it away.

Chapter Seventeen

Kenya

Kenya hadn't run since college, and her body was letting her know that it had been a while. She'd found herself running with Gideon every morning at the crack of dawn for the past few days. It came easy for him. He was in shape. She, on the other hand, couldn't remember the last time she'd done anything physical, except maybe if you counted the yoga class she took occasionally on Saturdays at the YWCA. It was pathetic, because she'd always been an athlete; had always been active. That is, until life had caught up with her. Now that Gideon had waltzed into Lu's Seaside Inn, she was motivated again. In fact, she'd found herself doing many things she wasn't used to doing.

Lu and Natalia were both skeptical when they'd heard about this new pastime—*running*. They'd done a three-way call that morning just to catch up on all that had been going on in each of their lives.

"Wait a minute, you're running now?" Lu asked.

"Yes! I realize I've picked up a few extra pounds this past winter, and I need to get them off. Your wedding is coming soon and . . ."

"Mmm-hmm," Lu interrupted. Her voice was riddled with skepticism.

"Maybe I should run with you," Natalia offered.

"Gideon is a runner," Lu interjected before Kenya could respond to Natalia. "Is that who you're running with?"

"Well . . . yes, but . . ."

"Who's Gideon?" Natalia asked.

"He's Zach's best friend."

"Oh yes, the best man," Natalia remembered.

"He's staying at the inn," Lu responded to Natalia and then turned her attention back to Kenya, "Are you sweet on him?"

"I wouldn't say that I'm sweet on him . . . *necessarily*. We have been spending some time together, yes. A little bit. It hasn't interfered with my duties at the inn . . ."

"You think I care about that? I trust that you're going to take care of the inn, but . . . I never thought to pair you with Gideon."

"Wait, so you have a new boyfriend?" Natalia seemed so confused.

She'd been spending so much time at the inn and with Gideon, she hadn't gone antique shopping or to lunch in the city with Natalia—something they did quite often.

"I don't have a new boyfriend, Nat Pack."

"It's actually kinda cute, though. He's single. You're single. You're both professionals. Both very attractive people. Why didn't I think to pair the two of you myself?" Lu asked to no one in particular.

"We're just hanging out, Lu. Nothing more."

"This man has got you running up and down the beach on Cape May. I would say it was a little more than hanging out." Lu laughed. "Running? You don't run!"

"She's right, Kenya. You don't run," Natalia added.

"I run . . . *now*."

"Is he cute?" Natalia asked.

"Very," Lu answered for Kenya.

"He *is* cute. And charming. He did this whole dinner-on-the-beach thing the other night. Had Lorenzo prepare a meal, with the whole bonfire, white tablecloth, soft music playing." She'd been wanting to tell them about Gideon and the things she thought she was beginning to feel. Instead, she tried to will those feelings away.

"Wait, what?" Lu asked. "He had dinner prepared for you on the beach? Okay, this is more serious than I thought."

"Do you like him, Kenya?" Natalia asked. "Because if you do, I'm rooting for you."

"There's no rooting for anyone. We're just friends hanging out."

"Glen would want you happy," Lu said.

"Okay, ladies. I must go get my run on. Then I have an inn to run in the absence of my friend. Is there anything else?"

"I miss you both," Lu said. "As soon as I'm back, I'm going to have Lorenzo whip up something extraspecial for us. We need to catch up."

"Indeed we do," Kenya agreed.

"Natalia, enjoy your day at the winery. And Kenya . . . I want to hear all about Gideon Harper and how he's managed to turn your world upside down since I've been gone."

"He hasn't turned . . . you know what? I have to go."

"We'll talk soon." Lu laughed. "I need details."

"Goodbye." Kenya chuckled.

She hung up, but their conversation lingered for a moment. *Had he turned her world upside down?*

"Heck no," she whispered as she laced her sneakers and then stood to stretch before meeting Gideon downstairs.

After running the stretch of the beach with Gideon, she bent over, panting, tried to catch her breath. She wiped sweat from her brow with the inside neck of her T-shirt.

"You okay?" He slowed his stride.

"Yes. You go on ahead. I'll catch up."

"No, just take a minute. Breathe."

Kenya did just that, breathed in and then out again. Then she stood straight up, veered up ahead—the inn was no longer in sight. "I'm okay."

Gideon stretched his hands and caressed Kenya's arms. "We're done for the day. Did a half mile and then we'll do a half mile back. That's good."

"We're a half mile short, and I'm no slacker."

Gideon smiled, shook his head, and mumbled, "Strong-willed."

"What?"

"Nothing. Come on, Counselor. Let's finish strong." He took off, slowly.

Though her legs felt like lead was weighing them down and her feet seemed to be stuck in the white sand, she willed them to move, one in front of the other in a slow jog at first, then her stride quickened as she caught up to him. As they approached the second half of a mile, Gideon slowed to a jog. Kenya slowed, too. Proud, because she had pressed on, challenged herself not to give up. She suddenly felt a burst of energy.

"Yes!" She leaped into the air. Before she realized it, her arms were wrapped around Gideon's neck.

"You did it."

She pulled away, embarrassed. She'd invaded his personal space.

He reached for Kenya's hand and pulled her back to him. He wrapped his arms around her shoulders. His nose touched hers as he looked down into her eyes. His lips touched hers, and she tasted the sweetness of his kiss. Her head told her to pull away, to take off running back to the inn, but she couldn't move. She was paralyzed. Instead, she relaxed inside of his embrace, found comfort there. Her heart was beating uncontrollably, her breathing off. Kissing Gideon was everything she didn't want but was everything that she wanted at the same time.

Gideon caressed her face gently. "Come on, let's get back. You have an inn to run."

"Yes, I do."

His fingers intertwined with hers as they walked back toward the inn.

"Tell me something about you, about your life," she said. "Something I don't already know."

"I cheated on my wife. That's why we're divorced."

"Wow. Okay. That was very . . . transparent."

"We were in a slump. The marriage, I mean. She was working a lot, traveling . . . a lot. And I'm not making excuses, but she wasn't present, and it just sort of drove a wedge between us." He sighed but held her hand a little tighter. "I started seeing someone at the hospital."

"Did you love her—the woman you started seeing?"

"I thought I did."

"Your wife found out," Kenya determined.

"Yeah, something like that," Gideon stated. "I know, I know. I'm a terrible person."

She judged him for a moment, but then resolved that she had no right to. "People make mistakes."

"Terrible ones. Life-changing ones," Gideon wrapped his arm around Kenya's shoulders. "What about you? Tell me something about you that I don't already know."

"I was the cause of my husband Glen's death."

"What? Did you shoot him?"

She hadn't shared this information with anyone. She closed her eyes, wondered why she was sharing it now—with a stranger. Well, he wasn't quite a stranger anymore, but still strange nonetheless.

"No, I didn't shoot him." Kenya laughed at Gideon's candidness. It was one of the things that attracted her to him. "He died in a car accident. He drove his sports car on the wrong side of the street and right into an eighteen-wheeler."

"Purposely?"

"He was depressed about something."

"I'm sorry. I don't quite follow. How was it your fault?" he asked.

"The night before his accident, he wanted to talk to me . . . needed to get something off his chest, he said. I told him to let me finish writing this brief and then we could talk. When I finished, he was already fast asleep. I didn't want to wake him, so I just slipped an Afghan over him and went to bed myself. When I woke up the next morning, he was already gone."

"Did you ever get a chance to talk to him about it?"

"The next day I was in court. He left me a message on my phone, saying he needed to talk. Needed to get something off his chest . . . I, um . . ."

Tears came out of nowhere, causing a lump in her throat, filling her eyes, chills rushing up and down her spine. Gideon stopped her from walking, pulled her into an embrace, and wrapped his arms around her and held her tight. He didn't offer any advice, no words of encouragement, no *let me fix this for you*. He just held her, and she was so grateful that he just allowed her to *be*. He wiped the tears from her eyes.

"When I got the news that he'd pretty much run his car into that truck, I knew . . ."

"You are not responsible for his death."

"I still have that message saved on my old cellphone. I still listen to it from time to time. Not as much as I used to, but . . ."

"Did you hear me?" He pulled away from her, pulled her chin up, and looked deeply into her eyes. "You are not responsible for his death."

She heard his words, took them in—every syllable. They

soothed her like salve on a wound. It was almost as if his words freed her, gave her permission to free herself. *Almost.*

"I've felt so guilty all these years. I should've stopped what I was doing that night and listened to what he wanted to say. He might still be alive today."

"I can't say whether he'd still be here . . . or not, but I know you can't blame yourself for other people's choices." His lips brushed against her ear and he whispered, "Forgive yourself."

She exhaled. Breathed in. Exhaled again. Then she collapsed in his arms. "I've never shared that with another human being."

"Thank you for trusting me." He kissed her tears away.

When she'd regained her composure, he placed an arm around her shoulders. She placed hers around his waist. Together they continued the walk toward the inn.

When they stepped up onto the veranda, she looked deeply into his eyes. "Thank you."

"I did nothing."

She kissed his cheek. "Got to get back to work."

No doubt their lives had changed since they'd first started their stride.

Chapter Eighteen

Natalia

Natalia wrapped her arms tightly around the brown paper bags, juggled them as she stuck in her key and unlocked the front door. She used her rear end to push the door open and then made her way to the kitchen before dropping the bags on the counter. She returned to the door, pulled her key out of the lock, shut the door, and locked it. She removed her sneakers in the mudroom, her bare feet pitter-pattering across the hardwood as she headed back to the kitchen, grabbed the remote, and hit the Power button. The CNN news correspondent's voice echoed across the quietness of the house as Natalia opened the back door to let fresh air in.

She unpacked the groceries, emptying the brown paper bags and beginning to put things away. On the drive home, she'd already decided on Portuguese rice and chicken—an old family recipe. One chicken breast would suffice, she thought, but if she made a little more, she'd have leftovers. She was quickly becoming accustomed to cooking for one. The quietness of the house was becoming customary, too. There was no loud music playing the moment she opened the door, or sports commentary on the television in every room of the house, no need to remove sneakers from the kitchen floor or fuss about clothing being scattered about the house. Dishes weren't stacked in the sink. The house was just as she'd left it that morning in fact—spotless.

She needed to get her groove in things. A pattern. A life, *without Nic.* As painful as it seemed, she needed to think about moving on. The garlic sizzled in the saucepan as she tossed in a mixture of colorful vegetables—red peppers, tomatoes, onions. She started a pan of basmati rice. Although Lu had returned from Sacramento and Lorenzo was preparing a special Friday night meal, as promised, she still prepared something for later. She poured herself a glass of Pinot Grigio, took a long sip, and closed her eyes as she savored it.

"Hello, Natalia."

The glass slid from her hand and shattered as it slammed against the floor. Her voice shrieked loudly; her body stiffened, but she managed to turn slowly to confront the familiar voice that had just scared the holy crap out of her. Nic stood there, hands stuffed in the pockets of his sweatpants. He was growing a beard. And he needed a haircut.

"You scared me."

"I'm sorry. I didn't mean to."

"What are you doing here?"

"Last I checked, I still live here." Nic gave her a half-smile.

"You haven't been here in a very long time." She bent down and started collecting the pieces from the broken glass.

Nic bent down and helped Natalia pick up the pieces of broken glass. Their faces in proximity, she inhaled all of him—the familiarity of his cologne. She could feel his breath against her face. The anxiety of having him so close caused her heart to beat briskly, her stomach to flip-flop.

"I'll clean this up. You need to get to whatever you got cooking over there." He motioned toward the stove, where a cloud of smoke had quickly formed.

"Portuguese rice," she whispered.

"Your grandmother's recipe."

She stood, rushed over to the stove, and turned the fire down beneath the pan. She faced Nic. "We need to talk."

He stood, pieces of glass in his hand as he tossed them into the trash can. "I know."

"The last time we spoke . . ."

"Before we talk, do you mind if I clean up a bit first? I had a long journey today. I really need a shower."

"And you didn't return to your corporate apartment in the city?"

"No, I didn't. I wanted to come here."

Natalia looked at Nic for a long moment before returning to the stove. "Um, yeah. Okay. Go get cleaned up. I'll finish up here. Are you hungry?"

"Yes. I haven't had your Portuguese rice in a very long time." He gave her a light smile before leaving the kitchen.

She stood there for a moment, head cocked to the side, a wrinkle in her brow. *Why the change of heart?* She listened as his footsteps made a clumping noise as he climbed the stairs. He was home, which was what she'd wanted—*had prayed for*, right? She dismissed the thought of it, returned to the stove, and finished cooking. Then she poured herself another glass of wine, pulled a plate from the shelf, and placed it on the island.

Alina Baraz's voice suddenly filled her space, the bass from Nic's stereo penetrating Natalia's chest, providing a bit of normalcy to her life again. A touch of a smile danced against her lips as she remembered how they once were. *He was home.* She couldn't wait to get to Lu's to share the news with her and Kenya. They would be overjoyed. The smile made its way to her heart. She looked up and saw him standing in the doorway of the kitchen, observing her. He was wearing a pair of distressed jeans, his bare chest glistening from the baby oil he'd undoubtedly rubbed all over his chiseled upper body. His feet were bare.

"I know how much you like that playlist." He walked over to the cabinet, grabbed a wineglass from the shelf, and poured himself a glass of the Pinot.

"It's my favorite."

"Mine, too."

"We played it so much that first year. I played it while you were gone, too," she admitted.

"It's good to be home." Nic took a sip of his wine, pulled out the chair from the island, and took a seat.

"I must ask why you're home, Nic. I mean, just last week you didn't know if you'd ever come back. And now, here you are."

"I've had a lot of time to think. And I realized that I wasn't being fair to you. You deserved more."

Natalia scooped spoons filled with Portuguese rice onto a plate, slid it in front of Nic. "Those letters . . . they were very troubling."

He sighed deeply; his eyes fluttered. "I can imagine that it was very hurtful for you to read them. I must admit, Angelina has always loved me, still loves me."

"She wants you to leave me, to be with her. And it felt like you had left me."

"I left because I was angry."

"Angry about what?"

"You were obsessing about things, about the baby. About everything. The miscarriage. And then, when Lu told me about the prescription medication, the one you took while you were pregnant . . . that caused the miscarriage, I think I just lost it . . ."

"W . . . wait. Lu told you about the prescription meds?"

"Yes. It's why I left," he said matter-of-factly, as if all of it were perfectly normal.

"When did you talk to Lu?"

"One night, when I was on one of my walks. She was at the inn, and I stopped, and we chatted. Wait, she didn't tell you that we talked?"

"No, she didn't. That was something I told her in confidence!"

"Why didn't you tell me?"

Natalia closed her eyes and shook her head. "I didn't know how. It was all . . . so . . . daunting."

"Well, you don't have to worry. I'm over it now. I know that you didn't intentionally kill our baby. You're not that type of person."

"Of course I'm not that type of person. But I can't believe you didn't talk to me about it before leaving. And I can't believe Lu betrayed my trust like that."

"There was no malice in her intentions. In fact, I had to drag it out of her. If I hadn't pressed, she'd never have told me."

"You left because she told you."

"Well, yes, but also because you were obsessing. Natalia, you were . . ."

Natalia grabbed her phone from the kitchen counter. She aggressively dialed Lu's number. The call went straight to her voicemail. She paced the floor back and forth, her mind racing. She was shaking uncontrollably. She would've cried if she weren't so angry. Nic moved swiftly and wrapped his arms tightly around her. He squeezed her until she stopped shaking, kissed her forehead. The tears betrayed her, consuming her. She collapsed in his arms.

"You should've just told me," he whispered.

Her voice shook. "How do you tell someone that you killed their baby?" She cried—a loud, ugly cry.

"Shhh," Nic comforted her. "Don't cry, baby. Everything is going to be okay from here on out. I promise."

His lips touched hers. Then his tongue danced inside her mouth. She missed his kisses, his touch. She searched his eyes. *Was he certain that everything would in fact be okay?*

Maybe it would.

Chapter Nineteen

Lu

Lu lit candles and placed fresh tulips in a vase. She chilled a bottle of Riesling—something to pair with the seafood gumbo she'd had Lorenzo prepare for her Friday night dinner with the girls. Zach and Gideon had disappeared into town to catch up over a few beers. The girls needed their time. Their space. And Lu needed answers about this Kenya-and-Gideon thing.

Kenya was the first to arrive, and Lu couldn't help but notice the glow that danced across her face. Her braids were pulled up on her head and she wore a short white halter dress with embellished sandals on her feet. Something was different about her friend, yet she couldn't quite put her finger on it.

"You look pretty. Kenya, you're glowing." Lu grinned wide at the sight of her best friend. She pulled her into an embrace, held her longer than usual.

"Look at you. I've missed you, my friend," Kenya said.

"Feels like I've been gone forever."

"I can agree with that."

Lu pulled out her chair and sat. "Where's Natalia? The two of you usually walk the beach together—arm in arm."

"I tried calling her before I left. She didn't answer. I figured she was changing into something comfortable, unwinding after leaving the winery."

"Yeah, I guess so. Let's have wine while we wait." Lu handed Kenya a glass of wine as she took a seat across from her at the table. She poured herself one. "Left your computer at home, I see."

"I did tonight. Figured I'd give you my undivided attention. I want to hear all about this trip to California and all that you've learned about Papa John, and Yana, of course."

"Girl, brace yourself."

"Really?"

"Yeah. I don't even know who the heck my mother is anymore."

Kenya laughed. "You know your mama is a whole trip."

"Let's just say I'm pacing myself before I see her. *Confront her.* I learned a lot on that trip. Needless to say, my emotions were all over the place. I can't even put into words what I'm feeling right now. There are so many layers to this emotional roller coaster—things I learned about my mother, John's health, attempting to connect with my siblings. My sister Milan." Lu shook her head.

"You mean Satan's spawn." Kenya laughed.

"She could benefit from some therapy. She seriously has some deep-rooted issues." Lu raised her glass in the air. "But I don't want to think about all that tonight. I just want to catch up with you two. I need to know why the heck you're glowing."

"I'm not glowing."

"Have you looked at yourself in the mirror lately? You're glowing. I don't think I've seen you like that since . . . you know."

"I must admit, I like him."

"Wow, she admits it. Oh my God, I should've recorded it."

"Don't blow it out of proportion. I like him, and I'm just waiting for him to do something to make me not like him."

"You know, what's messed up about that statement is, you're serious."

Kenya chuckled, but Lu knew her friend well. She knew that she wouldn't give herself a chance to be happy.

In the distance, Lu could see Natalia tramping toward Lu's Seaside Inn, a fast, intentional pace. Lips pursed, eyes wide, her arms swung aggressively from side to side. Her strapless sundress blew in the wind. In fact, the wind was so forceful it caused her steps to quicken.

As she got closer, Lu raised her glass in the air. "Well, we're glad you could join us. As you can see, we've started without you, my dear."

"Yes, we've been waiting forever." Kenya giggled.

"Lorenzo is preparing a special dinner for us," Lu announced.

Natalia didn't smile at their playfulness. Nor did she reply to their comments. There was a crease in the center of her forehead, a frown on her face. She almost looked as if she might burst into tears. She stepped onto the veranda and stood there, refusing to sit. Her eyes bulged; her nostrils flared.

"What's wrong, honey? Is it Nic again?" Lu grabbed a glass, poured wine into it for Natalia. "I know you need this."

"I don't want wine." Natalia stood in front of the table in a defensive stance, hands on her hips. "I just have one question, Lu. Did you tell Nic that I took prescription meds and killed our baby?"

Lu's eyes widened. Her breathing sped up. She was speechless. The question hit her hard, caught her off guard, made her tremble. Had she known it was coming, she'd have been better prepared. She'd have searched for a response. Instead, she lowered her glance.

"Well?" Natalia begged. "Did you?"

Lu whispered, "Yes, I did. And I'm sorry."

"What are we talking about here?" Kenya asked. "What prescription meds?"

Natalia disregarded Kenya's question, peered at Lu. "I told you that in confidence! I trusted you!"

"I know, honey, and I . . ."

"I thought you were my friend."

"I *am* your friend, Natalia." Lu stood. She wanted to reach for her, hug her. "Natalia . . . I am your friend."

"Friends don't repeat what's told to them in confidence."

"He came over one night . . . and . . . and . . . he was a mess. He wanted to understand why you were obsessing about having a baby. I thought I was helping."

"Well, you weren't helping, and it was *not* your place to tell him."

"It wasn't. And I'm so, so sorry." Deep regret pierced her heart. There had been so many times she'd wished she could take that moment back—the moment she'd opened her big mouth.

"It was the reason he left, you know." Natalia paced the stretch of the veranda as if she was in deep thought, as if she was reasoning with herself. "I kept thinking it was me. Thinking that I had run him away. Tormenting myself—examining every conversation we had leading up to the day he moved his things to Atlantic City, just trying to see if it was something I said or did. But all the while it was *you*. You were the one who ran him away. My so-called friend."

Kenya interrupted. "Why don't you sit down, sweetheart, have some wine, and let's hash this out. We're friends. Sisters."

"I don't want wine. And I don't want to hash out anything."

"I don't really know what Lu told Nic, but I know Lu. And I'm sure it wasn't her intention to hurt you. She loves you, like I do, Nat Pack," Kenya tried to soothe Natalia.

"When were you going to tell me that you'd betrayed me?" Natalia asked Lu. "I've talked to you plenty of times since then. You came to my house, read those letters. You pretended you were so concerned, and all the while you knew you'd betrayed me."

Lu covered her face with the palms of her hands. Tears filled her eyes. "I'm sorry."

"I hope that Nic comes back home," Kenya said. "But don't you think you're overreacting just a little bit? I mean, we all know how much you wanted a baby. How you were obsessing about it . . ."

"For your information, he's already home, Kenya. Thank you," Natalia announced sarcastically. "He came home last night, as a matter of fact."

Lu's eyes bulged when she heard the news. She was happy to hear that Nic had returned but devastated to know that he'd revealed her secret. She said, "Well, that's a good thing, huh? It's what you wanted, right?"

"Is it?" Natalia spat out, hands on her hips again.

"At least he's home. Just to put it all in perspective, mine won't ever come home." Kenya's eyes saddened. "At least I've forgiven myself for it, though—for causing him to die."

"What are you talking about, Kenya?" Natalia asked.

Lu had the same question. Kenya's revelation seemed to come out of left field.

"I was the one who killed him. I caused him to die. He needed to tell me something the night before he died, and I was too busy to listen. The next day he took his life. I know we all want to make it seem like it was an accident, but I've come to terms with it. He drove right into that eighteen-wheeler, on the wrong side of the street no less. Had I listened, made time that night . . . let him get whatever it was off his chest, I don't know, he might still be here."

"Kenya, it was not your fault that Glen died." Natalia took a deep breath. She seemed agitated. "Glen had cancer."

Lu and Kenya went silent for a moment. Shock overtook their faces. Simultaneously, they said, "What?"

"He had cancer," Natalia repeated it.

"Natalia, what the hell are you talking about?" Kenya stood this time.

Natalia spoke in almost a whisper. "Glen had stage four lung cancer. That's what he wanted to tell you that night."

"And you know this . . . how?"

"I overheard him talking to Nic on our patio one night. Nic urged him to get treatment—chemotherapy, radiation—whatever, to preserve his life, but he refused, saying that he didn't want to put you through all of it. He wanted to protect you. He didn't believe in chemo. Kenya, he was already dying before the accident."

Lu wrapped her arm around Kenya. She wanted to ease the blow that Natalia had just thrown.

"You knew about this and didn't tell me?" Kenya peered at Natalia.

"I wanted to tell you. So many times, I wanted to tell you. I just didn't want to compound your pain."

"Everybody wants to lighten Kenya's load, not put her through things." Kenya spoke about herself in third person. "News flash, people! I'm strong and I'm capable of handling things. I don't need to be coddled."

"Yes, you're one of the strongest people I know, but this, Kenya, was different. You were grieving," Natalia explained.

"I can't believe you kept this from me . . . for all this time . . . for three freaking years!"

"I tried calling you that day. I was going to tell you when you got home from the firm. But before I could reach you, I saw the footage on the news about Glen's accident. After that, it was just never a good time."

"In three years, you couldn't find one single good time?"

"It just seemed like it would cause you more pain. I'm so sorry. I thought I was doing what was best."

"What gives you the right to decide what's best for me?" Kenya gave Natalia an icy stare. "Do you know how long I've blamed myself for his death?"

"I didn't know that you were blaming yourself."

"You walked up here all high-and-mighty, intending to give Lu a piece of your mind. Wanting to blame her for betraying *you*. Well, you betrayed me. I don't know if I can forgive you for this one. This cuts deep."

Tears appeared in Natalia's eyes and crept down her cheeks.

"Kenya," Lu called. "Come on, Kenya. I'm sure she had your best interests at heart."

"My best interests? So, you agree that she should've kept this from me?" Kenya asked Lu. "You'd have kept it from me, too? Did you know about it, too?"

Kenya didn't wait for a response. She pushed past Natalia and headed toward her house.

"No, I didn't know. And I'm not saying that I would've kept it from you. I'm just saying . . . you were in a bad place for so long," Lu said.

Kenya threw her hand in the air, kept walking. A few seconds later, she stopped. Then she came back toward the inn with intention.

"You know what . . . since you two think it's okay to keep secrets, and since we're having this whole come-to-Jesus meeting tonight, Lu, you might as well know, I, too, have betrayed *you*."

"What?"

"Yeah. I saw your fiancé in Atlantic City a few weeks ago. Yes, the day he was supposedly performing an emergency surgery at his hospital on Cape May—at least that's what he told you. Well, he was visiting with a well-known divorce attorney. Go ask him what he was doing with her." Kenya turned and started up the stretch of the beach again.

"What was he doing there?" Lu shouted. "Kenya Lewis, you get back here and tell me what you're talking about."

Kenya did not return.

In a huff, Natalia left the inn also. She headed toward her home, a few paces behind Kenya.

In an instant, their friendship had crumbled . . . without warning, and without any hope of piecing it back together.

Chapter Twenty

Lu

Lu sat on the steps of the inn, watching as the stars danced across the dark sky above the ocean. It was pitch-black out there, and she listened as the crickets chirped. Her face was a mess as mascara ran down her cheeks and there was an empty bottle next to her; she had finished the last of the wine *alone*. She felt as if she needed something stronger but wanted to have all her faculties about her when she confronted Zach.

She heard his and Gideon's boisterous laughter as they rounded the corner of the inn. She could hear them before she even saw them. She wished he wasn't intoxicated because she needed him to be highly alert when she read him his rights—didn't want any misunderstandings, no bewilderment, no fog. She wanted him to be fully aware. However, her angst wouldn't allow her to wait until morning. No, she needed answers tonight.

Suddenly she heard the most off-key, falsettolike voice belting out the chorus of Prince's "The Most Beautiful Girl in the World." On a normal night, she'd have burst into laughter, thought it endearing, but tonight she wasn't in the mood for Zach's playful serenade. He tried, though. The moment he saw her, he danced in front of her and sang the words as if they'd been written specifically for her. He stopped long enough to plant a kiss upon her pouting lips. She didn't budge. Her mouth didn't curve into its usual smile; her eyes didn't dance. In fact, her fixed stare, narrowed eyes, and flared nostrils should've been an indication that this wasn't an ordinary night. But he missed all of it.

"Did you ladies have a wonderful dinner?" Gideon asked as he plopped down on the steps next to Lu.

"No, we didn't," Lu exclaimed. "In fact, it was a horrible night."

"What?" Zach lost his balance and plopped down on the opposite side of Lu. "What's wrong, babe?"

"So much is wrong, but I can't talk to either of you right now." Lu stood up and closed her eyes. She felt the tears coming again, but she willed them away. She headed toward the door of the inn.

"Hey Lu," Gideon called just before she went inside. She turned to look at him, hoping he'd say something to stop her heart from aching. His eyes danced, and with a wide grin, he asked, "Did Kenya say anything about me?"

Lu groaned and went inside.

As the sunlight crept inside the window and danced against the white curtains, Lu handed Zach a glass of water with an Alka-Seltzer fizzing inside.

"Thanks, sweetheart. I'm never drinking again."

". . . says everyone who drank too much the night before."

"No, I'm serious. This is terrible."

"Okay," Lu stood with her arms folded across her chest.

Zach tapped the bed next to him, "Babe, have a seat. Talk to me."

"I'll stand."

"What's on your mind?"

"What's this about you visiting a divorce attorney in Atlantic City?" She just cut to the chase. "Are you sleeping with this woman?"

Zach's eyes widened. He lifted himself up to get a better position. "No, of course not."

"Kenya suggested that I ask you about why you're seeing a divorce attorney. Is there something you need to tell me?"

Zach's eyes averted to the opposite side of the room, as if searching for the answer there. He exhaled. "Actually, there is. Please sit down."

Lu eased her behind onto the mattress next to Zach, crossed her arms again, and stared off into the distance.

"A very long time ago—long before I met you, when I was fresh out of med school, in fact . . . I had a friend who I married."

"What?" She searched his face, hoping for the punch line of a joke. She'd thought their marriage would be his first and hers.

"Yes. She was an Ethiopian girl I knew. I married her so that she could gain her US citizenship . . ."

"And you're still married to her," Lu determined.

"I didn't think that I would ever get married again, so I never worried about it. But then I met you, fell in love, and everything changed."

"And you didn't think it important enough to tell me?"

"I thought I could handle it before the wedding, and then I would tell you . . . after it was all behind us."

"You mean after you got me to the altar and too late for me to call off the wedding."

Zach shrugged. "Well, I . . ."

"This is so messed up. I feel hurt, betrayed . . ."

"Wasn't my intention to hurt you, sweetheart."

"Well, you did. And I don't think that I can trust you anymore."

"Come on, Lu. You don't mean that."

"I mean it." Lu raised her eyebrows and gave him a scornful glance.

"I didn't lie to you."

"No, you just omitted the truth, which is worse." She rose to her feet. "I think you should pack your things and move back into your place."

Zach's home near the hospital was a quaint and modest space that he'd planned on selling once they were married. Though it was closer to work for him—walking distance, even—he only went there to water the plants and let fresh air in from time to time. He spent most of his free time at the inn with Lu.

She moved quickly toward the door. She had rehearsed what she would say to Zach once he had sobered up, but she knew she had to move quickly, get it all out—*without tears.* Otherwise, he wouldn't take her seriously. "The wedding is off."

"Lu." His heart was wounded; she could tell. He maneuvered his body, then tried to stand. "You don't mean it."

"I absolutely mean it." She removed the engagement ring from her finger, laid it on the antique dresser. She placed her hand on the door handle. "Don't come after me. I need my space."

Lu needed to stand her ground. She opened the door and moved swiftly to the other side of it. Then she shut it and leaned her back against it as she lost her fight with the tears. They welled in her eyes like an uninvited guest. Her heart raced with great intensity. She could barely breathe. She rushed down the stairs and retreated to the laundry room—the only place she could think of to hide. To cry. To think. To regain her composure. She locked the door and stood there as the sheets in the dryer spun in circles, humming a tune.

Her issues with Yana had suddenly taken a back seat to

last night's fiasco with her friends. How had things gone so wrong? The fear of Nic revealing her secret to Natalia had come to fruition. In a way, though, it freed her. She'd held on to it for so long, it had become exhausting—a burden of sorts. But now, at least she could breathe. However, the news of Glen having cancer had her off-balance. Her heart ached for her friend, but at the same time she was angry with Kenya for not telling her about Zach and the divorce attorney sooner.

So much had changed in just a matter of hours. If she thought that her life was in turmoil before with John Samuels's and Yana's antics, it certainly was now, and she didn't know how to begin to piece it back together.

Chapter Twenty-one

Kenya

The wind blowing against Kenya's face felt freeing, and the sounds of Earth, Wind & Fire's "Fantasy" soothed her soul as she relaxed in the passenger's seat of Gideon's steel-gray 1957 classic BMW. The tears had left her eyes blood-stained, her heart in shambles, and her mind disorganized. Gideon gave her hand a tight squeeze. She looked over at him and his smile warmed her heart as they drove up New Jersey's coast.

She needed to get away—*far away*—and he was happy to oblige. A baseball cap lodged on her head, a T-shirt hugging her breasts and a pair of flare-legged jeans, which she wore when she wanted to bring her curves to life, embracing her hips. Yesterday's shenanigans had her mind racing, her heart aching. She'd been up most of the night trying to make sense of it all, crying her eyes out because a friend had betrayed her trust and because she'd also betrayed a friend's trust. The irony of it sickened her—physically sickened her. She'd already vomited the moment she woke up and discovered that she hadn't been dreaming.

Yes, it was real. Natalia had in fact kept Glen's cancer a secret all this time. For three years, no less, she'd looked her in

the face and pretended to be her friend. Kenya had gone antique shopping, broke bread, drunk wine, swapped secrets
with this Benedict Arnold, and all the while she'd had no clue
that she was being beguiled.

With a pained expression on her face, she willed the thoughts
away. It was easier to avoid the heaviness of it. If she didn't
think about it, it couldn't harm her; at least that's what she
told herself. And so, with that, she decided to focus only on
today and the handsome man behind the wheel of this beautiful sportscar.

She thought about how Gideon had rapped on her door
early, causing Ralph to lose his mind. He barked until Kenya
had time to wrap a silk robe around her body and peek through
the blinds to see who was causing such a ruckus at her door
at such an ungodly hour. Gideon stood on her porch, wearing a pair of designer jeans, sneakers, and a Yankees jersey. A
baseball cap was turned backward on his head. In what universe did he think it was okay to pop up at someone's home
unannounced, and before she had a chance to toss her bon-
net aside and freshen up? She loosened the lock and swung
the door open. Ralph jumped around as if he was happy to
see their visitor, as if Gideon was his best friend. Secretly, she
was just as happy. Her heart had pitter-pattered beneath her
robe.

He stroked Ralph's golden mane but looked at her. "Are
you okay?"

"I'm fine." She was lying, mostly to herself, but definitely
to him.

"Get dressed. We're going for a ride."

*Who did he think he was, ordering her around as if she be-
longed to him?*

"I can't. Now that Lu's back, I need to focus on my case.
I'm headed back to the office on Monday and I have a ton of
work that I need to do today."

"I knew you would say all of that, but I'm not taking no for an answer." He was composed. Cool.

"You don't understand, I . . ."

"Engine is running, and with gas prices the way they are now, I can't let it run for long. So, whatever your routine is to spruce up or whatever you do, I'll wait."

Kenya looked past him to observe the car parked in front of her house, just to see if it was in fact running. All she heard was the birds chirping and the morning waves. She breathed deeply. *Spruce up,* she mused. This didn't seem like a fight she'd win—or even wanted to. In a huff, she turned to walk away, hoping he wasn't watching her. "Go turn off your stupid car. I need thirty minutes."

With a victorious grin on his face, Gideon walked out the door, Ralph in tow. Once in her bedroom, Kenya stole a glance out the window and watched as he tossed a ball for Ralph to fetch. A smile crept into the corner of her mouth.

"Ralph, you're so damn easy," she whispered and giggled to herself, then went into the bathroom and started the shower.

Gideon hadn't given her any details about the day's events. He had just instructed her to dress casually and to bring a jacket in case it became a bit chilly later. *Later.* Meaning they would be gone most of the day. Although June in New Jersey was delightful—mildly cool, but with a gentle breeze—she'd brought a jacket along anyway.

"So, the wedding's off," he asserted sorrowfully.

"I knew she'd call it off." Kenya stared out the window.

"Yet you told her anyway." Gideon grinned at Kenya's cattiness.

"You had to have been there. It was one of those moments where it . . . just . . . came out."

"Just like that, hmm?"

"Zach should've told her long ago. This is not on me." She looked over at him, determined to drive that point home.

"You're right. It was on him to tell her. He should've taken care of it before even asking her to marry him."

"That's what I told him!"

"Though he's pretty wounded right now. I hate to see him that way."

Kenya was silent. She had nothing to offer. Her need to put Lu *in her place* had caused all of this. Suddenly, guilt set in. She'd single-handedly ruined her best friend's wedding, and for what?

"We had this big blowup last night. I guess when I heard Natalia say what she said, and it seemed that Lu was taking her side—wasn't taking my feelings into account—I couldn't hold it in."

"What did Natalia say?"

Kenya grew silent again and stared out the window.

"Well?" Gideon asked again. "What did she say?"

The thought of regurgitating what was said caused pain in her chest, but she spoke the words again. "She'd overheard a conversation between her husband and Glen, in which Glen revealed that he had stage four cancer. This took place the night before his death."

"And you didn't know that he was sick?"

"No clue. And she kept this from me all these years, even after he died. Now that's shady. All these years I blamed myself for Glen's death."

Gideon reached for her hand again and gave it a squeeze. "I'm sorry. That must've been really hard for you to hear."

"It was devastating. One, because I thought she was my friend. Then Lu was taking her side, making it seem like *I* was overreacting. She didn't have my back, not like I have hers."

"And so, because you were hurt and Lu wasn't taking your side, you wanted Lu to hurt, too."

"It sounds bad when you say it aloud. But yeah, something like that."

"I understand how you must've felt." She could tell that Gideon was choosing his words with great care. "Perhaps you all just need some time apart to sort things out."

"Perhaps."

She'd already decided she was never talking to either of them again.

Gideon found suitable parking on the street at the Asbury Park boardwalk. They'd talked nonstop during the hour-long drive from Cape May. He let the convertible top up, hopped out and rushed around to the passenger's side. However, Kenya had already opened her door and had one foot on the pavement.

"Just forget about chivalry," Gideon said sarcastically.

"Oh, were you coming to open my door? I'm so sorry." Kenya grinned, stuck her foot back into the car, and shut the door.

Gideon shook his head, opened her door, and reached out his hand to her.

She rested her hand in his. "Thank you, sir."

"Don't mention it." Gideon smiled, shutting her door, and hitting the locks with the remote.

The pair strolled down the boardwalk, her fingers intertwined with his. Her heart soared from his touch. His scent delighted her nose. She loved how he took control, led the way. She squeezed his hand at the thought. He gave her a gentle smile.

"This was a great choice. The boardwalk is one of my favorite places to visit. So much history here."

"Really?"

"Yes. This is where Bruce Springsteen, Jon Bon Jovi, and Southside Johnny all found their muse. But after the race riots, Asbury Park became a ghost town. For decades, it was virtually abandoned."

"This place?"

"Yeah, this place," Kenya explained. "Then, all of a sudden, this multibillion-dollar company came in and turned the place around, returned all of its magic."

"It's charming."

"Of course, it's not the Hamptons by any means, and it's certainly not Cape May, but it does have its charm."

Gideon pointed at the restaurant ahead. "I thought we'd have brunch at this place."

"Cardinal Provisions! Best chicken and waffles in Jersey," Kenya raved. "*If* we can snag a table."

"I have a friend who knows a friend." Gideon held the door as they stepped inside the crowded eatery. "We'll get a table."

They indeed got a table and enjoyed breakfast.

It was in the bleachers at Yankee Stadium that Kenya found herself completely in awe of Gideon. She thought his energy and whimsicality was infectious. He'd taken the time to pull together a full day of events—everything from brunch and tramping about at the Asbury Park boardwalk to driving all the way to Yankee Stadium to take in a baseball game, where they hooped and hollered for a Yankees' win, ate hot dogs, and chugged cold brews together. The excitement of it all made her heart feel good. She couldn't remember the last time she'd had so much fun. Kenya couldn't remember when she'd last attended a Yankees home game, yet here she was, unaware that a drive to the Bronx was even on the day's itinerary. The thrill of Gideon's inhibitions gave her a rush.

After the game, the moon glistened over the Jersey Shore

as Kenya and Gideon made the drive back to Cape May. With permission, she propped her feet up on his dashboard and rested her head against the headrest in the vintage BMW. This time the drop top wasn't dropped. Instead, the windows were rolled all the way up to block the chill from New Jersey's night air. She struggled to keep her eyes from fluttering as sleep threatened to overtake her. She reflected on her day and the fun she'd had—how she'd almost completely forgotten about the fact that her two best friends were no longer friends at all. The memory of it stung. It saddened her.

As Luther Vandross sang "Here and Now," Kenya's eyes rested beneath his voice. Soon sleep found her. By the time she awakened, the BMW had pulled in front of her house. She sat straight up, attempted to gather herself.

"You had a nice nap," Gideon teased, shutting off the engine.

"I did, didn't I?"

He jumped out of the driver's seat and made his way around to the passenger's side of the car. This time, Kenya didn't move. She awaited his arrival as he swung open her door.

"I remembered this time. That chivalry thing you do." Kenya stepped out of the car.

While walking, she searched her purse for the house keys. Gideon followed close behind. Kenya stuck the key into the lock, opened the door, and stepped inside. Ralph sprinted toward them, jumping up and down. She ignored him and turned to face Gideon.

He moved a dangling braid from her face. "How did I do today? Did you have a good time?" Gideon asked beneath the door's threshold.

"I can't even begin to express how amazing today was."

"I'm glad." He moved in closer.

Before she had time to analyze whether he would kiss her or not *or whether she wanted him to, for that matter,* his nose had touched hers, then his lips followed. He grabbed her waist with both hands, pulled her closer, and completely sealed the space between them. He walked inside, still holding on to her waist, careful not to allow their lips or bodies to part. He shut the door with a free hand and then lifted her. She obliged by wrapping her legs around his waist. She inconspicuously glanced over at Ralph, who had stretched his body across the cool hardwood. As if watching a movie on Netflix, he gazed upon them as Gideon carried Kenya up the stairs and to her bedroom.

Chapter Twenty-two

Lu

"Lualhati!"

She recognized the voice but was in no mood to respond. Her eyes were swollen, her nose red, and her head was thrashing. She rubbed her eyes and then glanced at her watch. It was seven o'clock in the morning and she hadn't slept a wink. She was slumped with her back rested against the headboard, and her knees were pulled into her chest with her arms wrapped tightly around them. She'd been in that position for hours. A box of tissue rested next to her in the bed.

"Lualhati!" the voice called again. Yana opened the door and stuck her head inside. "There you are."

Lu wiped her face, attempting to remove any traces of tears. "What are you doing here, Ina?"

"I was worried about you, my darling."

"Zach called you," she said knowingly. Mentioning his name made her heart hurt even more. She gazed downward.

"Yes, he did, and thankfully so." Yana gathered the used tissues and placed them into the trash can. "What is this about you calling off the wedding?"

"Didn't he tell you? He's already married."

"Yes, he told me." Yana placed her palm against Lu's face.

Then she grabbed her daughter's chin, lifted it, and gave her a smile. "Darling, this is nothing that can't be fixed."

This coming from a woman who fell in love with someone else's husband, Lu thought. Surely her idea about love and relationships would be skewed. She couldn't be trusted, Lu decided after replaying all that John Samuels had filled her brain with.

Yana slid onto the bed, facing Lu. She brushed Lu's hair from her eyes and then dried the tears with her fingertips. "He's already started divorce proceedings."

"That isn't the point. The point is that he lied to me in the first place."

"Did he lie or did he withhold information? There's a difference, you know."

"Like you withheld information?"

"Darling . . ."

"Why are you taking his side, anyway?" Lu asked as she stared deeply into her mother's eyes.

"I'm not taking anyone's side, sweetheart. I just don't want you to overreact about something that can be fixed with a conversation."

"Yes, a conversation that should've taken place long before he asked me to marry him. I should've known that he was a married man before we became involved."

"You're right." Yana moved closer to her daughter, wrapped her arm around Lu's shoulder. "But you know this woman is no one special. They were never romantically involved."

"So he says. How can I believe anything he says now?"

"I agree, he should've told you."

"Yes, he should've told me. My best friend knew, and she also should've told me."

"Kenya?"

"Yes, Kenya. Or should I call her Judas?" Lu rolled her eyes upward and crossed her arms over her chest.

"Now, Lualhati." Yana gave her a half-smile.

"No, seriously. I feel like everyone in my life has betrayed me or kept things from me. All the lies and secrets. I'm so over it. Even you have kept things from me."

"What? What do you mean?"

"I learned a lot while in California, Ina, about you and John Samuels's relationship, and *your lifestyle.*"

"What about my lifestyle?"

"You always told me that you were a waitress. You weren't a waitress when you met John."

"I *was* a waitress."

"Yes, but you were more than that."

"He had no right to tell you that. It was my place."

"Well, when were you going to tell me that you were a lady of the night?"

"There's really nothing to tell. It was a way of life."

"Because you were poor, right?"

"Very much so."

"Being a hooker was your only choice?"

Yana looked at Lu squarely in the eye. With her voice raised, she said, "Watch your mouth and your tone with me, young lady. I'm not proud of things in my past, the choices I had to make. Sometimes our lives aren't pretty, and our decisions are based on things beyond our control. You don't understand this because I've always shielded you from my past and things that were of no concern to you."

"It seems you shielded me from a lot."

"It was for your own good."

"For my good, or for yours, Ina?"

"There were some things that you just didn't need to know. Things that have had no impact on your life whatsoever. I took care of you, raised you to be a wonderful young woman. You graduated from law school and joined one of the most prestigious law firms in the country. Now you're the owner of a very successful inn. And I'm still your mother who loves you with everything in me. My past didn't change any of that."

Lu was silent for a moment, trying to digest what her mother said. A slight frown formed on her face and she pursed her lips. She couldn't think of one reason that her mother's past impacted her life. Yana was right; her past hadn't changed one thing. But she couldn't let it go. "Why did you go after a married man? Were there not any suitable single sailors in all of Manila?"

"I didn't know that he was married right away. And truthfully, Lualhati, I don't even know that I cared. We had our own life in Manila, John and me. We were in our own world. By the time I discovered that he was married with a toddler, I was already in love and already pregnant with you."

"But after you found out, you still followed him to the States."

"He was my ticket out, plain and simple," she said. "Don't get me wrong, I wanted him to choose me. But he didn't."

Lu breathed in deeply and then out through her mouth. Her eyes stared at Yana, but her shoulders relaxed, her stance softened. She felt sorry for her mother. She couldn't fathom what it was like to want a man and to watch him choose someone else.

Yana gently stroked her daughter's arm. "You have a good man, my darling. One who has chosen you, and only you. I urge you not to throw it away. Give him a chance to fix this. Don't become an old woman with many regrets."

"What are your regrets, Ina?"

"I don't regret my love affair with John Samuels, because I have a beautiful daughter as a result of it." Yana slid from the bed and stood up. "I have to go. But I hope that you'll think about what I said."

Yana kissed Lu's forehead and touched her cheek with the palm of her hand. Lu looked deeply into Yana's dark brown eyes, took in her smooth, flawless tan skin—not a wrinkle in sight. The crow's feet in the corners of her eyes were the only indication that she'd seen more than sixty-seven summers.

She'd worn the same candy apple red lip color since Lu was a child, and the same fragrance—Chloé. Over the years, Lu had tried buying her a variety of other colognes—expensive ones. Still, she preferred Chloé's 1975 honeysuckle and lilac scent.

Lu watched as her mother walked toward the door and touched the handle. Yana looked back before exiting, giving her a gentle smile. Lu didn't smile back, but her heart did. She loved her mother. Life hadn't always been easy for them, but she couldn't remember one single day that she went without eating or without the things that she needed. Yana had made sure of it. After talking to John Samuels, she had lost respect for her mother, had even rehearsed the conversation she had intended to have with a woman who had fed her nothing but lies her entire life. However, as she watched Yana leave the room, suddenly the things that John Samuels had shared didn't seem so important. What was most important at this moment was that her heart ached, and she couldn't seem to make it stop.

Chapter Twenty-three

Natalia

Natalia crawled out of bed and slipped the silk robe onto her naked body. She stood there for a moment, admiring Nic's chiseled arms and legs, the white sheet barely covering his midsection. Light snores escaped from his mouth as the morning sunlight gently crept across his face. He was home. Despite everything that had transpired with her friends, she was at least happy about that. Her heart was overjoyed. She smiled, pulled her robe tighter, and headed into the bathroom.

In the shower, she closed her eyes. As much as she wanted to block the thoughts of the other night—*the night that changed everything with Lu and Kenya*—she couldn't seem to get the conversation out of her head.

He came over one night . . . and . . . he was a mess. He wanted to understand why you were obsessing about having a baby. She kept playing Lu's words repeatedly in her head. She'd said, *I thought I was helping.*

Did Lu really think that she was helping?

And Kenya's *I was the one who killed him. I caused him to die* craziness was what caused Natalia the most pain. Why hadn't she just been brave enough to tell Kenya the truth? She'd told herself that she was protecting her, when really, she was protecting herself. It was easier to wish it away than tell her friend the truth. Natalia decided that it was she who had been a coward, and it hurt. Kenya wasn't picking up any of her calls. Natalia wasn't sure of what she'd say if Kenya picked up anyway. She was at a loss.

She hung her head, her eyes tightly shut. She only opened them when she felt strong arms wrap themselves around her waist. She was so deeply enthralled in her thoughts, she hadn't heard Nic enter the bathroom, nor had she heard him open the shower door and step in. He kissed the nape of her neck, and then her shoulders. His touch made her heart race, caused her to blush even though he couldn't see her doing it. She relaxed in his arms, rested her entire body and head against his bare chest.

"Natalia, you worry too much about things you can't change," he whispered. "Soon, you three will be friends again, and all of this will be behind you." He knew her well, knew that she wouldn't let what happened rest. She would stress herself to no end.

His words caused her sadness—deep concern for Kenya. She certainly wanted to repair her friendship with Kenya. As for Lu, she didn't know if she could ever forgive her for poking her nose where she shouldn't have. Though Nic was home now and had given up his condo in the city, the pain of him leaving in the first place still penetrated her heart and mind. The thought that Lu had watched her suffer, yet never revealed that she had been partly responsible for his leaving, that was something she couldn't forgive. She'd listened to the seven messages Lu had left on her phone, begging for her forgiveness, but hadn't returned any of them. She didn't know if their friendship would survive this.

"I'm headed into the city. Meetings all day today." Nic

washed Natalia's back with a lathered loofah sponge, and
then washed his own body.

She turned to face him. "Should I wait for you for dinner?"

"Go ahead and eat without me."

She was used to his long hours and unpredictable work
schedule. She didn't mind it, was just happy to have him
home.

"I'll keep it warm," she promised.

"Thanks." Nic rinsed his body and then slapped Natalia
on the rear end as he stepped out of the shower. "I need to
get going. The drive into the city will be murder."

"I'm leaving soon, too. The winery has been busy lately.
But I'm not complaining; busy is good, especially now."

"Yes, busy *is* good. Focus on the winery." He stood in
front of the mirror, quickly brushed his teeth, and then
spread shaving cream onto his face. He faced her with his
white foam beard. "Try not to obsess about it."

His words, *obsess about it*, took her back to an uncomfortable place, causing her to tense up. Her obsessing had
been the reason for Nic leaving in the first place. And here
she was, obsessing again, this time about what had taken
place with her friends. Her obsessing needed to end or it
would certainly ruin every relationship she ever had. She
exhaled and took a deep breath before stepping out of the
shower.

Chapter Twenty-four

Kenya

Kenya smoothed her skirt as she entered the law firm, a cup of coffee from her favorite café in hand.

"Good morning." She gave Alecia a wide grin.

Alecia handed Kenya a stack of handwritten messages. "You look rested. Vacation looks good on you."

"And I loved every minute of it."

"You should do it more often," Alecia said, and then got right down to business. "Your client, Mr. Charles—the great deacon—is in your office."

Kenya frowned and lowered her voice. "Already?"

"Been here since seven. Bright and cheerful fellow," Alecia teased.

Kenya groaned. "Get me his file, please."

She had hoped to have a few minutes to herself before dealing with Deacon Charles to enjoy her coffee while catching up on emails. But here he was, an entire forty-five minutes early. She gathered herself and shook her head.

"It will be okay." Alecia gave her a light smile and then started searching for the deacon's file.

Kenya sighed. She made the stride toward her office,

breathed deeply before opening the door. She forced a smile into the corners of her mouth, "Deacon Charles. Good morning."

"Good morning, Kenya! I hope you don't mind me coming a little early. I had business in the area, so here I am."

Business in the area before seven o'clock in the morning?

Dressed in a brown suit and shiny two-toned shoes, Deacon Charles looked as if he'd just stepped out of a magazine. His hair and beard were precisely trimmed, and there was a Rolex watch on his wrist and a diamond earring in his ear; he was picture-perfect. Alecia tapped lightly on the door and then entered. She placed the file on Kenya's desk.

"Thank you, Alecia." Kenya gave her a light smile and then watched as Deacon Charles stared at Alecia's rear end until he couldn't see it any longer. He smiled sheepishly when he caught Kenya's eye.

"Deacon Charles." Kenya leaned back in her ergonomic chair and sighed heavily. She placed a hand on her forehead before saying, "You're talking to the press again. How many times have we gone over this? You cannot talk to the press without me being present, or at least coaching you first. It's just not good for our case."

The night before, Kenya had caught a snippet of comments that Deacon Charles had made to a reporter regarding the video of him. Kenya had shrieked when she heard him say, *The evidence will show that it wasn't me who killed Julian, but quite possibly that wicked woman he was dating. You should ask about her alibi. The devil has certainly reared his ugly head. Check your facts. And talk to my attorney from now on. She's going to make sure I'm acquitted of all these charges. Count on it!*

"I know. They were just coming for me all at once. I didn't know what to say."

"You say, *I decline to respond to any of your comments*

without my attorney present. Or you simply don't say anything. You're making it very difficult for me to represent you."

"I apologize."

"You've apologized before, and the time before that. This is
your final warning regarding the press and anything else that I
ask you to do. I am the professional. If you are not going to
follow my instructions, you should fire me and get someone
else to represent you. Better yet, I'll have myself removed from
the case."

"I don't want anyone else, Kenya. You're the best. And I
promise, I will follow your instructions from here on out."

"Good." The wrinkle in Kenya's forehead grew. She shook
her head, then regained her composure. She was tired of dis-
ciplining him like a child, and she wouldn't continue. She
was fighting a losing battle with him. "Now, let's talk about
your impending trial. I want you to be fully aware of what to
expect."

After the preliminary hearing, the prosecutor was ready to
move to trial, and so a date had been set. The case was moving a bit faster than she'd anticipated. In a few days, they'd
be selecting a jury. She had her work cut out for her. She
spent the next hour going over the key details of the case
with Deacon Charles. After which, she escorted him from her
office. He followed her to the reception area of the law firm,
where he handed Alecia a wide grin and then exited.

"Creep," Alecia whispered after he was gone.

"Sorry about that." Kenya chuckled.

Alecia shook her head and then nodded toward the breath-
taking bouquet of flowers that was perched on her desk. "By
the way, those just arrived for you, ma'am."

Kenya beamed at the sight of them. "Really?"

"They're certainly not mine. That old fart I have at home
ain't sending me flowers."

"Well, he might if you start being a little nicer to him,"

Kenya teased as she got closer and leaned in to smell the flowers—a vibrant medley of pink lilies, orange roses, lavender cushion poms, and hot pink carnations. She plucked the small envelope from the bouquet, slid out the card.

> *What an amazing woman you are! Can't wait to see you again when I return to Cape May in a few weeks. Gideon.*

A smile crept into the corner of Kenya's mouth and her eyes danced, all without her realizing that Alecia was observing her closely.

"Well?" Alecia asked with a raised brow.

"Well, what?"

"That vacation must've been really nice."

"It was okay." Kenya blushed.

"You do know you're blushing, right?"

She grabbed the glass vase and headed back to her office with it before Alecia could ask any more questions and anyone else saw her with the bouquet. Her heart thumped rapidly as she took refuge inside the office and shut the door behind her. She stood with her back against the door and closed her eyes. Fear consumed her entire body. She liked Gideon, in a friends-with-benefits sort of way—at least that was what she told herself. But whatever this was—this public display of *whatever*—it would require her to explain things to people, and she didn't need that in her life. Her life was simple. If she and Gideon were tiptoeing around Cape May, all was well in the universe, but now that he was sending bouquets of flowers to her place of business, it complicated things. This was moving too fast.

She placed the vase on her desk, stared at it for a moment, admired its beauty. *Damn, that man had great taste*, she thought. She grabbed her portfolio and headed down the hall to the conference room for a staff meeting. She would text Gideon when she found a moment to thank him for the flowers. Before doing so, she needed to find the words to tell him that this thing they had going on, it wouldn't last. Couldn't last. Maybe a text would be too inappropriate for that conversation. Perhaps she'd wait to call him on her drive home.

After work, she merged onto the Atlantic City Expressway, the sounds of Earth, Wind & Fire filled her ears. She sang along, and then rolled up her window to block the wind. The lyrics of the song caused her to think of Glen, and those old records that he kept in a milk crate. His record player was still on the shelf in her family room. After his death, she'd played those records over and over until she couldn't stand them anymore, until she came to the realization they wouldn't bring him back. For a while, they comforted her, made her feel as though he was still with her, but eventually she grew tired of them.

She thought about his last days, trying to remember if she'd missed any red flags or signs that he was sick. Had he lost weight? Had his eating habits changed? She couldn't think of one thing that seemed different or out of place. Had she just been too busy to notice? Tears crept into her eyes as she thought of him battling his demon, this terrible illness—*alone.* Her chest tightened, her heart ached, her palms were sweaty as she grasped the steering wheel. Visions of the mangled sports car suddenly filled her head. She'd managed to block those visions out of her mind for so long, but now they'd begun to resurface. She thought of Natalia. How had she managed to keep such an awful secret for so long, and why had she?

The ringing of her phone interrupted the music and her thoughts. *Gideon.* She contemplated not answering. So deeply enthralled in her thoughts, she didn't want to be interrupted.

Not yet. Not until she'd cried every single tear. Not until her voice stopped quivering and wasn't so thick with grief. Not until she regained her composure. She needed to talk to him, though. She answered.

"Good evening," she said.

"Good evening yourself. Sounds like you're driving."

"On my way home from the firm. Had a beast of a day." She blew air from her mouth. Her day had been long and exhausting.

"I wish I was in Cape May to rub your feet when you get home."

She leaned her head against the back of the seat, thought of how nice a good foot rub would be when she reached Cape May. She quickly refocused. He was distracting her.

"I received the flowers today. They were drop-dead gorgeous. Thank you."

"Why do I hear a *but* coming?"

"Had everyone in my office asking questions that I didn't quite know the answers to. I wasn't ready for that. Honestly, I'm not quite ready for this."

"This, as in *us*?"

"I think we should slow things down a bit. We're moving way too fast."

The silence was thick and awkward. Though it was only a few seconds since either of them spoke, it seemed as if hours had passed.

With a deep laugh that seemed to come from his belly, Gideon finally said, "It was just flowers, Kenya."

"It's not just the flowers. I can't think straight when you're around. You get in my head and . . ."

"It's called *infatuation*. Some even call it *love*."

The L word. It caused her to tremble. Sweat beamed against her forehead even though the air was on full blast. Surely he wasn't saying what she thought he was saying.

"I . . . uh . . ."

"Kenya, just because someone you love died doesn't mean that you can't fall in love with someone else. It's perfectly normal to move on with your life."

"Whatever this is that we're doing can't work. First, you live too far away, and long-distance relationships don't work."

"We can make it work, if it's something that we really want."

"And . . . I can't help wondering . . ." She stopped in mid-sentence.

"Wondering what?"

She blew air from her lips. "I work a lot. If I'm not there when you need me, will you be unfaithful to me like you were in your previous marriage?"

"Ouch. That was a low blow."

"I'm sorry. I wasn't trying to be cruel, just want you to see the reality of things."

"No, don't be sorry. You have a valid point. It's true. I was unfaithful. I had an extramarital affair. Not only did I creep with someone else, but I allowed this person to destroy my family. I destroyed my family—not her. It was my decision. She gave me an ultimatum, and like a fool I left my wife and children, thinking that I had a future with her."

"Wow." Kenya was startled by his revelation. He'd told her more than she asked, and much more than she was ready for. She knew that he'd been unfaithful. He'd told her that much, but she had no idea that he'd abandoned his family. "What happened to this woman?"

"After I left my family, she got with someone else."

"Gideon," Kenya whispered.

"I'm not proud of it. I made a mistake that I have spent years trying to correct. I kicked myself for years, only to come to terms with the fact that there was just no fixing it.

My wife was never coming back. I would never have my family again, not like it was. I would never live in the same home with my children again. So, I just made the best of it by fathering them from a distance."

Gideon's revelation caused Kenya even more pause. She couldn't fathom being with someone who would abandon his family like that. How could she trust him, particularly if they lived in different states? It only solidified that it would never work, even if she wanted it to. Secondly, she had no intentions of feeling what she felt when she lost Glen *ever again*. She wouldn't survive that type of pain for a second time.

There was a long, uncomfortable silence between them. All she heard were her tires treading the highway.

"I really need to go," she finally said.

"Can I call you later?" Gideon asked.

"I really just need some space, some time to think."

"I see," Gideon said matter-of-factly. "Well, after you've had time to think, you know where to find me."

Before she could respond, he'd already hung up. She'd wished him gone, and suddenly he was. She was better off without him anyway.

Chapter Twenty-five

Lu

Six weeks later

Lu's head sank into the pillow. Her eyes fluttered; her breathing slowed; her head hurt. Exhaustion consumed her entire body. It had been days, even weeks since she'd had a good night's rest. But tonight she was determined to sleep. The week's remaining guests had checked out earlier in the afternoon, so the inn was unusually quiet, which was exactly what she needed. Now, lying awake in her bed, the only sound to be heard was the chirping of the crickets outside her window—that and the waves crashing against the shore. The sheer white curtains danced as the wind blew and the scent of her petunias crept inside the open window and tickled her nose. Zach's unanswered calls and text messages had finally stopped days ago, and she was left with her own thoughts—which were driving her crazy—wondering what he was doing when he wasn't at the hospital, and *who he was doing it with*. She stared at the ceiling in her bedroom, consumed by heartache. As angry as he'd made her, she had to admit his absence was felt—caused her pain.

Her ringing cell phone broke the silence. She glanced at the screen. It was John Jr. calling. She sighed deeply. A part of her wished that Zach would call again. She wouldn't answer, but she wanted him to try again, give her the satisfaction of knowing she was still in his thoughts. As Lu looked at her phone again, she wasn't certain that she wanted to talk to John Jr. either. He would hear the pain in her voice and ask questions that she didn't have answers to or didn't want to answer. He would ask about Zach, and she wasn't ready to reveal they were no longer together and, moreover, that she had called off the wedding. While in California, she and John Jr. had vowed to keep in touch, yet neither of them had called the other in weeks. Perhaps this call was an attempt to keep his end of the bargain, but his timing couldn't have been worse. She was in her feelings. Her heart raced and she closed her eyes, squeezed them tightly until the ringing stopped. She would call him back when she was in a better place. She made a mental note of it.

When the phone rang a second time, her heart started beating even faster. Her eyes widened in the darkness of the room. She sat straight up, grabbed the phone from the night-stand, and took a deep breath before answering.

"John Jr. Hi." She tried to make her voice sound normal. Jovial, even.

"Lu." He sighed long and hard, his voice dripping with melancholy. He sounded as if he was short of breath. "Doctors are saying that Dad won't make it past a day or two, maybe not even through the night. He's dying, Lu."

It felt as if time stood still; her heart had dropped from its place in her chest and was now at the bottom of her stomach causing turmoil there.

"What?" It was all she could manage to say before tears began to well in her eyes. Though she already knew he was dying—he'd been very sick on her last visit—hearing those words caused her great anguish, as if she was hearing the words, *he's dying*, for the first time. She was heartbroken by the thought of him leaving so suddenly.

"He took a bad turn this afternoon," John explained. "He's been asking for you."

"Really?" Her ears perked up, and for a split second her heart danced.

"Yes. This afternoon. Then he was in a lot of pain after that. They have him heavily sedated right now, so he's sleeping. But if by chance you wanted to come . . . you know, to say your goodbyes . . . now is the time."

"I want to come, but I don't know if I can. I have the inn, and I don't know if I'd be able to get a flight out in time. There are so many things to consider . . ."

"I understand. I just thought you should know."

"Thank you, John Jr. Thank you for calling me."

"No thanks needed. He's your father, too."

Indeed he was—*her father*. A father that she'd known for a very short time, but her father nonetheless. Her heart was shattered in pieces. She had lost so much time with him, and now there was a chance that she wouldn't have any more time with him. If Zach were there, he'd comfort her. He would hold her until the pain settled. He always knew just the right words to say. He knew how to ease her fears about things. The reality of his absence only caused her more grief. She scanned the phone for his number and pulled up his profile. His beautiful face graced the screen of her iPhone, greeted her with his award-winning smile—the one she loved so much. It was the same face that had popped up on her screen with every single call she had ignored. Her finger lingered just above the digits of his phone number, not really touching the screen, just lingering, contemplating. She leaned her head against the headboard as she began to have a full-blown conversation with herself. What if he rejected her call? What if he was with someone else? What if he answered and berated her for ignoring his calls? What if . . . what if . . . what if . . .

She tossed the phone onto the bed. To call would be admitting that she was wrong, or that she needed him. She closed her eyes, chill bumps racing up and down her arm, and not from the breeze that was blowing through the open window. She thought of John Samuels and the pain he must be enduring. The pain from his illness but also the anguish of knowing that he would soon leave this life and his family behind. It had to be terribly frightening. Tears strained her eyes.

She picked the phone back up from the bed and pulled Zach's number up again. She tapped the number on the screen, turned on the speakerphone. She was willing to take whatever lashing he dished out. Maybe she even deserved it, but the truth was, she needed him.

"Hello," he answered on the second ring.

"I'm sorry to call so late, but . . ." Her voice quivered. She didn't want it to, but it did.

"Lu, what's wrong?" Zach's voice dripped with concern.

"It's my father, John Samuels. He's dying. Doctors are saying he won't make it more than another day or two." Saying the words aloud caused such a tightening in her chest that she could barely breathe. "I don't know. I'm just really, really sad right now, and . . ."

"My shift is over in an hour. I can come over, Lu. Do you want me to?"

She was silent for a moment. Her heart rejoiced at the gentleness of his words. She exhaled. She contemplated his question: *Do you want me to come?* She hadn't seen or spoken to Zach in over six weeks. Though she hadn't answered any of his calls, she'd listened to his voice messages—all seventeen of them—twice. She missed him.

In almost a whisper, as if it was a struggle for her to admit it, she said, "Yes."

"Don't worry, I'll be there soon. Try to be strong until I get there, okay?" His words were like the antidote that her aching heart needed.

"Okay." Her voice cracked.

After he hung up, she held the phone against her chest and exhaled deeply.

The sight of Zach made Lu tremble. He was handsome, she thought, but his hair and beard were a bit disheveled. His eyes were weary. He'd been picking up extra shifts, she was sure of it. And he looked thinner. His olive-green scrubs were wrinkled. He stood on the veranda of her inn, didn't speak, just pulled Lu into him. He wrapped his strong arms tightly around her shoulders and held her there for a few long moments. She relaxed in the comfort of his arms. He smelled of expensive cologne. He placed his hands on each side of her face, forced her to look into his deep brown eyes.

"What do you want to do? Do you want to go there to say your goodbyes?"

"I want to so badly, but I don't have anyone who can watch the inn, since Kenya and I, you know . . ."

"You two still aren't talking?" Zach's eyes bulged as he stepped away from her. He placed his hands on top of his head in frustration, a wrinkle formed in his forehead. He paced the stretch of the veranda, but then turned to face her. "Lu."

Lu dropped her head low. There had been times when she had wanted to call her best friend, make things right, but they were both as stubborn as mules. Neither of them had wanted to give in to the other.

"I don't think she can take another vacation anyway," Lu explained. "And she has her big murder case and all . . ."

He was never one to dwell on things, just simply moved on to the next thing. "What about Yana?"

Lu smiled, shut her eyes, and shook her head. "Can you seriously imagine Yana running the inn? She'd be gone somewhere in the middle of the night, probably back to Atlantic City to one of the casinos, leaving the guests here to fend for themselves."

Zach laughed. "I think she'd be fine. You said that you don't have any guest reservations ahead for a day or two. Maybe you could just let her take care of things for a few days."

She shook her head, pondering his suggestion. "I don't know, Zach. What if someone pops up, a new guest or something else? I'm not worried about the regulars. Most of them know Yana anyway."

"A few days wouldn't hurt."

Yana had never run her inn before. She'd never even been there for more than a visit. She wasn't tech savvy, had no idea of how to make reservations or take credit card payments. She also talked a lot and might get on the guests' nerves. She'd be telling the staff how to do their jobs. But she was all that Lu had now.

As much as it pained her to say the words, she managed to say, "She might be okay."

"I think she'll be fine. Marissa, Max, and Lorenzo, they all know their roles. All Yana would have to do is answer the phone and check in any arriving guests. Teach her how to do it manually, so that she doesn't have to run the system."

"True." Minimizing what her role might be made it seem practicable.

"If you want me to go with you, I could get someone to fill in for me at the hospital. I've worked enough extra shifts that I'm sure someone would take mine. We could catch a red-eye . . ."

She interrupted him, astounded by his words. His disregard for the fact that she'd broken up with him and ignored all his calls moved her. "You would do that?" she asked.

Zach grabbed her hand and pulled her close to him. "Are you kidding me? I would go to the ends of the earth for you."

She tried to fight the tears, but they were persistent, burned her cheeks. There was a lump in her throat, preventing her from speaking.

"This is one of the most important moments of your life," Zach whispered in her ear. "I'll call my friend at the airline to see if I can get us on standby first thing in the morning."

"Okay, I'll see if I can get Yana on the phone. See how quickly she can get here."

She inhaled and then exhaled. Even when things were upside down, Zach always managed to bring them right side up again.

She dialed Yana's number, and she answered on the first ring.

"Hello, my darling."

"I need you, Ina."

"What is it? What's wrong?"

"John Samuels has been given only a day or two to live. He's been asking for me, and I'd like to see him while there's still time."

"I'm really sorry to hear that, about John."

"Are you, Ina?"

"Of course, Lualhati. He's someone I once loved. I would never wish suffering upon him."

"Well, I'm headed to California . . . first thing in the morning."

"That soon? Wow. Who will take care of the inn?"

"That's why I'm calling." She swallowed hard and contemplated before saying the words. "I was wondering if you could take care of things here while I'm gone."

Yana was quiet for a moment. Was she also contemplating? Checking her schedule, maybe? Her hesitance made Lu nervous and rethink her idea—*no, Zach's idea*—of her running the inn.

"Really? You want *me* to run the inn?" Yana finally spoke.

"If you have time."

"Of course I have time."

"How soon can you get here?" Lu glanced at her watch, took note of the time.

"I can be there in a couple of hours."

"Good. I'll be waiting for you."

"Wow," Yana said. "Sweetheart, it means a lot to me, that you would entrust me with your precious baby—Lu's Seaside Inn. I've never really . . ."

"Never really what?"

"I've never really been invited to come for more than a quick visit. Never stayed overnight."

Lu dwelled on her mother's words for a moment. She sighed heavily as guilt rushed through her. It was true; Yana had never stayed overnight, but Lu had no idea that she felt *uninvited*. The discomfort of the moment made her sad.

She changed the subject. "You can't be running up and down the highway, abandoning the place. You have to sit still, Ina."

"I know, I know. I wouldn't do that. I know how important the inn is to you. I would run it as if you were here. I promise, you won't regret it."

"I hope not." Lu closed her eyes and said a little prayer. If she was thinking of changing her mind, she certainly couldn't at this point. "Get here as soon as you can."

"I'm on my way." There was a smile in Yana's voice, and then immediately a bit of sadness. "And honey, I really am sorry about John. I know the two of you have grown closer over the past several weeks. I had hoped that he would beat the cancer."

"Me too, but he's taken a turn for the worse. That's why time is of the essence."

"I understand. I'll be there soon."

"Thanks, Ina."

Lu held the phone against her chest after she hung up. What had she just done? She hoped she wasn't making a grave mistake, leaving the inn in Yana's hands. Her mother certainly had a mind of her own.

Chapter Twenty-six

Lu

Lu secured the seat belt and tightened the strap around her waist. She peered out the small window. Zach's fingers were intertwined with hers as the jet ascended into the air. Lu's mind raced at a hundred miles per minute as the flight attendant gave her safety spiel. She glanced over at Zach with his head rested against the leather seat, his eyes shut tightly. Soon light snores escaped gently from his lips. She dug out earbuds from her carry-on bag and placed them in her ears, listened to soft jazz—something to calm her nerves. Though the music was loud in her ears, it couldn't drown out her thoughts as she revisited her conversations with John Samuels.

After she'd left California and returned to Cape May, they had begun to talk just about every single day. He loved to call her in the early mornings before her day got started, before the sun had a chance to rise over the ocean. They were both early risers, both morning people. He wasn't much of a texter, though, which was a problem because she would text an entire paragraph without ever picking up the phone. He, on the other hand, would call before ever typing a single word.

In fact, if she texted him, he'd respond with a phone call. It drove her crazy. It was the thing that drove her crazy about Yana, too. She assumed it was just a normal practice for their age group—a baby boomer thing. Despite all that, occasionally, John would send her well-wishes for a prosperous and peaceful day by text. He'd even learned how to add emojis.

She reflected on one conversation she'd had with him.

"What do you do for fun when you're not running the inn? What are your hobbies?"

She considered his question for a moment and couldn't think of a single thing she did for fun, nor one hobby. "Well, I have dinner with my two girlfriends every Friday night. We drink wine and catch up on our week. I look forward to that."

"That's what you do with them, but what is it that you do for yourself?" he asked, and then waited patiently for an answer.

She didn't have one.

"I guess I'm a workaholic," she admitted to him, and to herself.

"Well, you should strongly consider changing that. Find something that you love to do and do it!"

She silently agreed.

"What is or *was* your hobby?" she'd asked him.

"For years, I played golf. And tennis. And don't laugh, but I thoroughly enjoy jigsaw puzzles."

Lu laughed inside, tried to picture him working a jigsaw puzzle. "No judgment here," she said.

"When my children were younger, I forced them on camping trips that they had no desire to go on." He chuckled. "I wanted to teach them to do something more than work, to enjoy life. We should wake up each day, appreciate the morning sunshine, and live every moment of every day to its fullest. At the day's end, we should be exhausted from living, not working."

"Running the inn doesn't feel like work, though. I enjoy it."

"That's good to hear. I would love to see it someday. I can only imagine how beautiful it must be."

"Maybe you can come for a visit, when you're able to travel.

"Perhaps. I'll put it on my bucket list."

They both laughed.

Lu maneuvered her body in the seat a bit, then stretched. The FASTEN YOUR SEAT BELT sign flashed above her head. She pulled up the playlist that John Samuels had shared with her when they first met—a compilation of some of his favorite jazz artists—Miles Davis, John Coltrane, Thelonious Monk, Ella Fitzgerald, Duke Ellington. Some of them were some of her favorites, too. She'd named an entire room at the inn, her Harlem Room, in remembrance of the Harlem Renaissance jazz artists.

"I've always been an old soul," he'd told her once. "Those artists were geniuses. Even though they were before my time— really in my father's era—I appreciated them. That's when music was good."

"What was your father like?" she asked him.

"My father, Garrett Samuels, your grandfather, was a very stern man. He expected a great deal from his three sons. I disappointed him when I joined the navy. He wanted me to do something else with my life. He wanted me to go to law school, become a lawyer like him and my two brothers."

"Wow, an entire family of attorneys?"

"Isn't that something? You see, it's in your blood. You took after your grandfather and your uncles." John laughed. "But then, you followed in your father's footsteps when you quit, started doing something that you love. When you went against the grain, became a rebel, that's when you were channeling me."

"So, you were a rebel?" she asked.

He had laughed heartily that time. "Let's just say that I danced to my own music."

As the plane experienced a bit of turbulence, she listened as John Coltrane's "My Favorite Things" played in her ears. She could see why he loved those artists so much. Their music was flawless. A tear crept into the corner of her eye as she listened and thought of her father. She'd spoken with John Jr. just before boarding the plane. Their father was still alive, still breathing, and had awakened only to ask for her again. She hadn't prayed in a long time, but today she found herself praying that she'd make it to him in time to hear his voice again. To say her goodbyes. She closed her eyes and whispered her wishes to God.

The California sunshine kissed her face as they stepped out of the Uber at Mercy General Hospital. Zach grabbed their bags out of the trunk of the car and gave the driver a strong handshake.

"Thanks, man."

"My pleasure. Enjoy your stay."

He had no way of knowing that their stay would be anything but enjoyable. He obviously hadn't noticed the pain in their eyes, the slump in their shoulders, or the fatigue on their faces. The driver gave them a light smile and then hopped back into his Toyota Prius and pulled away from the hospital's circular drive. Lu slipped the strap of her bag over her shoulder. They'd only packed for a couple of days, hadn't planned on staying any longer than that, just long enough for Lu to show her face, make her peace, and return to Cape May and her inn.

The familiar smell of the hospital, with its shiny, buffed floors, greeted her at the door. They made their way to John's room. She gave the heavy door of his room a strong push.

The room was in semidarkness, the only light from just above John Samuels's bed. He slept peacefully, a breathing tube attached to his nose. His chest heaved up and down rhythmically. Balloons and bouquets of flowers adorned the windowsill and the end tables. She took a seat in the chair next to him.

"Why don't you go find something to eat," she whispered to Zach.

"What about you? Aren't you hungry?"

"Not really. I'd just like some coffee."

"Okay, but you should eat something, too. Maybe a piece of toast?"

She nodded a yes to appease him, though she didn't have an appetite for food.

"Be right back." Zach walked quietly from the room.

Lu stared at her father for a few moments and really observed his features. She wanted the picture of him to be ingrained in her mind. Lu wanted to remember him exactly in that moment, from the thick brows on his forehead, the way his mustache danced ever so lightly against his top lip, the dimple in his chin, and his large brown hands, which rested against his chest.

"They have him on morphine," she heard a soft voice say. "He'll be asleep for a while."

She didn't know how long Lillian had been in the room watching her watch him. Lu gazed at the woman. She wore khaki culottes and a short-sleeved cashmere sweater. Her hair was a beautiful mess on her head. She was pretty, Lu thought—an older version of Milan. Her eyes were sad, though, and her shoulders slumped. She looked tired.

"I didn't mean to intrude. John Jr. called me," Lu started to explain.

"I know. He was asking for you yesterday. As much as I hate to admit it, he wanted you here."

Lu's eyebrows raised at Lillian's candor. *As much as she hated to admit it?*

"John hurt me some years ago, when he had an affair with your mother. I thought my world had ended when he told me that he'd fathered a child outside of our marriage. When he left for Manila, I was eight months pregnant with Milan. He wasn't even here for her birth. I thought he was over there fighting for his freaking country, but he was doing much more than that. It took us years to work through that. I know that he wanted you in his life, but your mother wasn't having it. It was something that hurt him deeply for many years. Because of it, he was never able to give of himself to us, his family, not completely. He always felt like a piece of him was missing."

"I'm sorry," Lu whispered.

"Don't apologize. It's not your fault. John is many things, but if nothing else, he's a good provider and a wonderful father. His children love him dearly. I'm sure you do as well, even though you've only known him a short time."

Lu nodded her head. "I do."

"After connecting with you, I've seen him happier than he's been in years. The phone calls back and forth between you two brought him joy. He wanted to walk you down the aisle at your wedding, you know? He was really trying to get better so that he could fly to Jersey and do just that." She chuckled. "Had Milan trying to find a husband in order to beat you down the aisle."

Lu laughed, too. She didn't have the heart to tell her that the wedding had been called off and that Milan might in fact beat her down the aisle. Though Zach had accompanied her on the trip and had been her knight in shining armor, *as always*, the truth was, they weren't a couple anymore.

"It's too bad that things didn't work out. That he hasn't gotten better."

"Yes, I agree." Lillian grabbed her purse from the chair she'd obviously been sitting in. She pulled the strap over her shoulder. "I'll give you some time with him."

As Lillian quietly left the room, Lu glanced at her father again. He was still sound asleep. She leaned back in the chair. Her body ached; her head hurt from exhaustion. Her stomach was topsy-turvy. She wished she'd asked Zach for a ginger ale instead of coffee. Her eyes fluttered as she tried to make out what the news reporter was saying on the mounted television. Soon, sleep found her.

When Lu awakened, she squinted as she tried to remember where she was. Zach was slumped in a chair across the room, sound asleep. A cup of coffee rested on the table next to her, now cold. Two slices of wheat toast were wrapped in cellophane. When she looked over at John Samuels, she was met with a set of bright eyes. He attempted to smile.

She rushed to his side. "Hi," she whispered.

He spoke with his eyes, took her hand in his and squeezed it tightly. "Lualhati. I was praying that you would come."

"I was determined to get here."

He shook his head in agreement. "I'm glad."

"Do you need anything? Some water, something to eat?"

He shook his head no. A tear crept into the corner of his eye. "I'm sorry that I wasn't able to get better, that we lost so much time. But I cherish the time that we had."

He spoke in past tense, and it pierced her heart. *The time that we had.*

"Me too." She attempted to fight back tears. "The time that we will continue to have, right?"

She was hopeful. Doctors didn't always know how much time you had; it was merely a guess based on statistics, she reasoned.

John neither agreed nor disagreed about their time together, just continued to ramble. "You should always cherish the good things in life. Try not to waste time on things that don't matter. Be quick to forgive and live your life fully."

"I will."

John Samuels coughed, and soon he couldn't stop. The coughing spell seemed to last forever.

"I'll go get the nurse. See if she can bring you some water, okay?" Lu didn't wait for him to give her permission or to decline. She walked out of the room and went directly to the nurses' station.

"Good morning," the blonde-haired woman greeted her with a cheerful smile.

"Good morning. My dad is having a terrible coughing spell." *Her dad.* It was the first time she'd referred to him as that. "He needs water. Can someone get him some?"

"Of course. Right away." The nurse stood and moved quickly from around the desk.

"Thank you." Lu gave her a smile and then headed back to her father's room.

John's eyes were lightly closed.

"She's coming with some water," she said to him.

He didn't respond or open his eyes. The machine that he was attached to beeped loudly.

"Did you hear me?" she asked him, but he didn't budge. "Dad, did you hear me?"

She stood a few inches from his bed, her arms folded across her chest. She felt a strong tightening in her chest. She closed her eyes for a moment, her whole body tensed, and her breathing felt impaired. She hadn't even realized she was crying, intensely. She didn't know what else to do. She was stuck; her feet felt like lead. As soon as she felt Zach's hands rub up and down her arms, she knew that the inevitable had happened. If there was any doubt in her mind, it was proven then. She needed to get someone, tell them that John was gone, but she couldn't move. The nurse walked in with a pitcher of ice water, set it on John's tray, and then walked over and stopped the machine from beeping.

She offered Lu a sympathetic look, her eyes saddened. Lu knew that she was searching for the right words. "I'm so sorry."

Lu buried her face in Zach's chest. She knew that she would be the one making the painful phone call this time to John Jr., a call that she really didn't want to make.

Chapter Twenty-seven

Natalia

Natalia turned up the music—Sinead Harnett's vocals filled the house. She danced around the kitchen as she prepared the arroz de marisco, a Portuguese seafood rice dish. It was one of her favorites, and Nic's, too. She shook her booty to the music while rinsing the clams and mussels that she'd found at the seafood market. She peeled onion and chopped garlic. She'd already chilled and opened a bottle of Sauvignon Blanc.

Cooking made her happy. In fact, she felt as if she'd missed her true calling. She'd taken a few culinary courses as a young woman in Portugal and had dreamed of owning a restaurant or working in the food industry in some capacity, perhaps becoming a renowned chef at one of those five-star hotels or upscale restaurants like Fortaleza do Guincho, a French restaurant that sat on a rocky cliff above the Guincho Beach in Portugal. It had always been one of her favorite restaurants. Working in the culinary industry hadn't quite worked out for her. Her presence and services were needed at her family's winery, so she'd come to the States at a

young age. Her life was here. She enjoyed cooking, nonetheless, especially for the man she loved.

The first few weeks that Nic was home, she'd prepared a
home-cooked meal every night. They'd also taken frequent
late-night walks along the beach and made love in just about
every room of the house. They'd played music, sipped cognac
on the balcony, and talked until the wee hours of the night. It
reminded her of the way things used to be before everything
went wrong. He was saying all the things she needed to hear,
which eased her fears about things that had caused her to be
unsettled, put her insecurities to rest.

Her husband had come home, and she was delighted about
it. And now she needed him more than ever, considering her
best friends were absent from her life. It had been weeks
since she'd talked to Lu or Kenya. She hadn't quite forgiven
Lu for the betrayal that nearly destroyed her marriage. She
didn't know if Kenya would ever find it in her heart to forgive her for keeping Glen's illness a secret. She sighed at the
thought and tried to erase it from her mind. It was easier to
imagine that it didn't exist than to face it. She sipped the wine,
savored the medley of flavors—the lime green apple, white
peach, and passion fruit danced in her mouth.

The past few days, Nic had been working late, arriving
home in Cape May well past ten. But today he'd promised to
make it home at a decent hour, in time for a nice dinner.
Maybe they'd even walk the stretch of the beach, as they'd
done so many nights before, or retreat to the balcony for
some cognac. Maybe they would even puff on the cigars that
she'd picked up at one of the local cigar shops in town. She
wasn't really a sister of the leaf, but she enjoyed an occasional puff with her husband. She went into the dining room.
Even though there wasn't a need to light the jasmine-scented
candle as the aroma from the arroz de marisco filled the entire house, but she lit it anyway. She set the dining room table

with her grandmother's stoneware—pieces that had been passed down through the generations. She was never one to pull china out for special occasions only. No, she believed that delicacies should be enjoyed often.

Natalia returned to the kitchen, turned the fire down on the stove, and allowed the food to simmer. She stepped out onto the patio just to feel the Jersey sunshine on her face and breathe in the scent of the fresh saltwater. The wind blew gently as she sipped her wine. She glanced over at Kenya's deck and wondered if she'd already made it home after fighting the traffic from the city. She wondered if she'd picked up takeout from her favorite Chinese place and was perched on her sofa watching one of her shows. Natalia missed Kenya. Had they been on speaking terms, she'd have invited her over for dinner. Even as mad as she was at Lu, she missed her, too. Their Friday night dinners had been a tradition—an escape, a place of refuge. But now everything was different. The last night they were all together had been explosive. It had changed everything between them.

When she stepped back inside, she heard the chirp from her phone—a text message.

Sweetheart, I'm sorry. Looks like another late night Nic texted.

She typed, **Oh no!**

I know, I'm sorry. This meeting is running a lot longer than anticipated. I haven't even left the city yet.

Natalia glanced at her watch. It was already seven thirty.

I cooked arroz de marisco, she typed.

Yum! A woman after my heart and stomach. LOL. Keep it warm for me. I'll be another hour. Maybe two.

Okay. She added a sad face emoji.

With a huff, she tossed her iPhone onto the countertop, walked into the dining room, and blew out the jasmine candle. She collected the stoneware from the dining table and placed it

back into its place in the china cabinet. She grabbed the silverware and headed into the kitchen, stopping in the doorway. In midstride, an idea popped into her head. Instead of
waiting for Nic to come home, what if she took dinner to
him? They could eat right there in his office at the architectural firm and sip a bottle of wine. If work held him hostage,
prevented him from coming to her, she'd go to him—problem
solved.

What started as an idea quickly became a full-blown, plan
and she began to put it into motion. She pulled out her
wicker picnic basket from the top shelf in the pantry, the one
that she and Nic used when they frolicked along the beach on
Saturday afternoons, or when they drove into Atlantic City
for one of the summer concerts. She packed the basket with
storage containers filled with shrimp and rice, disposable
plates, cutlery, napkins, wineglasses, and a chilled bottle of
Riesling. Once Natalia had everything she needed packed
into the basket, she rushed upstairs and changed into a pair
of flare jeans and a T-shirt. She also slid a pair of embellished
sandals onto her feet. She did something with her hair and
freshened her lip color. Once back in the kitchen, she grabbed
her keys from the nook on the wall and picked up her leather
purse. She rushed to the garage, tossed the basket into the
back seat, and hopped into her sedan, hoping she had enough
gas to make it into the city without having to stop. The odds
were in her favor because she'd filled her tank two days before.

She relaxed in the leather bucket seat, drove—no, *sped*—
up Garden State Parkway, all while singing all the words to
Beyoncé's "Cuff It" loudly. She was feeling good. It seemed
that her life with Nic was back on track again, and she couldn't
be happier with her home life. He was present in her life again
and they were enjoying each other. Though she desperately
wanted to try again, she'd decided that she wouldn't obsess

about trying to have a baby. Instead, she would just allow Mother Nature to have her way. They'd been given a second chance and she wouldn't mess it up, not this time.

The sun had already begun to set over Atlantic City by the time she pulled into the parking lot of Nic's firm. There were a few cars left in the parking lot but not many. She immediately spotted his gray Audi. In fact, she parked in the spot right next to it. That way, when they left, it would be convenient for her to follow him home or vice versa. She stepped out, reached into the back seat, and grabbed the picnic basket, locked her doors, and headed into the building.

The night security officer buzzed her in as the doors had already been locked to the public.

"Good evening," he greeted her once she was inside. "Can I help you?"

"I'm here to see Nicolai Oliveri." She gave him a wide, friendly smile.

"Is he expecting you?"

"He's not." She giggled. "I'm his wife. I brought dinner since he's working late. I'd really like to surprise him."

"I'm sorry. I will need to check your picnic basket. And I must call him to let him know you're here. Can't let you up without his permission."

"Really?" Natalia poked out her lip. She hadn't visited Nic's office in years, and it seemed they'd tightened security since the pandemic. And this officer was new. The others knew her well, knew that she was Nic's wife.

"Yes. Sorry." The officer was apologetic.

"Natalia! Is that you?" Ryan Neal, Nic's old friend and colleague, stepped off the elevator. "What are you doing here?"

"Nic is stuck in the office working late and I wanted to surprise him with dinner. But I'm told I can't go up without his permission."

Ryan turned to the officer. "Carl, I've got this. I'll take her up."

"Okay, I just need to check her purse and her picnic basket," said Carl.

Natalia opened her purse to give him a view of what was inside. She opened the picnic basket. "It's just food and wine."

"Smells wonderful." Carl gave her a warm smile. "Okay. Go ahead."

She followed Ryan to the steel-gray elevators. The tail of his dress shirt had already crept from inside his pants, his tie loosened, a tattered briefcase in his hand. It seemed he'd been burning the midnight oil, too.

"How is Val doing? I haven't seen her in forever." Natalia filled the silence with small talk as they both stepped into the waiting elevator.

"She's doing great. She's working on her master's right now, trying to juggle that and the kids. Her plate is full." He was unenergetic and his eyes were puffy underneath. "Mine too."

"I'll bet. How many children are there now?"

"We have three. Mallery's going to middle school this coming year."

"No!" Natalia exclaimed. "I remember when she was born."

"They're growing so fast, Natalia. You wouldn't recognize her with the purple streaks in her hair and the attitude. Whew!" He blew air out of his mouth. "So much attitude."

"Teenagers." Natalia giggled. "Time flies, doesn't it?"

"It certainly does," said Ryan as he stopped just short of one of the offices. "Well, there you are. Nic's office. Looks like he's still in there."

"Yes, it does." Natalia gave Ryan a smile. "Thank you so much. And it was great seeing you. Please give Val my love."

"I will, Natalia. And it was great seeing you, too." Ryan headed back toward the elevators.

Natalia walked the few steps toward Nic's office with the picnic basket in tow. The food was still warm and very fragrant. She turned the knob, opened the door, and stepped inside. From the ceiling-to-floor window she could see that the sun was setting over the Atlantic Ocean. There was such an amazing view from his office. She weaved past the rows of drafting tables and made her way to Nic's area. She heard his laughter, which she knew very well. He wasn't alone; someone else was also working late. Then she heard the woman's giggle. She stopped a few feet short of his area and immediately zeroed in on the brunette who was perched atop his desk. She couldn't see her face, only the long brown tresses that danced down the length of her back. Nic was facing the woman, his tie loosened, his shirt unbuttoned. He brushed a stray hair from the woman's face and then gently kissed her lips.

So deeply captivated by each other, neither of them heard Natalia approach. She stood there for a moment, quietly, wanting to just observe; grasp the magnitude of what was going on. Her heart pitter-pattered underneath her T-shirt. She breathed deeply. It was as if she was having an out-of-body experience, or perhaps her eyes were deceiving her. He couldn't have just kissed another woman's lips with the same ones that had kissed her goodbye that morning in the shower. Surely she was dreaming. She closed her eyes for a moment, and then opened them again, just to see if she'd been hallucinating. She wasn't. Her husband—*the one who had just told her to keep his dinner warm because he was working late*—was still very much there with another woman.

"Nic?" she called to him.

He looked up and saw her, his eyes as round as saucers and a bewildered look on his face. "Natalia?" He moved away from the woman quickly, putting space between them.

He tried to button his shirt, adjust his loosened tie, regain his composure. "What are you doing here?"

"I think the question is, what are you doing?" She stood a few feet away for fear of what she might do if she was closer. Her eyes quickly scanned the desks around her, looked for something that could be hurled at him.

The woman slowly turned around to face her, and a pair of soft gray eyes met with Natalia's, a sly grin on her face.

"Angelina?" Natalia's eyes narrowed, a frown formed in the center of her forehead. The anger inside of her caused her blood to boil. She wanted to break something, scream, choke the shit out of Nic!

"Natalia, it's not what you think." Nic quickly moved away from Angelina, making his way around the desk and closer to her.

"Isn't it?" Natalia's breathing changed. Her chest heaved up and down intently, and she no longer trusted herself. "What is she doing here, Nic?"

Angelina hopped down from the desk and walked around to the front of it. She stroked her swollen belly; her baby bump was the size of a small watermelon.

"Hello, Natalia." Angelina gave her a wicked grin. "It's so good to see you again."

Natalia ignored the greeting and instead gave her husband a scornful look. She thought her legs might betray her and give out. She trembled from the thought of it. Instead, they were stuck; she couldn't force them to move. And she needed her legs to move so that she could escape from this nightmare. Her anger turned to hurt; a sharp pain encompassed her chest. She hoped that Nic would explain what she already knew to be true, but he didn't. She wanted him to tell her that her eyes had deceived her, that she'd only imagined what she'd seen. Natalia wanted him to tell her that he had not impregnated his child's mother *again*. Perhaps it was someone else's child. But he stood there, speechless—dumbfounded. His eyes begged for her forgiveness, but she wouldn't give it to him. Not now. Not ever. She would never give it to him for this!

"Natalia," his voice quivered.

"Fuck you, Nic." The expletive slipped from her tongue with as much contempt as she could impart. Her legs were finally mobile, and with a huff, she walked briskly from his office, almost ran. She needed to get away from them both as quickly as possible. Natalia wished she didn't still have the picnic basket in her hand; it was slowing her down.

Nic ran after her, "Natalia. I'm sorry. I don't really know what to say."

"Don't say anything. Isn't that what you just did?" Natalia made it to the elevators, pressed the button, and then turned quickly to face him. "Is that your child?"

He sighed deeply, looked to the ceiling as if the answer was up there.

"All this time, you're calling me insecure, telling me those letters meant nothing to you. Making me feel as if I'm the one who's freaking crazy. Blaming me for wanting desperately to have a child, and all the while . . ."

"I didn't even know until a few days ago."

"That's why suddenly the late hours, arriving home at an ungodly hour." She willed the tears not to fall. She wasn't going to cry. Not yet. Not in front of him. And certainly not in front of Angelina, the home-wrecker who was now standing in the doorway of Nic's office, arms folded across her chest, observing her pain. "My God, I feel so stupid! Thinking that we were really making things work. That we had a second chance. We were starting over."

"I really wanted us to . . . start over." He reached for Natalia's hand.

She pulled it away quickly. "Don't touch me!"

She was grateful that the elevators opened. She stepped in, while he stood there with his hands stuffed into the pockets of his slacks, watching her. *Such a pitiful sight*, she thought.

"You deserve each other," she spat out. "Don't bother coming back to Cape May. I'll toss your shit into the canal and hope that it somehow floats here to you."

When the doors shut, she exhaled. At last she was free. Free to allow the tears to flow this time.

Chapter Twenty-eight

Lu

John's home was filled with several family members, colleagues, and friends. Pans filled with fried chicken and fish, casseroles, freshly baked desserts, sodas, bottled water were all delivered to the house. It seemed that people were bringing food every five minutes. There was barely room in the kitchen to hold it all. It was evident that he was a well-loved man.

Lillian had been busy greeting guests who had assembled after John's memorial service. Milan had finally pulled herself together after nearly having a nervous breakdown. Jess was silent since the day she'd heard the news of her father's death and John Jr. blamed himself for not being there during his father's final moments.

"I just went home to shower and catch a quick nap. I was on my way back," he said. "I can't believe I wasn't there."

"Stop beating yourself up about it." Milan rolled her eyes at her brother. "Don't you know, he was waiting for *her* to show up."

"Not now, Milan," John Jr. warned.

"It's true. He was asking for her, and then she showed up. After that, he had permission to die. End of story."

"Why do you always have to be such a brat?" John Jr. asked, and then the two of them went back and forth about the timing of their father's death.

Milan's words struck a chord with Lu. She couldn't help thinking there was some truth to them. It seemed that he had been awaiting Lu's arrival. He'd somehow stayed around until she'd arrived. She neither agreed nor disagreed with Milan. However, she kept quiet about it because she didn't want to give her the benefit of gloating. Instead, she glanced over at Zach, who was deeply engaged in a conversation with one of John Samuels's navy buddies, who had been a medic in the military. The two of them had been talking shop for most of the afternoon. Zach gave her a wink, his eyes asking if she was okay. She gave him a light smile to let him know that she was.

She was grateful the memorial service had already been planned prior to John's death. He had played an integral part in his own memorial service, insisting that it be celebratory and not sad. He had written some things that he'd wanted to be read and created a list of the music he wanted played. He wanted it to be swift, not a long, drawn-out event. He also wanted it to take place quickly after his death. Since he was being cremated, there was no need to wait. If someone couldn't make it, then they'd—in his words—*see him on the other side*. The timeliness of it allowed Lu to extend her stay just a few days longer. Albeit she and Zach had to purchase new clothing, as they'd only packed for two days. Lu was grateful that it took place sooner rather than later.

"I'm going to see if your mom needs help in the kitchen," Lu excused herself.

Lillian held a pan of food in her hand as she forced a smile and seemed to be trapped in a conversation with a woman who wouldn't set her free. Lu gently took the pan from Lillian's hands.

"I'll take this." She gave Lillian a gentle smile.

Lillian exhaled, offered a thank-you with her eyes.

Lu asked, "Would you like something to eat?"

The woman that Lillian was talking to observed Lu with inquisitive eyes. It was clear that she wanted to know who she was and would probably ask Lillian once they were alone. There were several observers at the memorial and at the house afterward. Particularly since Lu's name was listed as one of John's children on the ceremonial program, and none of them had ever met her. Surely people were curious, had questions. One of John's brothers, Jared, had introduced himself after the service. He had known about Lu for years and had even seen her once when she was an infant.

"John was quite fond of you. Quite fond of your mother, too." Jared's smile was identical to John's. He was a thinner version of his brother. "How is Yana anyway?"

"She's fine," Lu said.

"I wish she had allowed him the chance to be your father. It tormented him for years, you know."

Lu kept her comments light, didn't offer too much. "It was a difficult situation."

"Yes, I suppose it was," said Jared. "Well, it was good to see you again. I would like to stay in contact with you, if that's possible."

John had spoken about Jared often. They were close.

"I'll make sure we exchange information before I leave for Jersey."

"That would be great." He pulled her into an awkward hug. She hadn't seen it coming, but she hugged him back.

*   *   *

Lu wasn't sure who the woman who wasn't allowing Lillian any peace was. She was watching them both like hawks.

"Maybe later. I don't really have an appetite," Lillian told Lu. "But you should eat something."

"I will," Lu assured her. "I'm going to try to arrange things in the kitchen."

"Thank you."

Lu was grateful for the reprieve, the opportunity to escape. She set the pan of chicken on the counter and started organizing the other containers of food. She busied herself by placing the meats together, the sides together, and organizing the desserts. She tossed empty paper plates and cups into the trash can. She turned on the faucet and filled the sink with water, added some detergent. She stood there, her hands grasping the edge of the sink, closed her eyes for a moment, hoping the tightening in her chest would ease up. She thought of her last moments with John and remembered the things he'd said to her.

Cherish the good things in life. Try not to waste time on things that don't matter. Be quick to forgive and live your life fully.

Be quick to forgive. Those were the words that she couldn't quite shake.

"You wash and I'll dry." The familiar voice shook her from her thoughts.

She turned and her eyes locked with Kenya's. She was dressed in a black sheath dress that accentuated her curves. Her hair was in a bun on top of her head. Lu exhaled. Her friend was certainly a sight for sore eyes. They reached for each other at the same time and hugged tightly.

"What are you doing here?" Lu asked.

"I knew you needed me." Kenya smiled and gently kissed Lu's forehead.

"Oh my God. You have no idea."

"Yes, I do." Kenya began searching the kitchen drawers for a dishcloth and a drying towel. She found them and handed Lu the dishcloth. "You wash, I'll dry."

Lu turned back to the sink and started washing glasses. "I'm so sorry for the way I behaved . . . you know . . . that night. Everything just seemed to explode . . ."

"We don't have to talk about any of that right now. Let's get you through this."

Lu's heart warmed. She was on the verge of tears. "Thank you for coming."

"I'm still your best friend, honey. That won't ever change." Kenya took the clean glass from Lu, dried it, and found a place for it on the shelf.

"Have you talked to Natalia?"

"No," Kenya said. "Not a word."

"Truthfully, I'm worried about her," Lu admitted as she washed another glass, rinsed, and handed it to Kenya.

"I know. I am worried about her, too, even though I'm still very angry with her." Kenya pointed a finger to drive her point home.

"I know, honey, but you have to realize that she would never intentionally hurt you."

"I know that, but you have to understand . . . she kept this from me for three years. Three freaking years!" Kenya said.

"Now that was wrong," Lu agreed.

"Darn right it was wrong." Kenya's voice was filled with angst.

"But I hope that one day you'll find it in your heart to forgive her."

Kenya breathed in through her nose and out through her mouth. "I don't know that it will be anytime soon, though."

"I hate the way everything happened."

"She called me a few times, left a few apology messages on my phone, but honestly, I'm not ready to talk to her yet."

"You will, in your own time. I know that you love her."

Kenya nodded a yes and then moved closer to Lu. From the sink, they were both facing the living room. She whispered, "Now tell me, which one of them is the devil's spawn, Milan?"

Lu giggled; she hadn't expected Kenya's candor. "She's the one in the gray dress, long hair."

"Did you know that you have the same face? She's your twin!"

"Unfortunately, yes." Lu laughed at her friend.

Kenya looked at Lu, then at Milan, then at Lu again. "I mean, she looks like a darker version of you. That is incredible."

"Okay, yes. We favor a little bit."

"A little bit?"

Lu changed the subject, moved the focus from Milan. "My sister Jess is the one wearing the black A-line dress."

"The quiet one."

"Yes, and my brother John Jr., he's over there in the gray suit, multicolored tie."

"Oh now, he's a cutie! Is he single?"

"What do you care? You have Gideon."

"Well . . ." Kenya looked sheepish.

"Tell me you didn't run him off already, Kenya."

"Things were moving way too fast. Besides, he lives a million miles away."

"He's not all that far away."

"Well, maybe not that far. But you know long-distance relationships never work."

"Kenya, you have got to stop this madness. Gideon is a great guy."

"A guy who cheated on his wife and left her for another woman. Who does that?"

"Zach told me all about it. That was years ago. And he's been kicking himself over it ever since."

"And rightly so. He should kick his own ass." Kenya grabbed the plate from Lu, dried it.

"Kenya!"

"Next subject. What's up with you and Zach? Are you two back together or what? Is the wedding back on?"

Lu sighed deeply. "We haven't talked about getting back together, nor the wedding. He's just been here for me through this and that's all."

"He's a good guy. As much as I wanted to punch him in the face and throw him out the window, I must admit, he genuinely loves you."

Lu had already resolved that very fact in her mind, but she neither agreed nor disagreed with Kenya. She just grabbed the next plate, washed, and rinsed it thoroughly. "I'm glad you're here, friend. But did you have to take another vacation at my expense?"

"I just took a couple of personal days. I'm back in Jersey tomorrow. Unless you need me for longer."

"We're leaving tomorrow also, after the reading of the will."

"Hmm . . . the reading of the will? Papa John left you something?" Kenya asked.

"Yes, and I told him I didn't want anything. I don't want to fight with his other children over money or property, or any of it."

"There shouldn't be a fight, sweetheart. It sounds like he was very intentional with his estate. Whatever you get is rightly yours and you deserve it."

"I suppose."

"Should I stay with you for the reading of the will? I can move my flight to a later time. I'll act as your attorney through this matter."

"I think I'll be okay. Plus, you're not a civil attorney."

"They don't know that."

"Anyway, you need to get back. You need to prep the deacon for the trial."

"Girl, that deacon is working my last nerve, you hear me?" Lu giggled.

"No, seriously, he's stressing me out. I warned him that if he talks to the press again, I'm dropping his case."

"Did he hear you?" Lu asked.

"I don't know. We'll certainly see."

"Don't drop him," Lu said playfully. "You're all he has."

"He's on a short leash." Kenya grabbed the plate and dried it. "If you change your mind and want me to stay, just say the word."

"Thank you, friend." Lu dried her hands with the dish towel. "I'm glad you're here. Today was hard."

"I know it was," said Kenya. "You want to get out of here, go find some cocktails?"

"I would love that."

Lu hung the dishcloth on the sink and walked out of the kitchen. Kenya followed. She found Zach, who was chatting with John Jr.

"I'm glad you made it, Kenya," Zach said once they approached.

"I wouldn't have it any other way. Thank you for letting me know." Kenya gave Zach a hug.

"Kenya and I are ready to get out of here. How about you?" Lu asked Zach.

"I'm ready, too. Where are we going?" Zach said.

"To find a cocktail or two," Lu told him.

"Hello, I'm John," John Jr. interrupted them and held out his hand to Kenya.

"Kenya." She took his hand in hers. "Pleasure."

"It's all mine." John Jr. lifted Kenya's hand to his lips and kissed it.

"I'm sorry. Excuse me for being rude," Lu said. "Kenya is my best friend."

"Good to meet you, *Best Friend.*" John Jr. gave Kenya a wide grin. "My sister has told me absolutely nothing about you."

"She's told me everything about you." Kenya smiled at John Jr.

"Really?" John Jr. returned an award-winning smile. "I hope it was all good stuff."

"Rest assured, it was all good stuff."

"Good." John seemed to exhale. "I know a great place for cocktails."

"I just need some air," Lu explained. She felt contained, smothered.

"I understand. Let me just say goodbye to my mother and I'll meet you all outside," John Jr. said.

"I should say goodbye to her, too." Lu followed John Jr. to the den, where Lillian was entertaining guests.

He hugged his mother, kissed her cheek. "I'm leaving, Mother."

"Where are you going? It's still early." Lillian frowned.

"I'm taking Lu out for a few drinks."

"I see." Her eyes veered toward Lu, giving her a sideways glance.

"I wanted to say goodbye," Lu interjected. "The memorial service was beautiful."

"Thank you for cleaning the kitchen. Milan, Jess, and I will try to find somewhere for all that food."

"It's really a lot of it. It's very apparent that John was well-loved."

"He was indeed," said Lillian. "I'll see you both tomorrow for the reading of the will, right?"

"Yes, Mother. We'll both be there," John Jr. interjected.

"Okay, good. Don't be late. And don't drink too much."

"I love you, Mom. I'll come back later and stay with you again tonight, okay?"

She touched John Jr.'s face. "Thank you, sweetheart."

Lu felt sad for Lillian. She knew that tonight would be another hard night for her. Learning to live without John Samuels would be a difficult road, she presumed. Good, bad, or indifferent, he'd been her husband for more years than Lu was on earth. She thought of her life with Zach, and how she had only been apart from him for a few weeks after their breakup. However, his absence was very real; she'd discovered that she could barely breathe without him. She couldn't imagine having to live the rest of her life without him, like Lillian would have to live the rest of hers without John. She couldn't fathom the woman's pain, having to say goodbye to a man she had loved for so long.

"Good night," Lu said to Lillian.

"Good night, Lu. I'll see you tomorrow."

John Jr. grabbed Lu's hand and led her through the crowded living room and out the door. It felt good to be outside, the California air blowing through her hair; the mild temperature was perfect. She exhaled. She could breathe.

Chapter Twenty-nine

Kenya

Kenya's flight had landed at an ungodly hour of the morning. She quickly retrieved her bag and tossed it into the trunk of her car. Had she been dressed appropriately, she'd have stopped by the firm to get some work done, but she decided to head home to Cape May instead. She could work from home. Her late night of cocktails with Lu, Zach, and John Jr. had left her exhausted. She nearly overslept and missed her flight. John Jr. had walked her to her hotel room, wanting to come inside for a nightcap, which she vetoed. He was charming and handsome but clearly not her type.

She'd always told herself that *her type* was Glen. It was something that kept other men at bay—*in her mind anyway*. However, lately, Gideon had popped into her thoughts and dreams way too often, unwarranted, unannounced, like an uninvited guest who hadn't called before showing up on her doorstep. Too often, she found herself wondering what he was doing and even considered dialing his number a few times but fought the urge each time. She didn't want to send Gideon mixed signals, giving him false hope. Besides, it was a good probability that he wasn't interested in talking to her anyway, probably wouldn't answer the phone if she called. Their last conversation hadn't been a pleasant one, though she had to admit she missed him like hell. In just a short time, they'd connected on a level that she hadn't connected with anyone in a long time. She missed his smile, his touch, his conversation. Hell, she just missed him. But none of it mattered.

Kenya pulled into her Cape May neighborhood, and just before driving past Natalia's home she couldn't help thinking of her. She figured she was probably at the winery, just getting her day started. Had they been on good terms, Kenya might've popped her head in at the winery just to say hello. Might've called to ask if she wanted a breakfast sandwich or a cup of coffee from their favorite café on the island. She'd have picked up a cup for Natalia and one for herself. The truth was, they weren't on good terms, and besides, Kenya was exhausted. She couldn't think of anything more than getting home to her comfy bed. She would leave Ralph at the kennel for a few more hours while she caught some shut-eye before working. She'd pick him up later.

Her eyes veered toward Natalia's two-story beachfront home as she passed. She squinted, trying to make out exactly what it was that was strewn about on the front lawn. It appeared to be trash, or maybe laundry. Kenya slowed down. It was definitely clothing. For some reason, there were clothes all over Natalia's front yard.

"What the hell?" Kenya whispered to herself.

The garage was open, and the trunk of Natalia's sedan was lifted. The back doors of the car were open as well. A few seconds later, Natalia emerged from the house carrying an armful of clothing that she tossed carelessly into the trunk of the car.

"What are you doing, girl?" Kenya whispered to herself.

Natalia was so consumed by what she was doing, she

hadn't even noticed that Kenya was watching. She seemed to be on a mission. For what, Kenya had no idea, but she sat there for a moment in hopes of finding out. Soon Natalia emerged from the house with another armful of clothing, which she also tossed into the trunk of the car. Kenya pulled up next to the curb, placed the car in Park, turned off the engine, and stepped out of the car. She approached just as Natalia emerged with another armful of clothing.

"What's going on, Nat Pack?" Kenya asked.

Natalia finally noticed her, looked up at Kenya with red, glazed eyes, but she didn't stop what she was doing. She tossed the clothes into the back seat and went back into the house without saying a word. Kenya followed. Clothes were strewn about on the kitchen floor and made a path from there to the garage. Natalia grabbed another armful, pushed past Kenya, and went into the garage. Then she returned.

Kenya stopped her when she walked past this time. She grabbed her arms. "Sweetheart, what's going on?"

"I'm headed to the Cape May Canal!"

"Why, honey? What for?"

"This is everything. All his clothing, possessions, everything. I'm going to toss it all into the canal."

"Whoa! What?" Kenya asked. "You mean Nic's things? Why?"

"Because he's a liar. And a cheater. And I hate his guts!" Her entire body trembled, an enraged look on her face. She cried—not a sad cry but a wrathful one.

Kenya grabbed her and held her tight. "Oh, Nat Pack. Tell me what's going on."

Natalia was too choked up to speak at first. Kenya allowed her to cry, get it all out. Her eyes observed Natalia's usually meticulous kitchen. Dishes were stacked along the countertops, two empty wine bottles resting near the sink.

When Natalia regained her composure, her eyes found Kenya's. "She's pregnant."

"Who's pregnant?"

"Angelina. He got her pregnant."

"You mean the one who wrote all those freaking letters, *Angelina*? The mother of his child, *Angelina*? The chick who's in Sicily, *Angelina*?"

"She's not in Sicily. She's here. In Jersey."

"What?" Kenya's breathing increased, a bewildered look on her face.

"I saw her at his office. Yeah, walked in on them. He was kissing her, and then she turned around and . . . that's when I saw her belly. She's pregnant with his child."

"That low-down, dirty dog!" It was Kenya who was infuriated now, but she had to remain calm for Natalia's sake, and in order to gather all the details. "What did he have to say for himself?"

"Nothing. He said nothing. He just looked at me. Just stood there. And she also stood there with a smug look on her face, gloating. She loved every minute of it."

"I'm so sorry you had to go through that." Kenya gave her a half-smile.

"It was so painful." Natalia cried harder.

Kenya felt helpless. She wanted to relieve her of the pain, but she had to remain levelheaded. "You know you can't throw his things into the canal, right, sweetie? You'll go to jail."

"I don't care. I give up."

"You can't give up either, Nat Pack. You give up and you relinquish your power to them. Don't give them that. I know you're hurting right now, but trust me, this too shall pass."

"I won't get past this."

"I know it feels that way right now, but you will. You'll get through this. Just like you did when you had the miscarriage. Just like you did when he moved out of the house. Just like you did when you read those freaking letters. You will get past this."

"This is much more painful than any of those things. She's giving him what I never could—a child."

"I know it sounds crazy, but because you don't have a child with him, it makes it that much easier for you to move on *without him*. You don't have any ties, except maybe this house. And we'll fight his ass in court for you to keep the house."

"I feel so stupid. All this time, I thought I was the one who was overreacting. Thinking that I was insecure."

"You're not stupid. Your intuition was spot-on. He wanted you to think that you were overreacting or being insecure, so that he could continue to do what he wanted to."

"I know now. I sincerely thought we were starting over, thought God had given us a second chance."

"Don't blame yourself for *his* shortcomings. You're a beautiful, strong, capable woman. You're smart. Successful. You'll be okay, my friend."

"Am I? Your friend still?" Natalia asked. "I haven't been that great a friend to you, Kenya. And I know that now. To keep something like that from you for three years . . ."

"I'm sure you had your reasons, concerns. I don't like it, but . . ."

"I would never hurt you intentionally. I hope you know that."

"I do know that. It didn't make it better, but I know who you are as a person. You wouldn't hurt a fly."

"I had planned on telling you the day of the crash. I was waiting for you to get home from work. I had contemplated calling you at your law office but didn't want to tell you something like that over the phone. I needed to tell you in person. Then I saw Glen's crash on the news. After that . . . I don't know . . . it was just so hard. I kept telling myself, *I'll tell her after the services*. Then, it was, *I'll tell her when she stops grieving*. The longer I waited, the harder it became."

"I understand. I was in a bad place for so long. So fragile. I can't imagine that anytime would've been the right time."

"I didn't want to compound your pain. I wanted you to heal first. Thought it was too much to lay on you all at once."

"Sometimes we must have those hard conversations with each other, Nat Pack. Even when we know that it will hurt someone we love."

"I was gravely mistaken and I'm so sorry. And I'm sorry you thought Glen's death was your fault."

"It was," Kenya said matter-of-factly. "I could've been there for him, but I was too busy. Maybe I could've stopped him from committing suicide because we both know that's what it was."

"We don't know for sure that it was suicide, Kenya. Maybe he just lost control of the car, for whatever reason."

Kenya had already thoroughly examined every single detail of the accident. She'd gone over every possibility with a fine-tooth comb. She'd studied both the coroner's and the autopsy report. He hadn't had a stroke, or a heart attack. He had not been impaired. She knew, because she'd obsessed about it for far too long.

"There's no other rational explanation."

"You can't blame yourself for the actions of others. Whatever Glen did or *didn't do* was his choice—not yours. He had an obligation to bring you into the fold. You should've had a say in his treatment, or his decision not to be treated. Nic urged him to tell you, but he refused." Natalia dropped her head. "But that doesn't excuse my actions. The minute I overheard them talking, I should've gotten you on the phone. You're my friend, my sister. I had an obligation to tell you. I owed you that much. Please forgive me."

Kenya grabbed Natalia and hugged her tight. She whispered, "I forgive you."

Natalia collapsed in her arms. Kenya could tell in that moment she desperately needed to hear those words and had yearned for them, no doubt. "You don't know how much that means to me."

"I think I do." Kenya smiled. "Now, girl, let's get those clothes off your front lawn before the neighbors start to whisper. Let's unload those clothes out of your car. And then we're going to clean this kitchen."

Natalia laughed for the first time. "Those neighbors are probably already whispering."

"Screw them! They don't know what you've been through in the past twenty-four hours. Nor the past several months, for that matter."

"True," said Natalia as she led the way out to the garage and then into the front yard. "Where were you coming from anyway? Why aren't you in the city, at your law office?"

"I'm coming from the airport. I went to Sacramento to be with Lu. Her father, John Samuels, died this week."

"Oh no." Natalia stopped in her tracks and covered her mouth with her hands. For a moment, it looked as if she might cry again. "That's so terrible. I had no idea."

"Yeah, she and Zach flew out there on Monday, but I figured she could use a friend, so I flew out there on the day of the memorial service."

"I didn't know. I'm really sorry to hear this news. Is she okay?"

"She's okay." Kenya began picking up Nic's clothing from the lawn.

"Who's running the inn?"

"You won't believe it. Yana."

Natalia laughed. "Are you kidding? I can't believe she trusted Yana with her baby."

"She had no choice. She and I were at odds. You and she were at odds. She had to make a hard decision. I'm going over there in a little bit to make sure Yana's doing okay and hasn't hightailed it back to Atlantic City for a bingo game."

Natalia laughed. "Or sitting in front of a slot machine."

"You know, friend, forgiveness works multiple ways."

"What do you mean?"

"I mean, you now have to forgive Lu for what she did to you. Just like you deserved forgiveness, so does she."

Natalia lowered her head, contemplating Kenya's words. "I know."

"She feels terrible about telling Nic about the baby. She thinks that she destroyed your marriage."

"Well, that couldn't be further from the truth. Nic destroyed us."

"It would do her heart good to hear that from you. Release her from that burden."

"I will."

"Good. Now, let's get this lawn and kitchen cleaned up. Then I gotta go check on Yana and go pick up Ralph from the kennel."

"Kenya, I love you." Natalia's arms were filled with clothing. "You're a great friend."

Kenya exhaled and gave her friend a warm smile. "I love you more."

Chapter Thirty

Lu

Lu smiled as she listened to Kenya's message for a second time.

"I'll have you know that Yana, your mother, has that inn in tip-top shape. You won't recognize it." Kenya laughed. *"When you get home, have Lorenzo make one of his famous Friday night dinners for us. We're going to sit on your veranda and talk about some things. There is a lot that we need to catch up on. All I can tell you is, brace yourself. Natalia and I will both be there, and all will be well in the universe. I promise."*

"What are you up to, Kenya Lewis?" she whispered, and then glanced over at Zach, who was sleeping in the seat next to hers. Then she glanced at her watch. It was three o'clock in Jersey, and she hoped that Lorenzo was able to prepare a meal by seven. When he prepared their usual Friday meals, he spent a great deal of time shopping for the right ingredients at the market, choosing the best wines. Some meals took time, preparation, thought. She would message him the minute their flight landed, but there were no guarantees. The excitement of them getting together had her giddy, though, even if he just whipped up something simple. It had been weeks since they'd gathered on Friday. She couldn't help but wonder how Kenya had managed to get Natalia there, but she was grateful. She needed to see her face when she apologized profusely for the umpteenth time.

She gazed upon the clouds outside her window. She thought about the meeting that had taken place at John Samuels's attorney's office that morning—the reading of his will. Her stomach had churned as she sat across the table from Milan, who had scoffed at her the entire time, with flared nostrils and a clenched jaw.

". . . and to my daughter's mother, Yana Ábalos, I leave the sum of $214,000. This should satisfy my half of tuition for Lualhati's undergraduate studies, as well as her tuition for law school. I have already instructed my attorney to write her a check and ensure that she receives it immediately upon my death. To my daughter, Lualhati Samuels, I leave my vacation home in Napa Valley, California. The property's last appraised value was $985,000. She is not allowed to sell the property for profit but must use it as a vacation home or as a second location for Lu's Seaside Inn, should she choose to expand. Should she choose not to expand, the property currently nets a significant amount of income each month as a vacation rental. The property will remain in the Samuels family and can only be passed down as an inheritance."

Lu had been blown away by John's generosity toward her and Yana. She was amused by the way Milan's and Lillian's eyes had bulged as John's attorney read that part of the will.

"That's our family vacation home." With a huff, Milan crossed her arms over her chest.

"It's been years since we vacationed there. The last time we were there, I was in my first year of college," John Jr. said.

"Still, it should remain in the family," Milan argued.

"Lu is family, Milan. Whether you like it or not." John Jr.'s brow had raised, and he gave Lu a wink of the eye from across the table.

Zach had squeezed her hand beneath the table. Lu's mind had raced rapidly, a mile a minute, as she tried to sort things out, make sense of what was really happening. She'd told John that she didn't want anything. After hearing the thought and care that had gone into how he'd distributed his will, he'd given her much more than money. He'd invested in her future. He'd gained her respect.

As the wheels on the jet hit the runway and began its taxi to the gate, Lu took her cell phone off airplane mode and sent a quick text to Lorenzo, asking him to prepare a special dinner for her and the girls.

His response was swift. "*I know just the thing. Headed to the market now.*"

Zach opened his eyes and gave her a smile when she looked at him.

"We're home," Lu said.

"Finally." He grabbed her hand. "Are you okay?"

"I'm good. Lorenzo is going to prepare dinner for the girls and me."

"You mean you and Kenya?"

"And Natalia."

"Wow, she's coming, too? That's good news. Maybe you all can finally squash your differences. Reconnect."

"Yes. I'd like that more than anything."

"I'm going to drop you off at the inn and then head over to the hospital for a bit, but I'd like to come back later, after the girls leave, so we can talk. Is that okay?"

"I'd like that."

She'd insisted on separate rooms in Sacramento, so that there would be no lines crossed, vision blurred. She didn't want there to be intimacy while she grieved John's death.

However, Zach had no idea that every single second that she lay awake in her bed, in the adjoining room next to his, she thought of him, yearned for him.

She crept into the Vintage Hollywood suite, the one with the portrait of Ginger Rogers on the wall and peeked her head inside. Yana was humming a song that she used to sing to Lu as a child. "Paru-Parong Bukid," an old Filipino folk song, was one of Lu's favorites. It reminded her of Lolo, and how he would fill her head with stories and their rich family history. Though Lu had never visited the Philippines, Yana and Lolo made sure she knew everything there was to know about it. She would visit one day—it was on her bucket list. She stood there listening to her mother and watching as she folded towels.

"Well, something's got you in a good mood this evening." Lu startled her mother.

"Ooh! You scared me." Yana jumped and then reached for her daughter, hugging her tight. "How are you, sweetheart?"

"I'm fine. The guests are down there asking for you. They have been raving about how wonderful you've been to them. *Your mom is so sweet. Your mom is the cutest little thing. She's been so good to us.* Lu giggled. "Max told me that you tried to take over his kitchen."

"I did not try to take over his kitchen. I taught him to make turon." Yana mentioned her best dish, a Filipino treat made with plantains and jackfruit. It was something she made often when Lu was a child. "He was bragging about his French toast. But now he'll be making turon for your guests and they'll be bragging about it."

"You're something else."

"Thank you for trusting me with the inn. I've really enjoyed myself."

"I'm glad."

"Now tell me about your trip. What was John's memorial service like? Was it sad?"

"It was really upbeat. John insisted on it being celebratory, not sad. He pretty much planned it all himself."

"What's his wife like? Is she nice or snooty?"

"She's okay. Nothing special."

"Is she still pretty? I saw pictures of her years ago, but she was much younger then. Did she age gracefully?"

"She's still very pretty, Ina." Lu changed the subject. "I stayed for the reading of the will."

"Really?"

"Yes." Lu reached into her purse and handed Yana a check folded in half. "This is from John's attorney."

"What? What is it?" Yana unfolded the check, observed it. "What is this, Lualhati?"

"It's from John Samuels. It's reimbursement for half of my school's tuition—my undergrad as well as law school."

"What? Why would he do this?"

"Because he wanted to do his part, as my father, as a man, Ina. He wanted to die admirably."

"I told him that I didn't want his money. This is much too generous."

"Yes, I know. But you denied him an important part of his life—*me*."

"You can send this right back to that fancy attorney of John's in California. I don't want it."

"Give it here." Lu grabbed the check from Yana. "I'll just deposit it into your account. You denied him a relationship with me. You must allow the man something, Ina. Let him rest peacefully, knowing that he took care of his responsibility."

Yana opened her mouth to say something. "I . . ."

Lu interrupted. "I don't want to hear anything more about it. You and I both know this would be a great help to you."

Yana smiled. "And what did he leave to his precious Lual-hati?"

Lu walked over to the window, gazed at the ocean, and thought of John. "He left me a vacation home. He gave me the choice to either keep it as a vacation property or to transform it into another inn."

"Did you see it?"

"Not in person. I've only seen it in pictures. It's a beautiful Victorian home in the Napa Valley, about an hour and a half from Sacramento," Lu explained. "Apparently, the family vacationed there in the past because his daughter, Milan, was in a tizzy about him giving it to me. She went on and on about it having sentimental value. Blah, blah, blah. She's such a brat."

"She's a daddy's girl." Yana laughed.

"They hadn't vacationed there in years. He has only rented it out, which means it already has a significant stream of income. It has six bedrooms and a huge kitchen. It's very beautiful. I can't wait to see it in person. There just wasn't time during this trip."

"That's great, my darling. I know you will do the property justice."

"Thank you for taking such good care of the inn, Ina." Lu kissed her mother's cheek and then walked toward the door. "Now I have to get showered and changed. The girls are coming for our Friday night dinner."

"The girls as in Kenya and Natalia?"

"Yes."

"So, you've made amends?" Yana clasped her hands together.

"Something like that. Kenya flew to California to support me during John's memorial service. Natalia and I will talk tonight."

"That's good, sweetheart. I'm glad," said Yana. "What about

you and Zach? Have you two squashed your differences? Is he going to be my son-in-law or what?"

"Not quite. We haven't had a chance to talk. And as of right now, the wedding is still off, Ina."

"Oh, Lualhati, you're even more stubborn than your mother."

"By the way, Ina, you're welcome to join us for dinner tonight. I'm sure that Lorenzo is whipping up something spectacular."

"I can't, sweetheart. I need to head back to the city before sunset. Bingo tonight."

"Of course." Lu walked back into the room and kissed Yana's cheek. "Drive safe."

"I will."

"I love you, Ina."

"I love you more."

Lu stood in the doorway, watching her mother as she continued to fold linens for a moment, and then rushed to take a shower.

The fragrance from Lorenzo's Mediterranean shrimp swept through the entire inn. Lu set the table on the veranda with beautiful vintage china, lit candles, placed a vase at the center, filled with fresh flowers—a medley of scarlet pimpernel, California poppy, and fall phlox. She had chilled a bottle of Pinot Grigio and pulled it from the fridge. She grabbed three wineglasses. When she looked up, she could see Kenya and Natalia walking the stretch of beach, arm in arm, as they'd done so many times before. Watching them made her smile. She was giddy.

"Good evening, ladies."

"Good evening." Kenya smiled lightly. "I could smell the food before I left home. Smells so good."

"Me, too. Smells wonderful. I'm sure Lorenzo has whipped up something superyummy." Natalia smiled. "Hello, Lu."

"Natalia." Lu nodded at her friend. Things felt awkward. She poured wine into each of their glasses and handed one to each of them.

"Let's toast." Kenya held her glass into the air. Natalia and Lu did the same. "Here's to friendship. *No*, to sisterhood. Even though we go through tough things, we endure."

Lu tapped her glass against Kenya's, then Natalia's. She looked into her friend's eyes. "Sisters."

Natalia took a sip of her wine and then placed the glass on the table. She reached for Lu and hugged her tight. "Sisters."

Lorenzo emerged from the house carrying a tray with three bowls. "If you ladies would take your seats, we're going to start with the balela salad."

"What exactly is balela salad, Lorenzo?" Kenya asked.

"It's an ancient Middle Eastern chickpea salad. It's easy to whip up in such a short time; wholesome, colorful, and packed with flavor." Lorenzo placed a bowl in front of each of them.

The ladies took their seats at the table.

"This looks wonderful, Lorenzo." Natalia gave him a smile.

"Thank you. Please enjoy." Lorenzo vanished into the kitchen again to finish preparing whatever had the entire inn smelling like a four-star restaurant.

Lu smiled to herself. She was happy in that moment. The last time the three of them had been together at the inn, she'd thought for sure it would be the last. But it seemed the stars had aligned in the sky, and all was at peace in the heavens.

Chapter Thirty-one

Natalia

Lu looked Natalia square in the eyes. "I can't even begin to tell you how sorry I am . . . I mean, it's my fault that Nic left. I'm so glad he's home now."

Natalia sighed heavily. "That night was so . . . explosive, and incredibly painful. And you're not the reason Nic left." She bit her bottom lip, shut her eyes for a moment. The thought of saying the words aloud *again* caused a sharp pain in her chest. But she had to bring Lu up to speed. It was necessary to forgive her and release her. "So much has gone on since we were last together."

"That's an understatement." Kenya's eyes glanced at Lu and then landed on Natalia.

"You were not the cause of Nic leaving. He wanted a reason to leave." She swallowed, relived the vision of Angelina's swollen belly. Her heart fluttered. "It seems he's impregnated the mother of his child, Angelina. They're going to be parents again."

"What?" Lu frowned, trying to make sense of what Natalia said, as if she'd spoken in French.

"Yes, he's been a very bad boy. It seems he was doing

more than visiting family while in Sicily." Natalia sipped her wine.

"Are you kidding me? What in the entire fuck!" Lu became furious.

"My sentiments, too. He made me think I was overreacting, being insecure for no reason. He played the victim."

"How did you find out?"

"We were really connecting on a level that we'd never done before, at least I thought we were. It felt like . . . you know, like the beginning. Then, suddenly, the late hours started again. He'd call and tell me to keep his dinner warm. Well, I decided to pay him a visit, take dinner to him at his workplace. Thought I would surprise him. I drove all the way to the city, a batch of my arroz de marisco in tow. Needless to say, I was the one who was surprised."

"She was there," Lu shook her head

"Yes, big belly and all," Kenya added.

"Bastard!" Natalia exclaimed.

"What did he say? Did he have an explanation?" Lu's eyes bulged, her body stiffened.

"No explanation. Just behaved like a kid whose hand was caught in the cookie jar."

"Did you curse them both out? Tear his office apart? I would have," Kenya said.

"I ran away. I just wanted to get out of there as quickly as possible. I could barely breathe."

"Did he at least run after you?" Lu relaxed a bit.

"More of a jog. A very slow jog. I told him I was going to throw his things into the Cape May Canal." Natalia chuckled nervously, although inside she was dying. The pain of reliving it was slowly killing her.

"Um . . . yes. When I turned into the neighborhood after arriving home this morning, his clothes and belongings were all over the front lawn." Kenya laughed. "And she was stuffing the rest of them into the car. She was indeed headed to the canal."

"Good thing you pulled up in time." Lu laughed, too. "Or she'd be in jail right now."

"I thank God for Kenya. I was in a bad place."

"Yeah, we spent the day getting some things in order." Kenya gave Natalia a warm smile and touched her hand, then turned to Lu. "His things are now boxed up and in the garage. And when he comes to retrieve them, he'd better bring the sheriff!"

Natalia sighed. She was tired of discussing Nic. "So, enough about my dreadful life, how was your trip to Sacramento? I'm so sorry about John Samuels. Just when the two of you started to connect, this happens." Natalia shook her head. "Life sure does have a terrible sense of humor."

"Yeah, it kind of sucks, but I'm grateful for the time we spent together. The conversations we had." Lu took a sip of her wine. "I had a father for every bit of two seconds, but it was great while it lasted."

"I'm glad you were able to go and get your questions answered."

Lu solemnly took a bite of her food. "Me, too."

"Tell her what he left for you . . . in his will," Kenya urged.

"Do tell." Natalia squeezed her hands together.

"A beautiful piece of property in Napa Valley. A six-bedroom Victorian home that's currently being rented as a vacation home."

"Lu's Seaside Inn number two?" Natalia asked.

"Quite possibly."

"I'm so happy for you."

"I'm excited to see it in person. Maybe a girls' trip," Lu said.

"I'm in!" Kenya exclaimed.

Lorenzo emerged from the kitchen again. "If you're done with the salads, I'm ready to bring the entrées."

"We're ready, Lorenzo." Lu held her empty salad plate in the air.

Lorenzo collected their empty plates.

"So, Kenya, what's going on with you? Tell me about this fellow, Gideon," Natalia said after Lorenzo was gone.

"Nothing to tell, Nat Pack. He's ancient history."

"Not ancient history," Lu interjected. "He was just here a few weeks ago, rocking your world. He had you smiling and running up and down the beach. Then you gave him the boot. Although I'm not clear why exactly."

"Things were moving way too fast and I wasn't ready. Simple as that."

"You do realize that you sabotage every single potential relationship that comes your way, right?" Natalia asked.

"I admit, I have baggage."

Natalia understood Kenya's reservations and her thoughts about Glen. Though she hated that it existed, she understood. All she could do was give her friend some grace. "You will know when it's right. You won't be able to fight it any longer when it's right."

"And if it doesn't happen, I'm okay with that scenario, too." Kenya shrugged. "The last thing I need is someone else's baggage when I have my own."

Lu looked away toward the ocean while sipping her wine.

Natalia changed the subject. "How's your big case with the great deacon?"

Kenya rolled her eyes. "He's a thorn in my side. But we're in the home stretch now. Jury selection is next week and then we go to trial. Hopefully it's not a long-drawn-out trial and we can wrap it up quickly."

"Hopefully so. I don't even know him and I want to shake the living daylights out of him," Natalia teased.

Kenya laughed. "I think he's innocent. I just need to highlight some of the awesome things that he does in the community, and at the church. As annoying as he is, he does a lot of good. He's my father's very good friend, like family almost. I don't think he's a murderer."

"Well, I hope all goes well and that it wraps up quickly." Natalia clasped her hands together. "And then we can get back to the wedding plans."

Kenya and Lu looked at each other and then dropped their heads.

"What?" Natalia asked.

"The wedding's off, Nat Pack," Kenya spoke for Lu.

"What? Why?" Natalia reflected on the night that everything went wrong, the night of the explosion, and remembered that Kenya mentioned something about Zach seeing a divorce attorney. "Was Zach cheating?"

"Zach is married, Natalia. Married! To an Ethiopian woman who he married years ago so that she could remain in this country. He never divorced her."

"Wow. So, that's why he was seeing the divorce attorney." Natalia's head was spinning from all this new information. "So, the woman won't give him a divorce? Is that why the wedding is off?"

"The wedding is off because he lied. He wasn't forthright with me. Didn't trust me enough to tell me the truth," Lu interjected.

"Maybe he was just afraid," Natalia offered.

"Afraid or not, that's a terrible way to begin a new marriage, with lies and secrets," said Lu.

"I agree with that statement," Kenya chimed in. "Although I do believe wholeheartedly that Zach loves you and is completely devoted to you. He just messed up."

"He messed up big-time," Lu said.

"Such a shame that the wedding of the summer won't take

place. I was so looking forward to it. Have you canceled the vendors? The musicians? Have you told your guests?"

"Not yet."

Natalia exhaled. "Good, then there's still hope. I mean, in case you change your mind."

Lorenzo emerged from the kitchen with three plates filled with something fragrant and beautiful.

"Looks and smells wonderful, Lorenzo. What is it?" Kenya asked.

"It's Mediterranean garlic shrimp, cooked in a white wine and olive oil sauce, served over a bed of rice. I hope you enjoy. Bon appétit."

"Thank you, Lorenzo." Lu gave her chef a warm glance and then turned to Natalia. "Even if I did change my mind, it wouldn't matter. I can't wed a married man."

"She has a point there," Kenya added.

"Then we have to get him divorced! Kenya?"

"Don't look at me. I'm in criminal law, not family law."

"But you have lawyer friends who can help, right?"

"Zach already has an attorney. Her name is Danielle Curry, and as much as it pains me to say it, she's the best there is," said Kenya.

"That's if I were to change my mind. That hasn't been decided yet."

"Well, I certainly hope you do. This circle of friends, this island of Cape May, this world needs some goodness. So much bad has gone on, I need to know that real happiness and love and goodness really does exist."

Kenya grabbed Natalia's hands and held them tight. "It does exist, honey. It does."

Natalia hoped that someone could prove it because, at the moment, she wasn't the least bit convinced.

Chapter Thirty-two

Lu

After helping Lorenzo in the kitchen, Lu sat on the stairs of the veranda, a mug filled with herbal tea and lemon wedges in hand. She stared off into the darkness of the night, watched as the moon twinkled and the stars danced; listened as the ocean rippled against the shore. Ella Fitzgerald belted the lyrics to "Summertime" as it played softly on the stereo. She thought of John and hoped he was listening to Ella as well, *and dancing*. About this time on any given evening, they would've been engaged in a heated discussion about something or other, or she'd have been asking him a million questions, and he would answer every one of them ever so eloquently and honestly. He was one of the most transparent people she knew. It was what she most admired about him, the way he seemed to lay things all on the table or tossed things into the air, allowed the pieces to fall where they may. It was a wonderful trait, she thought.

A butterfly floated past her nose. She reached out her hand and allowed it to land on her palm. It flew away, but then a few seconds later it was perched on her knee. She reached out her hand and allowed it to rest on the curve of her finger.

"I know that's you, John Samuels," she whispered and then chuckled.

The butterfly, which flew past her nose again, its melanin— a blend of yellow, brown, and black—landed on her hand again, stayed there until she finished the last drop of her herbal tea.

She relaxed her back against the wooden railing and pulled up her legs to her chest.

"Hey." Zach stood at the bottom of the stairs, wearing blue scrubs and a pair of Crocs on his feet. He stroked his precisely lined beard and his eyes lit up when he saw Lu. "You're still up."

"Yep, just enjoying the night."

"How was dinner with the girls?"

"It was good. A lot has happened since we last spoke. It was great catching up."

Zach took a seat next to Lu on the top step. "So, everything's good. You all made up?"

"Yeah, we did." Out of habit, she stretched out her legs, rested them on Zach's lap. It was something she'd done many nights when they'd relaxed on the veranda steps, especially after one of his long shifts at the hospital.

He slipped her flip-flop from her foot, massaged her heel and then her arch, then slid his finger between her toes. She leaned her head back and closed her eyes for a moment. She exhaled as a moan slipped from her lips. Her inner thighs tingled, and she wanted to tell him to stop, but she couldn't.

"I'm sorry I didn't tell you about Nala. I realize now that it was a terrible mistake to keep my past from you. Honestly, I just never handled it because I didn't meet anyone, before now, that I wanted to marry."

"Her name is Nala," Lu said it emphatically. Before then, she'd never heard the woman's name. Didn't know that she'd even existed. "What's she like?"

"She's a nice person. She was a good friend at one time."

"Apparently, you were a good friend to her as well."

"We were a couple of silly kids making decisions that we had no idea would affect our future lives. She was facing deportation and I wanted to help."

"Did you love her?"

"I loved her as a friend. That's all we were. I didn't love her like I love you. I've not loved anyone like I love you."

"Is she pretty?"

"She's pretty." He looked into Lu's eyes. "Not as pretty as you."

"I guess I walked into that." Lu smiled.

"She was looking for a better life in the US. People in other countries aren't as fortunate as we are here. I wanted her life to be better."

"Kinda like John rescued Yana from poverty in the Philippines. I guess I can appreciate that. We all need our knight in shining armor."

"I'd like to be your knight in shining armor. I'd like to be your rescuer, your protector." He grinned. "Your baby daddy, if you change your mind and decide that you want children."

"Have you changed your mind about children?" Lu asked. It was the first time they'd talked about children since they'd both decided they didn't want to be parents.

"Well, after going through this whole John Samuels thing with you, it's had me thinking about some things. I mean, if I was ill and dying, I think I would like to have a family around me. As annoying as that sister of yours was, I bet John was still proud of her. Proud of all his children. It was beautiful to see how his eyes lit up when you were around him."

"So . . . how many children would you want . . . I mean, if you potentially had some?" Lu asked.

"I don't know, one or two. I'd definitely want a junior, I mean, if I ever decided I wanted children. Potentially." He slid off the flip-flop from her other foot and began massaging her heel. "What about you? Have you thought about it at all?" Zach stopped massaging her foot, long enough to hear her response.

"I must admit . . . I have. I mean, of course, not right away, but I'm not completely against it anymore, not like I was. I wouldn't mind a girl and a boy. Potentially." Lu motioned for him to get back to the massage.

"So, if we were to . . . say, continue with our wedding plans, and got married, we might have a little Zach Jr. and a little Lualhati running around Cape May? Potentially."

"Potentially." Lu giggled.

"My lawyer has located Nala, and she's been served with the divorce papers. I'm just waiting for her to sign," Zach offered.

"What if she doesn't sign?" Lu asked.

"She will. She has no reason not to."

Lu turned her head, looked out into the darkness of the ocean, watched as the waves played hide-and-seek against the sand.

"So, Lualhati Samuels, I have to ask you." Zach grabbed her hand in his and caressed her empty ring finger. He reached into his pocket and pulled out the three-carat princess-cut diamond engagement ring that he'd given her eight months before. "Will you still marry me?"

"You just carry that ring around in the pocket of your scrubs?" She smiled.

"Don't mess up the moment."

She placed her hands on each side of his face and caressed the stubble against his jaw. She looked into his tired eyes and then gently kissed his lips. She'd wanted to do that since the moment he'd dropped everything and come to her rescue, without pause or reservation. He'd already been with her through the better and certainly through some of the worse. She had no doubt, he loved her.

"Yes. I will still marry you," Lu touched his nose, "provided your wife gives you a divorce."

"Oh, you got jokes." He kissed her lips again and then slid the ring back onto her finger.

"No joke, sir. Get yourself unmarried or there will be a problem."

"Consider it done," he said.

"Good, because there isn't room for three of us in this relationship."

Zach chuckled. "I love you and I can't wait to be your husband."

The truth of the matter was, even after all that had gone on in her life in just a short time, she couldn't wait to be his wife.

Chapter Thirty-three

Kenya

Kenya sped from her downtown law firm all the way to the Chelsea Heights neighborhood where her father had built his church over ten years before. She still remembered the groundbreaking ceremony and then, eight months later, the ribbon-cutting that took place on those grounds. Walter Lewis had been so proud, standing next to the mayor and a few board members of the church. Deacon Charles had been at her father's side from the moment they'd signed the contract on the new church home and before that. He'd been there when they'd barely had a place to hold Bible study and resorted to holding it in her parents' den. After the ribbon was cut, she remembered how the two men had embraced; strong, genuine. It had been a proud moment for both. Kenya hated the predicament that Deacon Charles had found himself in now—facing second-degree murder charges.

She had just attended his church on Sunday. She had sung her praises and hugged and chitchatted with just about every single member in attendance. Even Sister Caroline, who talked more than anyone in the world, made it her business to corner Kenya every single Sunday, asking when she was going to *find a nice man to give her some babies.* Try never, lady! However, when she said it this Sunday, Kenya couldn't help but think of Gideon. He popped right into her head, as if it were perfectly natural for him to be there. Though she tried with all her might to erase him from her thoughts, lately he seemed to show up more often than she needed him to.

She pulled into the neighborhood and fought her way past the police cars lined up haphazardly along the street. Blue lights flickered and strangers had started to gather to see what the fuss was about. Kenya parked her black Mercedes a block away, stepped out, and locked the doors. She strolled down the block toward her father's church, her red bottoms click-clacked against the pavement. She spotted Walter chatting with a police officer. As she got closer, her eyes veered toward the church. The word *Murderer* was spray-painted on the mahogany brick wall in huge black letters, just below the steeple.

"Daddy." Kenya lightly touched her father's arm.

"Hey, baby girl. I'm glad you're here." He pulled Kenya into an embrace.

"What's going on?"

His tone emotionless and with a look of pain all over his seventy-two-year-old face, he said, "When I pulled up for afternoon prayer, I saw this. I canceled the prayer service, called the police, and then called you. I hope I didn't interrupt any of your meetings."

"It's okay. I'm glad you called."

"Who would do this?" Walter asked to no one in particular.

"Someone who clearly has no respect for the Lord's house." Kenya was saddened as she stared at the graffiti.

The officer handed Walter a business card. "If you think of any more information, sir, you can reach out to me at this number."

Walter took the card and glanced at it. "I certainly will. Thank you."

The officer walked away and joined his team, who were in search of clues.

"I'm sorry about all of this, Daddy."

"I'm just glad they didn't break in or burn the place down, you know? This is something that can be cleaned up."

"Have you already called someone?"

"Not yet, but I'm going to as soon as the cops are done." He gave Kenya a pointed look. "And listen, I do not want your mama knowing anything about this. It will only make her worry."

"Well, it's a little too late for that." Kenya nodded toward the swarm of news trucks that had already started pulling into the neighborhood.

"My word! They're like bloodhounds. I can't wait until this trial is over and Deacon Charles is acquitted of all charges so we can get back to the Lord's work."

"Tomorrow is the last day of jury selection and we go to trial next week. I'm hoping it's a quick trial. I'm anxious to get this over with as well. Your deacon is working my nerves."

Walter gave her a subtle laugh. "He means well."

"Yeah, yeah." Kenya shook her head. "Anyway, don't say anything to the reporters. I'll handle it."

The reporters and cameramen rushed toward them, microphones and cameras in hand.

"Work your magic, baby," Pastor Lewis told Kenya.

"Pastor Lewis, can you tell us anything about the graffiti on the building? Does this have anything to do with the charges that have been filed against your parishioner, Donovan Charles?" The blonde-haired woman stuck her microphone directly into Walter Lewis's face.

"Pastor Lewis declines to comment regarding this," Kenya intercepted.

"Wasn't Mr. Charles formally charged with murder just recently by the Atlantic County prosecutor's office?" another reporter asked. "And aren't you his counsel, Miss Lewis?"

"Yes, he was, and yes, I am," Kenya announced. "He goes to trial next week."

"Wasn't it Mr. Charles who was seen on the video footage retrieved from the bodega across the street from the victim's condo?"

Kenya grabbed her father's arm and ushered him through the crowd. "No further comment," she said.

"Do you think the graffiti is a message from someone with information regarding the crime?"

"I think that illegally spray-painting someone's property is vandalism, which is a punishable crime. And we have nothing further to say. Now, if you'll excuse us." Kenya and Walter pushed past the reporters until they reached her father's pickup truck. "Go home, Daddy. Call someone to clean up this mess."

"Okay, sweetheart."

"I'll call you later." She kissed his cheek, wiped the lipstick traces away with her fingertips, and then headed toward her car.

Once inside, Kenya grasped the steering wheel tightly and leaned her head back against the leather seat. She had represented many criminals over the years, some innocent, others she knew were guilty; precarious clients, some of the most unsavory characters in New Jersey, but never had her career crept into her personal life in this manner. This was the first time her family were involved—her parents, the church. She glanced over at the graffiti-ridden brick wall, stared at the spray-painted words splattered across the front of it. She needed to win this case and fast, so the world would know once and for all that Donovan Charles was not a *murderer*.

Chapter Thirty-four

Natalia

Natalia relaxed at the dining table, a glass of wine in front of her. She stroked her hair with her fingers and rubbed her temples. Her head ached just as much as her heart did, mostly from crying. She couldn't count the number of times she'd considered giving up hope that her life would ever resemble anything normal, hope that the pain in her chest would ever subside. She kept having disturbing visions of Nic making mad, passionate love to Angelina. She envisioned him holding her in his arms and caressing her face with his fingertips, as he had to her. However, she couldn't even envision herself with him anymore. Their life together had become a blur.

Her throat was dry, and she took a sip of the wine to quench her thirst, or maybe it was to rid her thoughts of Nic and Angelina. She wasn't sure anymore. The reasons were beginning to run together like one big blurry mess. All she knew was that the Cabernet Sauvignon was helping her to erase her troubles, and she had opened this second bottle for that reason. Kenya had assured her that *this too shall pass*, but she wondered how quickly it would, because it seemed to be taking its sweet time. Her emotions were in a whirl.

She lifted the papers and read through them *again,* for the third time since she'd left her attorney's office. She wasn't asking for much—didn't want anything from him—only the house on Cape May. And the furniture. Of course she wanted the furniture. Most of it included the Victorian antique pieces that she and Kenya had spent many Saturdays shopping for and restoring.

She had already changed the locks and left Nic's belongings in the garage. She had peeked through the window and watched as he'd loaded them into the back of his SUV the night before. He had rung the doorbell and knocked, wanting to speak with her, perhaps to try to explain his side. However, from her point of view, his side was quite clear the night she found him with Angelina. There was no denying what she'd encountered in his office. Had it been secondhand information, there would be reason for conversation, but she'd seen it with her own eyes, and her eyes didn't lie. She had declined to answer her phone and the door and instead watched as he pulled away from their home, quite possibly for the last time. He didn't need to return. Their lives together had come to a painful end.

She swallowed more of the Cabernet, and then stood up and paced the floor. She needed to eat something but didn't feel like the hassle of cooking. She hadn't eaten a real meal since dinner at Lu's on Friday night. When the doorbell rang, it startled her. Had Nic returned to torment her some more, to insist that she speak with him? Her heart started beating fast as she peeked through the curtains in the living room. *Kenya.*

"Hey." She swung the door open wide.

"Hello, my dear. I brought dinner." Kenya waltzed into the house and past Natalia, a brown paper bag in her hand. She headed for the kitchen.

"Hello to you, too." She shut and locked the door and then followed Kenya to the kitchen.

"I know you haven't eaten anything today." She looked at Natalia, raised an eyebrow. "Have you?"

"Well, no, but . . ."

"Nat Pack, you have to eat or you'll make yourself sick." Kenya picked up the empty wine bottle from the island, held it into the air. "You need more nourishment than this. How many of these have you had?"

"I've lost count," Natalia admitted and then hung her head.

Kenya walked over to the shelf and pulled down two plates. She handed one to Natalia. "I brought Chinese." She opened the silverware drawer and retrieved a fork, then began to pile pork lo mein and an egg roll onto her plate. She took a seat at the island.

Natalia fixed herself a plate and joined Kenya. "I saw that lawyer today; the one you referred me to."

"Danielle Curry."

"We drew up the divorce papers. He's going to be served at his office this week."

"Good." Kenya used chopsticks to load lo mein into her mouth. "Did he pick up his things?"

"Yesterday."

"You didn't let him in, did you?" Kenya asked.

"No. I didn't answer the door, or my phone. Finally, he stopped knocking and calling."

Kenya slid from the barstool, went to the fridge, and grabbed a bottle of water. Natalia went into the dining room and retrieved the copy of divorce papers and handed them over to Kenya.

Kenya slid back onto the barstool and scanned the paperwork. "You're not asking for much. You sure you don't want to ask for spousal support? Half his 401k or his savings? You're certainly entitled to it."

"I don't want anything from him. I have my own money. I

just want my home and my furniture. That's it." Natalia poured wine into her glass. "Wine?"

Kenya nodded a yes. "Sure, I'll have some."

Natalia pulled another wineglass from the shelf, poured Kenya a glass, and handed it to her. She slid back onto her barstool. "I feel so much hate and anger in my heart toward him."

"I know, honey. That's normal, even for you. What he did was despicable. I hate him for you." Kenya sipped her wine. "I can't believe he's the same guy who was such a good friend to Glen."

"Glen would be cursing him out right now!"

"Or talking some sense into him. They were close. Inseparable at times. I think Glen might've been the only one to get through to him."

"I don't think he ever stopped loving her. Angelina. Maybe I was his rebound."

"You were not his rebound. I have no doubt that he loved you and still does, Nat Pack. He was just being a man," Kenya assured her.

"Why wasn't I enough?"

"Oh no, don't do that. Don't give him your power. You were more than enough. Look at you! You're a beautiful, intelligent business owner. You're talented, sweet as can be . . ."

"And barren. I couldn't give him the one thing that he wanted so badly, another child."

"That's no reason to cheat!" Kenya sighed deeply, laid her chopsticks on her plate. "This is not your burden to bear, it's his. He made this bed. You were a perfect wife to his undeserving ass. Don't you dare blame yourself."

A tear crept down the side of Natalia's face. She wiped it away with her fingertips. "Thank you."

Kenya stroked Natalia's face. "I know it hurts right now, but I promise you'll get through this."

"I know I will."

"I hate that he came back at all. You were starting to re-cover from the last blow of discovering those stupid letters. I felt like you were healing from that, and then boom! He came back and disrupted everything."

"I had started growing accustomed to life without him. Got my groove back."

"And you'll get it back again. You'll see."

"Hope so."

After dinner, Kenya left. Natalia cleaned up, put the left-over food away. She washed the plates and empty wine-glasses, dried them and put them away. She glanced over at her phone lying on the counter and considered calling Nic. As the wine began to make her tipsy, she decided that she wanted answers to some of her burning questions, the first being why he had hurt her this way. Why had he led her to believe she was the one who was crazy? Why Angelina, of all the women in the world he could've chosen? She picked up the phone, pulled up his number. A few seconds later, she placed the phone back on the island.

"No," she whispered. Instead, she headed upstairs and started the shower.

She held on to Kenya's words. Made a mantra out of them: *This too shall pass. This too shall pass. This too shall pass.*

Chapter Thirty-five

Kenya

Kenya swayed down the hallway of her office and stepped into the conference room. Mitch was already there, engaging in small talk with Deacon Charles.

"Okay, let's get started." Kenya joined them, set her laptop on the table.

"Good morning, Kenya. Don't you look beautiful this morning, all bright and cheerful? You know, you're beautiful just like your mother. And I must say that red is definitely your color."

Kenya beamed at the deacon's compliments. She was indeed the spitting image of Melba Lewis; people always told her that. Though she looked like her mother, she was completely a daddy's girl. She'd always been. She had particularly chosen the gray suit with a silk red blouse underneath. Occasionally she stepped out of her conservative box and gave her wardrobe a bit of pizzazz, but today she needed to look professional and exude confidence. Red was her power color, and she needed all the power she could get for the first day of her high-profile murder case.

SUMMARY ON CAPE MAY   271

Kenya turned to Mitch. "Have we narrowed down our character witnesses?"

"My friend, Walter, your father, will make the best character witness of all. Don't you think?" Deacon Charles offered his unwarranted advice, as if he had joined the legal team.

"I'm not putting my father on the stand. I won't put him through that. There are other members of the church who can vouch for your character. Larry Davis, for instance, who you've served with on the deacon board. Edward Thompson, one of the community leaders who you've worked alongside in the community, feeding the hungry, doing your toy drive, and that back-to-school thing that the two of you head up every year. He's your frat brother, too. Right?"

"Yes, he is."

"You've been a member of the board at Rutgers University for umpteen years. We have to play up your strengths. Make sure the jury sees you as a normal contributing citizen."

"Put me on the stand, Kenya. Who's a better character witness than me?" Deacon Charles urged, wearing a brown tailored suit, adorned with gold cuff links and a crisp white designer shirt. He was always sharply dressed, even on Sunday morning. The tall, handsome middle-aged man kept his facial hair precisely trimmed. He often flashed the huge championship ring that rested on his finger, an indication that he was more than just a regular player on the team at Rutgers. No, he ruled the court during his college basketball days. He always made sure everyone knew that he had been *this* close to making it to the NBA.

"Absolutely not," Kenya vetoed his idea of taking the stand.

"Why not?" he asked, a frown in the center of his forehead.

"You're not ready and the prosecution will eat you alive. It would jeopardize the case. Too risky." Kenya opened her laptop and began typing some key points. "Besides, I hate to say it, but you're like a loose cannon, Deacon Charles. You talk to people when I tell you not to and, furthermore, I don't trust what you might say on the stand."

"Fair enough. I've handled things badly." He backed down, his stance relaxed now.

"I don't ever think it's a good idea to put the defendant on the stand unless it's absolutely necessary. And I think we're okay with the witnesses we have."

Mitch jumped in. "We need to go over your alibi. Make sure it's airtight. Your wife is going to corroborate your testimony that you were home all evening and did not leave the house, correct?"

"It's the truth, I was. I dropped by that Cuban restaurant on Pacific, ordered takeout, and then headed home."

"Mr. Charles, we know that at some point you stopped by Julian Miller's condo. And before you answer, let me remind you that you are under oath, and we have video footage of you."

"Yes, I dropped by Julian's place. I needed to drop off some papers that required his signature."

"Did you get him to sign those papers?'

"Yes, he signed them, and I left. Then I went home and spent the rest of the evening with my wife."

"Even though the time of death doesn't coincide with the time that the video placed you there, how do we know you didn't return later, catch him while he was sleeping, and smother him to death with a pillow?"

"That's ridiculous!" The deacon slammed his fist against the table.

Mitch remained calm and cool, continued his interrogation. "He died by asphyxiation. Maybe you returned later, came in through a back entrance, away from the cameras."

The deacon's posture became more rigid. He lowered his brow and squinted his eyes. "Julian was my friend. I loved him like a brother. I would never hurt him."

"You lied about being home all evening when you were questioned in the beginning. It was only later that we learned you went out to pick up dinner. You lied about seeing Mr. Miller that day. In your statement, you claimed that you hadn't seen him at all that day, when in fact there's video footage that places you at his home. How do you explain the discrepancies in your statements to us and to the police, Mr. Charles?"

"What I've told you today is the truth."

"How do we know you're not lying today, and yesterday, and the day before that?"

Deacon Charles shook his head profusely.

"If you'll lie about something as simple as picking up dinner, maybe you'll lie about anything. One could conclude, Mr. Charles, that you're just a liar," Mitch stated.

Deacon Charles disregarded Mitch's statement and turned to Kenya. "You've known me most of your life. I'm godfather to you, Xander, and Tricia, for God's sake. I'm not lying!"

"We just wanted you to see what will happen if we put you on the stand," Kenya told him.

The deacon exhaled. His breathing slowed a bit, and he relaxed in his seat after the interrogation.

"Are you willing to accept any plea bargains? The prosecutor will ask before trial," Kenya explained.

The deacon tapped his finger on the table with every syllable, "I'm not taking any plea bargains," and then pulled a handkerchief from his inside pocket, wiped his forehead. "I'm innocent, and the jury will see that."

"Okay, then let's do this," Kenya explained.

They spent the remainder of the morning talking about their witnesses and what to expect later that afternoon, when they appeared in court.

After meeting with the prosecutor in the judge's chambers, Kenya walked into the courtroom, where members of Cornerstone Baptist Church were sprinkled about, there to observe and support Deacon Charles. The deacon's wife, Eleanor, sat right next to Kenya's parents in the front row. Her brother, Xander, gave her a thumbs-up. She had hoped that her sister would've shown up, but she hadn't. She wasn't surprised, though. Her relationship with Tricia had been strained for so long. It was as if Tricia blamed her for continuing her education, leaving home, becoming successful— all the things she wasn't. Sometimes, Kenya found it hard to believe that the three of them had grown up in the same household.

Kenya took her seat next to Mitch and Deacon Charles.

"You okay?" she whispered to the deacon.

"As well as can be expected." Deacon Charles stared straight ahead, a wrinkle between his eyebrows. He wrung his hands together as his leg bounced up and down.

"Relax," Kenya told him.

"Counsel, are we ready?" the gray-haired female judge asked.

"Ready, Judge," said the prosecutor, Oliver James.

"Yes, Your Honor, the defense is ready," Kenya announced.

"Good." The judge nodded her head for the prosecution to begin.

Kenya watched intently as Oliver questioned the prosecution's first witness—Sophia Willingham, personal assistant to Julian Miller, who testified that the relationship between Deacon Charles and Julian was volatile at times. Everyone's relationship was volatile at times, Kenya thought. *Wasn't it?* She couldn't wait to cross-examine.

Kenya stood, smoothed her skirt before approaching the witness. "Mrs. Willingham, *or should I say Ms. Willingham,* you're recently widowed, correct?"

"Yes, ma'am, I am. But you can keep the missus on there, honey."

"I'm so sorry for your loss."

"Thank you, very kindly. I miss Harold more and more each day, God rest his soul."

"Have you been able to find a replacement for your deceased husband?"

"Beg your pardon?"

"Weren't you looking for a replacement when you came onto my client just a few weeks ago? Suggested that the two of you go out to dinner, have a few cocktails . . ."

"There's no harm in dinner."

"What about the after-dinner sex that you suggested to him? Was that harmless as well?" Kenya turned to face the courtroom with her eyes still locked with Eleanor's.

Eleanor blinked a few times, then dropped her head.

"Your Honor!" Oliver James stood, objecting to Kenya's line of questioning.

"Get to it, Counselor," the judge said to Kenya.

"Yes, Your Honor." Kenya turned back to the witness and approached her, "Isn't it true, Mrs. Willingham, that you came on to Mr. Charles within two weeks of your husband's death?"

"I admit, I did. I was just feeling a bit lonely."

"But when he turned you down, it angered you, didn't it?"

"No."

"It made you want to get back at him. Made you feel like a fool. Desperate. Pathetic. And the easiest way to get back at him was for you to join the prosecution's bandwagon and testify that he and Mr. Miller had a volatile relationship. Isn't that why you're here today, to get back at him for giving you the cold shoulder?"

"Their relationship had become very rocky, especially toward the end. That I know for sure."

"But isn't it true that every relationship is volatile at some point? I mean, aren't we all imperfect people?"

"I suppose so." Mrs. Willingham adjusted in her seat and smoothed the wig on her head.

"Wasn't your relationship with your husband rocky at times?"

"Yes, but . . ."

"You didn't murder your husband . . . did you, Mrs. Willingham?"

"Absolutely not! My husband died of a heart attack."

"Your Honor!" Oscar objected again.

The judge gave Kenya a warning glance.

"How long had you been Mr. Miller's personal assistant?" Kenya asked before the woman could regain her composure.

"Fifteen years."

"In fifteen years, have you had any arguments, disagreements with him? Heated discussions?"

"Of course. We hadn't always seen eye to eye. Julian could be quite stubborn, even cantankerous at times."

"I bet that just got under your skin."

"Sometimes, yes."

"Made you want to kill him, huh?"

"Well, no, not . . ."

"Maybe it was you who slipped into his condo well past midnight."

The judge warned, "Careful, Counselor. The witness is not on trial here."

"Withdrawn, Your Honor." Kenya turned to the jury, observed their faces, then walked back to her seat. "I have nothing further."

Day one.

She was ready for every witness that the prosecution threw her way.

Chapter Thirty-six

Natalia

She poured a taste of wine into each of their glasses and then slid them in front of them.

"Okay, ladies. Let's pick up your glasses. You want to observe the wine, its hue and intensity. Is it pale in color or more of a deep ruby red?" Natalia asked, not really expecting an answer. "Then we want to swirl it."

Each woman looked at the wine in her glass, observed the color, followed Natalia's lead, and swirled their glasses in a circular motion.

"Just looks yummy to me," the bride-to-be giggled.

The wedding party had popped into the winery for an impromptu wine tasting. Their intimate wedding was set to take place on the beach, much like Lu's and Zach's wedding would in September, at least she hoped there would still be a wedding. She hoped that their love and marriage would last forever, not like hers and Nic's. She wished for them a different outcome.

"Now, we want to smell the wine. I would say close your eyes, position the glass just below your nose, and take a quick whiff. Which fruits do you smell?"

"Berries—strawberries, raspberries," one of the ladies said.

"Does it have notes of herbs or flowers? What about aromas like vanilla, coconut, or chocolate . . ."

Natalia had conducted hundreds of tastings at her winery. She could do it with her eyes closed, knew everything about every bottle of wine in her cellar. It was something that she enjoyed—introducing patrons to new wines, new experiences. But today she was distracted. Her stomach was topsy-turvy, nerves on edge, hands fidgety. The wait was driving her crazy.

Today was the day.

The sheriff would serve Nic with the divorce papers today. She knew that he would call soon thereafter, frantic. He'd probably be angry because of the embarrassment of being served at his place of business. He might not agree with her terms and even decide he wanted to fight her for the house and all its furnishings. Or maybe he'd insist that they enlist a Realtor, sell, and split the proceeds. And this was a stretch—a huge one—he might not want the divorce at all. What if he just flat-out refused to give her a divorce altogether? Either scenario had her on edge.

The suspense was killing her.

She motioned for her assistant to take over the wine tasting while she stepped away, retreating to her office. She fell into the leather chair, rested her back and head against the leather. Her heart rate increased as she was about to dial Danielle Curry's number when she called.

"Natalia." Danielle was calm and reserved.

"Has he been served?" Natalia asked before her attorney could finish the sentence.

"I'm afraid not."

"Why? What do you mean?"

"He doesn't work there anymore. He resigned yesterday and left for Sicily this morning."

"He just up and left without warning?"

"That's what we were told," said Danielle. "Now, there are ways to get this done without him. Him being out of the country can actually work in our favor. You just say the word."

"I'm sorry, I . . . I just need to think this through." Natalia's eyes threatened to fill. She felt a lump forming in her throat. "Thank you. I'll get back to you."

"Okay, Natalia. We'll talk soon." Danielle ended the call.

Natalia sat there, her face covered with both hands, crying. How dare he disappear when she needed closure!

Chapter Thirty-seven

Kenya

Kenya waltzed into the courtroom, her head held high. In the previous days of the trial, she'd cross-examined every witness that the prosecution placed on the stand and left every testimony with a shadow of doubt.

"Wow, you're shrewd," Deacon Charles had whispered to Kenya the day before.

"I'm very good at what I do." Kenya's cockiness caused him to stare at her in awe—or admiration—she wasn't sure which. "Close your mouth, Deacon. Tomorrow will be trickier. Let's hope your witnesses come through for you."

She'd packed her briefcase, left him standing there with his mouth open. She rushed to her family and received hugs from them. The press had waited just outside on the courthouse steps. With microphones pressed in her face, she declined to comment on every one of their questions. Deacon Charles followed suit, also declining to comment. He'd been warned, and she was happy to see he had heeded her warning that if he recklessly spoke to them again, she'd drop his case immediately. He didn't want that, particularly after witnessing her performance during the trial thus far.

*   *   *

Today would be the hardest day yet, and she knew it.

Kenya walked into the courtroom. The members of Cornerstone Baptist Church were all there. Her parents were in the front row again, alongside Xander, who gave her his award-winning smile and his usual thumbs-up. Deacon Charles's wife, Eleanor, was not present, and Kenya thought that strange. She had warned them they should keep things as normal as possible, so she was alarmed that his support wasn't there. However, in Eleanor's place sat Tricia. Kenya's heart fluttered at the sight of her sister. She smiled at Tricia, and although she didn't return the smile, Kenya was happy to see her there.

Kenya took her seat next to Mitch and Deacon Charles.

"Is the defense ready to proceed with closing arguments?" the judge asked.

Kenya stood. "We are, Your Honor," she said, and turned to face the jury.

"Ladies and gentlemen, the prosecution wants you to believe that my client is guilty simply because he entered Mr. Miller's condo the night of the murder. They have no evidence other than the video footage of my client entering and leaving the premises. You've heard testimony from people who knew both men, and attested to their relationship—they were friends, partners, brothers. Did they argue over the years? Of course; all friends do. Arguing doesn't equate to murder. You've heard from the defendant's church members. He's an upstanding member of Cornerstone Baptist Church, where he's been a deacon for more than thirty years. He's active in his community, feeding the hungry, facilitating toy drives and back-to-school programs." Kenya paced in front of the jury. She tried to read their faces, wanted to make an impact. "The evidence must be so convincing that you can answer 'yes' to the question: Has the state proved the defendant's guilt beyond a reasonable doubt? There's a rear entrance to the building where Mr. Miller lived. The evidence showed the key to that door was missing from Mr. Miller's key ring." Kenya shrugged her shoulders. "Anyone could've been in possession of that key. Mr. Miller was a shrewd business-man. Any number of people might have had motive. I'm sorry, but there just isn't enough evidence to convict my client, and certainly not beyond a reasonable doubt. The prosecution has failed to prove their case, and I would ask you to keep that in mind when you deliberate, and that you return a verdict, the only verdict, of *not guilty*. Thank you."

Kenya returned to her seat.

"You may proceed, Mr. James."

"Thank you, Your Honor." Oliver approached the jury. "Members of the jury, his name was Julian Miller Jr., and he was born on April 12, 1953, right here in New Jersey. You met his parents and his sister, Leona Miller, yesterday, and heard about the special bond that he had with his family. You heard from his colleagues, who spoke about his work ethic and the people in the community who held him in high regard. Julian died from someone choking him to death. He couldn't breathe in his final moments. Asphyxiation is a horrible way to die. When he was found, he had no pulse. Ladies and gentlemen, you saw the video. That video unequivocally places the defendant at the scene of the crime and proves that Mr. Charles entered Ju-lian Miller's home on the night of the murder. He lied in his original statement, claiming that he hadn't been there. He retracted that statement after the video footage became public. No one was seen entering or leaving Mr. Miller's home that night but the defendant. Julian Miller was heart-lessly strangled to death by the defendant, his longtime friend and business partner. You heard testimony that in his final days, their relationship had become volatile. This case is exactly what you thought when you first saw that video. When you saw the defendant enter Mr. Miller's home and then exit, your eyes weren't playing tricks on you. This was murder. The defendant is guilty of murder in the second degree. Thank you."

Oliver rested in his seat as the judge gave instructions to the jury.

Kenya began packing up her briefcase. She didn't know how long the jury would deliberate. It could be an hour or twenty-four hours.

"What happens now?" Deacon Charles whispered.

"We wait."

"How long will it take?"

"It's in the hands of the jury now."

In the fellowship hall of her father's church, lunch had been prepared for the family and the congregation—fried chicken, macaroni and cheese, collard greens, and sweet tea. Loud conversations and laughter ensued. Deacon Charles paced the floor, wrung his hands. He rubbed the back of his neck and loosened his tie. Kenya observed him from across the room while eating.

"Well, I must say, you were a beast in that courtroom today," Tricia took a seat next to Kenya at the table, a plate of food in her hand.

Kenya smiled inside. She raised an eyebrow. "I guess that's a compliment."

"I was quite impressed," Tricia continued. "Proud, actually."

"Thank you. I'm glad you made it. Glad you were able to see me work."

"Yeah, me, too." Tricia smiled at her sister and Kenya's heart soared. "I'm going back to school. I've enrolled at NYU for the fall semester. Most of it online."

"That's great, Tricia." Kenya laid her fork down and faced her sister.

"Of course I'm not going to become a big-time lawyer like my sister or anything, but I am going to finish my degree."

"I think that's fantastic." Kenya gave her sister a hug.

"I'm pretty excited about it."

"You know what would be great? If you and Malik would come to Cape May and hang out with me for a weekend."

"You know you've never invited me there. After all these years."

Kenya tried to remember a time when she'd extended an invitation so that she could prove her sister wrong, but she couldn't think of one single time either. She'd always assumed that it was a given that her family could visit anytime, but she saw that Tricia had expected a personal invitation.

She thought about saying, *You've always had an open invitation,* but thought it best to say, "Well, I'm inviting you now."

"Figured you had your sisters, Lu and Natalia. Figured you'd forgotten that I was also your sister. Your blood sister."

"I haven't forgotten that. We will always be sisters, Tricia. No one can change that."

Tricia was quiet for a moment, ate her food in silence.

She looked over at Kenya. "Malik and I would love to come for a visit."

"Cool." Kenya grinned from ear to ear. "Pick a date when you're free, and I'd love to have you."

"I will."

Kenya saw Mitch approaching, his cell phone glued to his ear.

He whispered in her ear, "Verdict's in."

Everyone returned to the courthouse. Kenya, Mitch, and Deacon Charles took their places. The jury piled in and took their seats. The bailiff handed the verdict over to the judge. She looked at it and handed it back. The foreperson stood.

"Will the defendant please rise for the verdict?" the judge asked.

It seemed that Deacon Charles's legs were on the verge of giving out as he slowly began to stand. His shoulders were tight, and he stared at the juror who would be reading his fate.

"On the count of murder in the second degree, we the jury find the defendant . . . not guilty."

Kenya was elated to hear those words. Cries rang out loudly from Julian Miller's family. His mother covered her mouth, tears filling her eyes. She collapsed into her husband's arms. His sister yelled out in disagreement with the verdict. On the other side of the aisle, cheers rang out from the congregation of Cornerstone Baptist Church. Deacon Charles clasped his hands together as if praying. He reached for Kenya and embraced her.

He whispered in her ear, "Thank you. Thank you so much."

Kenya gazed at her family. Her father gave her a wink of the eye. Her mother smiled. Xander gave her his usual thumbs-up, and Tricia actually blew her a kiss.

She had won her case, made the congregation happy. Deacon Charles could sleep easy another night, and on top of it all, she had a sister again. All was well in the universe.

Chapter Thirty-eight

Natalia

Before Natalia knew it, she was booked on a morning flight to Cantania. She knew that it was extreme but decided that she needed to see Nic face-to-face. She had questions that she needed answers to, and she wanted to serve him with the divorce papers that he'd dodged by retreating to Sicily much too soon. She needed closure, but currently she had none. She was a woman scorned and wanted to confront the man who had left her heart tattered into pieces.

Her suitcase was packed and sitting next to the garage door. She slipped her sneakers onto her feet and grabbed a bottle of water from the refrigerator. Her purse hung on her shoulder, and she dug into it to make sure she had her passport. It was there. Her phone was lodged in the back pocket of her jeans. Her nerves on edge, her stomach topsy-turvy, she grasped the doorknob. Nausea and dizziness descended upon her, causing her to run to the hallway powder room at record speed.

With her head deeply immersed in the toilet bowl, she vomited. Just when she thought she was done, she vomited again. She stood up and then balanced herself against the sink. She turned on the faucet and rinsed her mouth, glared at herself in the mirror.

"Is this COVID?" she whispered to her reflection.

Natalia made her way upstairs to her bedroom. She sat on the edge of the bed for a moment, needing to collect herself. She went into the bathroom and stood over the sink, brushed her teeth, and rinsed with mouthwash. Her phone rang and she pulled it out of her back pocket. She glanced at the screen and saw it was Kenya. To answer would mean having to explain to her why she had done something so impromptu and irrational as booking a flight to Sicily without warning or permission. She didn't feel like explaining. She'd call Kenya once she'd arrived at her destination.

She heard the ding, an indication that Kenya had left a text message.

Where are you, Nat Pack? Pick up. I have good news. Need to celebrate!

She must've won her case! Natalia beamed. She was proud of her friend, but she couldn't tell her that just yet.

After collecting herself, she made her way back downstairs to complete her mission. This time she walked out to the garage, her luggage in tow. She tossed the bag onto the back seat of her car and then hopped into the driver's seat. Her stomach still topsy-turvy, she pulled out of the garage and made her way out of the neighborhood. As she slowly made her way to Route 47, she felt as if she might faint and pulled over on the side of the road. She grabbed the steering wheel and attempted to gather herself. When she looked in her rearview mirror, a car had pulled in behind her and a gentleman headed toward her car.

"Natalia, I thought that was you," he proclaimed once she let down her window.

"Zach?"

"Are you okay?" he asked.

"I just felt a little dizzy, so I pulled over. I just need a minute to get myself together."

A look of concern on his face, he asked, "Where are you going? Can I drive you?"

"No, no. That won't be necessary, Zach. I'll be fine."

"You don't look so good. You sure I can't help?" he continued to press.

Natalia needed air, so she opened the door and stepped out of the car. She hoped to catch a good breeze before continuing on her way. Her legs became weak and gave out on her. Soon everything went black.

Natalia opened her eyes and squinted to make sense of where she was. She glanced at the needle that had been lodged into her arm and held into place with medical tape. She followed the intravenous tube to its source—an IV drip.

"Well, hello, sleepyhead." Lu leaped from her chair and greeted her.

"What am I doing here? What happened?"

"Well, sister, you passed out on the side of the road. Luckily, Zach was there. He brought you here."

"Where's my car?"

"Zach came and got me, and I drove it here. We didn't want to leave it on the side of the road," Lu told her.

"Oh, thank goodness."

"Were you headed somewhere? You've got a suitcase in your back seat."

Natalia looked sheepish, turned her head away.

"I got here as quick as I could!" Kenya rushed into the room, nearly out of breath. "Nat Pack! Are you okay?"

"I'm fine. I just passed out." Natalia attempted to sit up. "Might be COVID or something. You both might want to put masks on."

A doctor walked into the room, a smile on his face. "Hello, Mrs. Oliveri. I'm Dr. Ramos. How are you feeling?"

"I feel okay." She swallowed hard, noticed that her throat was extremely dry.

"I have good news for you. The baby's fine," Dr. Ramos said with a smile, as if what he said was perfectly normal.

With a shaky voice, she asked the question that Kenya and Lu were probably asking too. "The baby?"

"Yes." He looked at her chart, and then up at her. "You didn't know there was a baby?"

Kenya walked over to the bed, grabbed Natalia's hand, and held it tightly.

"No, I didn't."

"Well, I hope that it's good news for you. You're eight weeks along."

Her body grew completely still and her eyes bulged. She couldn't believe her ears. Her free hand shook as it made its way to her belly. She touched it gently.

Lu walked over to the bed and touched Natalia's stomach, too. "Oh my goodness, Natalia."

"I'd like to keep you for a few more hours just for observation." Dr. Ramos walked toward the door. "But after that, you're free to go."

He walked out.

Natalia trembled. Her mind raced. "I know I should be happy about this, but . . ."

"Yes, you should be happy about this. You've wanted this for so long," Lu interjected.

"Isn't this what you've always hoped for . . . worked hard for?" Kenya asked.

"It is, but . . ."

"But what?"

"Nic's gone back to Sicily . . . for good. I'll have to raise this baby all by myself."

"Good riddance," Kenya exclaimed. "And how do you figure you'll have to raise the baby alone? What are we, chopped liver?"

Natalia looked away. A lump formed in her throat.

"We're here for you Natalia," Lu added.

"What's wrong, honey?" Kenya asked.

"I'm just . . . just really sad." Tears streamed down her face and she wiped them away with her hand. Her chest heaved up and down.

"Oh honey, don't cry." Kenya grabbed her hand again, squeezed it. "That baby has the best aunties on the planet, who will punch anyone in the face if they try to mess with her."

"Or him," said Lu.

"Or him," Kenya agreed. "It's probably a girl, though. She'll be a badass, like her Auntie Kenya."

Natalia couldn't hold in her laughter. Suddenly, she felt giddy. "I'm actually pregnant."

"You're actually pregnant," Lu repeated it.

Kenya lowered her voice, as if the nursing staff could hear. "You've got to put the bottle down, though, sister, because you've been drinking like a fish lately."

Natalia laughed heartily. "Kenya!"

"I'm just saying."

"What did you want to tell me? Your good news," Natalia said.

"You won your case, didn't you?" Lu asked.

"I won my case. The old man walked. The church is happy. My father's happy. All is well," Kenya quipped. "And now we have a new little girl coming . . ."

"Or boy," said Lu.

"Whatever it is, I just hope she or *he* is healthy." Natalia smiled.

"Indeed," Kenya agreed.

"Lu, to answer your question about the suitcase on my

back seat . . . I was on my way to the airport before I passed out on the side of the road. I was headed for Sicily to confront Nic and get him to sign the divorce papers."

"What?" Lu and Kenya asked at once.

"Are you out of your mind?" Kenya asked.

"I know. Bad idea, huh?"

"Incredibly bad idea. Nic has made his position clear. And as painful as it is, you have got to move on. Not just for you, but for your baby."

"I agree," Lu said. "Focus on your miracle."

She was amused by how much her life had changed since she'd left home that morning. A smile crept into the corners of her mouth. She liked the sound of that. *Her miracle.*

Chapter Thirty-nine

Kenya

The rehearsal dinner

Kenya made a mad dash for Cape May after work. A wreck on the Garden State Parkway, where an eighteen-wheeler had slammed into the back of a sedan, had traffic blocked for miles. She tried not to let the irony of it take her to a dark place, cause her grief. No, she needed to move past her grief. Finally, traffic was moving again, and she thought she might make it to Lu's rehearsal dinner on time after all.

Her phone rang, but she didn't recognize the number. She wondered if it was a client calling. If so, they were out of luck; she was officially off duty for the entire weekend. Her best friend was getting married tomorrow and she couldn't be happier. When her phone dinged, she knew that the person had left a long detailed message. Her curiosity got the better of her and she decided to listen.

Hello, Kenya. It's Eleanor Charles. You know, Deacon Charles's wife. I hope this message finds you well. I want you to know that you're responsi-

ble for setting a murderer free. Yes, your beloved deacon is a murderer. You see, Julian was threatening to tell me all about their love affair. Eleanor laughed nervously; her voice quivered. *Imagine that. My husband, the respected deacon at Cornerstone Baptist Church, was having a love affair with his business partner. Julian didn't get a chance to tell me in person because he was murdered, but we all know the things that are done in the dark always come to light. They say when you go looking for things, you're sure to find them. I thought I'd go looking for some information about that woman who testified in court. You know, the widow? I wanted to see if they'd been creeping around. But what I found was far more than I bargained for. Instead, I ran across a string of text messages between Donovan and Julian. It's why I didn't show up for trial on the second day. I couldn't bring myself to come. I couldn't sit in that courtroom, not after knowing the truth. Turns out, Julian didn't want to be Donovan's lover any longer. He wanted to pursue a relationship with a new woman in his life and Donovan wasn't having any of it. It appeared that Julian was tired of Donovan running his life, so he threatened to expose Donovan, destroy his reputation with the good church folk. As a result, Julian lost his life.*

There was a long uncomfortable pause.

He begged me to lie about his alibi that night, and like a fool, I did it. He wasn't home the entire night. When I woke up in the middle of the night, he was gone. Eleanor sighed heavily. *Anyway . . . I*

*just thought you should know. If anything happens
to me, you know that he did it.*

Kenya's body stiffened; her hands shook. Her mind raced
a million miles a minute. How had she missed the signs? Was
Deacon Charles really that cunning, or had she just turned a
blind eye because she'd wanted him to be innocent so badly?
She began to replay every conversation, every detail, every
movement, every mannerism in her head.

He was seeing a woman. Some . . . mystery woman. Kenya
replayed the deacon's words in her head, when he'd attempted
to place the blame on someone else.

She grabbed the steering wheel, shook it with all her might,
and yelled loudly.

"He played me," Kenya said aloud.

She felt unsettled. Her blood boiled as she fumbled with
her phone. She wanted to get Deacon Charles on the phone
and confront him. Had she been closer to the city, she might've
driven to his house, but to do that might place Eleanor at
risk. She felt imprisoned, stuck. She had to find a way to remove him from her father's life, the church, and everything
that was good and wholesome. He didn't belong there. She
needed justice for them but had to be careful about how she
went about it. He was dangerous when backed into a corner.
He'd proven that. She listened to Eleanor's voice message
again and experienced all the same emotions for a second
time. She wouldn't rest until Donovan Charles paid for mis-
leading her.

Finally home, Kenya remained in the driver's seat of her
car. She couldn't move. Her heart thumped quickly, loudly.
She dialed Mitch's number and told him about the awkward
voicemail that she'd received from Deacon Charles's wife.

"You're kidding, right?" he asked.

"Dead serious."

"Well, you know he can't be tried again, not for the same crime." Mitch sighed. "But I don't know, let me do some digging. People who do bad things usually have a pattern of doing them. Let me see what I can dig up."

"I would like for him to be ousted from the church and away from my father and my family."

"I agree. He's a bad apple."

"Indeed. Rotten to the core. I have to go for now. I have a rehearsal dinner to attend, but we'll revisit the subject later."

"Try to enjoy yourself, Kenya."

"Will do."

She hung up, and as soon as she was able to move, she stepped out of the car and went inside. She quickly showered and slipped into the red after-five, off-the-shoulder dress that she'd been dying to wear since its purchase. It was the one that accentuated her curves. The strappy, sexy sandals gave her outfit the perfect finishing touch that it needed. She hopped back into her car and rushed over to Natalia's winery for the rehearsal dinner.

One of the large tasting rooms at the winery had been transformed into a chic space with crystal and metallic décor. White tablecloths adorned the tables. White roses in gold vases were set at the center of each table. When she rushed into the room late, looking for a place to sit, she quickly realized that there was assigned seating. In fact, there were only two empty seats left. Hers and another one.

She plopped down, right next to Gideon, who was looking exceptionally handsome in his khaki trousers, an off-white crewneck shirt underneath a navy blazer. He gave her a hello with a nod. No words, no enthusiasm, just a nod.

"How are you?" she asked with a smile.

"I'm good. What about you?" he asked in return. He spoke to her as if she were a stranger.

"I'm good, too," she replied. She attempted to personalize the small talk. "You look good."

"Thank you." He didn't return the compliment. Just the thank you.

The server slid a salad in front of her. She was famished, hadn't eaten since lunch, so she picked up her fork and devoured her salad. When she finally came up for air, she did a quick scan of the room. Her parents were there, her father looking distinguished in his gray suit and her mother wearing a simple yet beautiful lace dress. She loved how they always complemented each other—she was the yin to his yang, and he hers. The way he looked at her, as if she was the most beautiful girl in the world, was something that Kenya always admired about her daddy.

Natalia was working the room, bouncing around, making sure that all the guests were comfortable and handling the staff and caterers. At the table, seated next to Lu, was John Jr. He'd made good on his promise to attend his sister's wedding, and that made Kenya happy. When he caught her eye, he raised his glass and gave her a wide grin. She smiled and raised her water glass. When Lu caught Kenya's eye, she smiled and waved. Kenya gave her a side-eyed glance but waved back. If there was any wonder as to why she was seated right next to Gideon, there was no doubt that the seating arrangement had been carefully orchestrated by the bride-to-be herself.

A beautiful woman wearing a formfitting, cream-colored jumpsuit appeared in the doorway, looked around for a moment as if she was searching for someone. She walked into the room, and Kenya couldn't help but notice Gideon's enthusiasm. He waved to her and grinned widely. She gave him a sweet smile, walked over to their table, and took her seat on the opposite side of him. He kissed her cheek.

"You look beautiful," he told her.

Did he just compliment her?

"Look at you, looking all handsome," she said as she stroked him arm. "Sorry I'm late. Flight was delayed."

"It's okay. We're just getting started with the salad." Gideon motioned to the server.

Kenya's body became tense. The smile that had graced the corners of her mouth just a few minutes before was gone. She was overcome with jealousy. *Who was this woman who had Gideon's undivided attention since the moment she walked into the room?* Kenya was so busy staring at them that she hadn't heard the server ask if she wanted something to drink.

"I'm sorry, yes, I'd like a Chardonnay, please."

"Yes, ma'am. I'll bring it right away."

Across the room, Zach stood and tapped his fork against his glass. "May I have your attention, please?"

The room quieted down and all eyes were on him.

"Lu and I would just like to say welcome and thank you all for agreeing to share in our special day. It's been a long time coming. And I must say, we've had a few challenges along the way, but we're here! Our big day is upon us, and I couldn't be more excited. I'm thankful to have this woman by my side." He looked at Lu, and the two of them smiled and gazed into each other's eyes for a moment. "Tonight, we want you to eat, drink, and mingle. Unwind. Tomorrow, we do the damn thing!"

The room exploded with cheers and applause. Kenya clapped, and her heart was warmed as she watched her friend from across the room. Lu had found her Prince Charming, and Kenya couldn't have been more elated. Even though she thought she might've had to drop-kick Lu's Prince Charming, she was happy that he'd managed to get himself unmarried just days before his wedding.

The live band began to serenade the guests with its smooth instruments. Gideon and the woman in off-white made their way to the dance floor and danced to the upbeat song. Her father tapped her on the shoulder. She was grateful, too. She had no intention of sitting and watching as Gideon waltzed someone else around the room.

"Let's dance, baby girl." Walter Lewis grabbed her by the hand and pulled her onto the dance floor.

"You're looking very handsome tonight, Daddy."

"Thank you, sweetheart. And aren't you just the prettiest girl in the room? Well, the second prettiest. Your mother is the prettiest." Walter laughed in his deep baritone.

"She is quite beautiful." Kenya glanced over at her mother as she held on to her father's hand while he swept her across the floor.

"I'm so proud of you. You were so great in that courtroom."

"Thank you, Daddy. Although I have some deep concerns about your beloved deacon, I'm glad I was able to get a win for you and the members of the church, but . . ."

"I think we all share some of those deep concerns right with you, sweetheart."

"Really? Like which ones?" She leaned back and looked at her father, wanted to know what he knew.

"I'm an old man, but I've been around the block a few times." Walter's eyes danced when he laughed. "I've already uncovered some things about my old friend, Donovan Charles. The board members have already begun proceedings to have him removed from the deacon board, among other things. But that's a conversation for another time. Let's enjoy your friend's big day. She's looking mighty beautiful over there."

They both looked over at Lu, who was busting moves with Zach on the dance floor.

"Yes, she is. She's genuinely happy, and I'm glad about it."

"Zach is a good man," her father asserted. "I can't wait to do the nuptials at their wedding tomorrow."

"Indeed he is a good man. And good for her."

Suddenly, the music slowed down, and the band began their cover of the Jackson Five's old tune "Who's Loving You," giving it a nice twist. Kenya was completely caught off guard when Gideon approached them, asking her father if he could cut in. Walter stepped aside and Gideon grabbed Kenya by the waist.

He pulled her closer, leaned in. "Hope you didn't mind me cutting in."

"I thought you'd still be on the floor with your little girl-friend over there."

He followed her glance to the woman seated at their table, who was watching them, a light smile on her face.

"Oh, you mean my sister Geneva?" Gideon grinned widely. "She didn't feel like dancing anymore."

"Your sister." Kenya dropped her head in shame.

"Jealousy is not your thing. You're much too confident for that." Gideon grabbed her chin, pulled her head up, and looked into her eyes. "And much too beautiful."

"I admit I did get a little jealous, hearing the man I love dote on another woman."

Did those words really just topple out of her mouth, and without warning?

"Ah, *the man you love*," he gloated.

"Yes. I've finally come to terms with it," she owned it.

"Come to terms with it?" He laughed heartily. "You make it sound like an illness or a burden."

"It's neither of those things, but I must admit that it is very scary and confusing for me. It's been a while since I've felt this way about anyone."

"I understand, and the last thing I want to do is make you uncomfortable."

"The only discomfort I felt was hearing you tell another woman how beautiful she was in my presence, all the while ignoring me." She was transparent with Gideon. She loved that she could be herself with him—no façades.

"Well, the *man you love* just happened to be doting on his baby sister. Besides, he only has eyes for the *woman he loves*. And she's standing right in front of him, wearing the hell out of that red dress, I must say. In fact, she took his breath away when she sashayed her way into the room."

"Sashayed?" She turned her lip upward, then frowned.

"Yeah, you sashayed into the room."

"I did not sashay! If anything, I walked in and commanded the room."

"You sashayed." She could feel the heat from Gideon's lips as he whispered in her ear.

"Shut up and kiss me," Kenya ordered him.

"You mean in front of all these people? You do know that's PDA, right? You know you don't engage in any type of public displays of affection."

Kenya grabbed Gideon's lapel, pulling him closer. Her lips found his and she kissed him with intensity. He grabbed her waist, pulled her into him, moved to the music. She followed his lead. Her heart was full, her emotions all over the place. In a single evening, she'd learned the most horrific information about one man, all the while giving another man permission to love her, deeply, unconditionally, and unapologetically.

Chapter Forty

Lu

The wedding of the summer

L u's nerves got the better of her as she stood there just inside the door of the inn. The backless, flowy white dress with lace detailing had given her all the feelings of a beach wedding while remaining elegant and sophisticated. Her body shook and her nerves were on edge as she awaited Kenya's stroll down the aisle ahead of her. Natalia stood on the veranda, and after everyone was in place at the altar, she motioned for her to exit the house. John Jr., who was handsomely dressed in a gray tuxedo, took her hand in his, and placed it in the fold of his arm.

When she heard Luther Vandross's "Here and Now" begin to play, she knew it was time. Tears stood at the edges of her eyes, threatening to fall and make a mess of her makeup but she willed them away. Yana fixed a hair that was out of place, then hugged her tightly. She straightened the tail of Lu's dress, smoothed it out before she stepped off the veranda. She was happy that Yana had graciously allowed John Jr. the honor of standing in for their father, a gesture that made Lu love her mother that much more.

They stepped off the veranda and made their way to the area of the beach where the guests were seated, tread through the sand, both barefoot, toward the altar. The arch was beautifully decorated with orchids, hibiscus, and plumeria. Kenya's father, Pastor Lewis, stood there with a Bible in his hand and a fatherly grin on his face. Kenya stood to his right; her peach-colored dress blew with the wind. Gideon and Zach stood on the left, both handsomely dressed in gray tuxedos. Zach inconspicuously dabbed his eyes with a handkerchief. He'd gotten choked up as he observed her.

She and John Jr. stopped just short of the arch.

Pastor Lewis asked, "Who gives this woman to be married?"

"I do, sir." John Jr. smiled, kissed Lu's cheek, and then took his seat.

Zach took her hands in his as Pastor Lewis performed the nuptials. She had visualized this moment a thousand times in her head, but it was surreal to see it all come together on that beautiful September day—the weather a perfect seventy-five degrees, the sun shining, and the waves whispering gently against the shore. After exchanging vows in front of her family and friends and God, Zach finally pulled her into his arms and kissed her deeply. And she became his wife on the beach on Cape May.

"I'm so happy for you." Kenya was the first to embrace her. "You're such a beautiful bride."

"Thank you. I can't believe we're finally here."

"It's been a long time coming." Kenya locked arms with her. "That was really sweet of Yana to allow John Jr. to walk you down the aisle."

"Yeah, it was. I feel like John is here, looking down on us."

"I think so, too."

Lu gazed lovingly at her mother. "Yana's going to be spending more time at the inn. Going to help out a few days a week."

"That's sweet." Kenya leaned her head against Lu's.

"I saw that you and Gideon were pretty cozy last night at the rehearsal dinner."

"Yeah, I'm in love with him."

Lu was taken aback by Kenya's revelation. She had to step aside to get a good look at her friend's face. "Wow!"

"Don't make a big deal of it." Kenya giggled. "I'm just going to throw caution to the wind. See how it goes."

"You deserve it, Kenya. I'm so thrilled."

"Yeah, yeah."

"Don't give the man a hard time, either. Give him some grace."

They both giggled and glanced over at Gideon, who stood there with a plate in his hand, nibbling on fruit. He gave Kenya a wink and she blushed. Lu's heart soared—her friend had finally given herself permission to love again.

Zach approached the pair, his hands in his pockets. "Kenya, would you mind if I steal my bride away?"

"Not at all." Kenya embraced Lu.

Zach took her hand in his and whisked her away to the dance floor. As she danced with her new husband to the sounds of Nat King Cole's "Unforgettable," she smiled and peeked over his shoulder at Natalia, who stroked her growing belly. Natalia gave Lu a gentle smile and blew her a kiss. Lu couldn't help thinking that it was a shame that she'd be going through the pregnancy without Nic. He had no idea that Natalia was pregnant, and she preferred it that way. However, Lu knew that she would be the best mother ever—*without him.* The baby would have the best three aunts—Natalia's sister and, of course, Lu and Kenya—who would be there from the moment she *or he* entered the world. Lu and Natalia both followed each other's glances across the terrace at their friend, Kenya, as she danced with Gideon. She kicked her leg into the air when he dipped her. When Gideon locked lips with Kenya for a long kiss, Lu's heart was filled with so much joy.

As the sun began to set on the beach, Lu pulled Natalia onto the dance floor and grabbed Kenya's hand—pulled her out there, too. The three of them held hands and danced to Lizzo's "Good as Hell." They had each endured their own challenges over the summer on Cape May, but with one another, they'd overcome. Life was everything they could've ever hoped for or imagined—and then some.

Chapter Forty-one

Natalia

October in Sicily brought with it beautifully warm temperatures, sunshine, and marvelous views of its prominent cliffs and mountains. Natalia had always loved it there, and autumn was the best time to visit, if that's what you wanted to call it—*a visit.*

The minute she saw him, her body shook and her legs trembled. Nic's eyes bulged when he walked over to the table, greeted Natalia, and saw her growing belly.

"Wow, you're pregnant," he said.

"I'm here because I need closure." Natalia ignored his statement, stuck with the script that she had rehearsed with Lu and Kenya on the flight to Sicily.

"I understand you need closure, and Natalia, I can't tell you how sorry I am . . ."

Natalia pulled the order for divorce from her bag, laid it on the table, and handed Nic a ballpoint pen. "I just need you to sign these and both of us can move on with our lives."

Her hand shook and her voice quivered, *just a little bit.*

Her breathing was off and her nerves out of control. She hadn't expected to be so off-center.

"What about the baby?" Nic asked.

"What *about* the baby?" Natalia forced the pen into his hand.

"Will I have any rights to the child?"

"No. My child will grow up without you, not knowing you. That's what I want. If he or *she* decides to look for you later in life, it will be up to them. But after you sign these papers, you will not ever see or hear from me again. Your actions have consequences."

"Truthfully, I've already begun to pay. My family has disowned me because of this."

Natalia turned her head away from Nic, a light smile dancing at the corner of her mouth. She found some satisfaction in hearing that he had already begun to reap.

"I would just like to know why. Why her, Nic? Why?"

"I guess we just never got . . ." He cleared his throat. "I guess we never got over each other. I wanted things to work between you and me, Natalia, I really did. But if I'm being completely honest, I still loved her."

Natalia's heart sank. She attempted to blink away the tears, tried to remain composed, but she was unsuccessful. She felt them coming, betraying her. The tears burned her eyes. She'd come here for answers, and as painful as they may be, she needed them. However, part of her wished he hadn't been so truthful. A little lie would've soothed her wounded heart.

"If you would just sign these, you can be on your way."

Nic gave the order of divorce a quick scan and then scribbled his signature on the last page—a signature that she'd seen many times, like when they'd purchased their home on Cape May, purchased their vehicles, applied for their marriage license—all the things that had mattered at one time. Yet here they were, in this beautiful restaurant in Cantania—his home—ending it all with a signature.

"You deserve everything you're asking for here: the house, your car, the furniture. I won't fight you for anything." He laid the pen on the table and rose to his feet. "I guess this is goodbye, then?"

"Yes, it is. Goodbye, Nic."

He looked as if he wanted to say something more, as if he needed to explain or apologize, maybe hug her. Instead, he hung his head. "Goodbye, Natalia. Please be good to our baby. But most importantly, be good to yourself."

She exhaled as he walked away. She could breathe again.

Natalia folded the papers and stuck them back into her bag. She glanced across the beautiful courtyard at Lu, who was lodged on a barstool at the cocktail bar, ordering another Corvo Irmàna Frappato, a Sicilian red wine. Natalia giggled at the fact that Lu had already overstuffed her luggage with too many bottles of the wine. Kenya whispered something to Lu, and the two of them laughed. Natalia smiled at her friends, took in the fact that they were both glowing. One was newly married and the other was surely headed for the altar soon, as Kenya and Gideon had become quite cozy. She was happy for them but suddenly felt alone—her heart ached.

Kenya spotted Nic leaving the restaurant as he passed the bar. She glanced at Natalia, gave her a look that seemed to ask if she was okay. Natalia gave her a light smile: assurance. When Kenya and Lu returned to the table, they embraced her.

"Are you okay, Nat Pack?"

"Yes."

"You did it." Kenya smiled at her.

"Yes, you did," said Lu. "So proud of you."

"I cried a little." Natalia giggled.

"It's okay. This was huge for you." Kenya gave her a squeeze.

"Do you feel like you got closure?" Lu asked.

"As much as I'm going to get."

Traveling to Sicily had been Natalia's greatest fear, but she'd conquered it. She was evolving, becoming someone she didn't even recognize. She'd managed to confront Nic about Angelina and served him with divorce papers. She'd all but gloated about their unborn child and all the while gained the closure that she needed and deserved.

The two of them plopped down at the table. Natalia scanned the handwritten menu that listed what was fresh from the market and off the boats that day. It had been a challenge getting a reservation at the popular restaurant in the seaside town of Trapani. She had to admit Sicily was gorgeous. It was no wonder Nic retreated here every chance he got. She decided that she would order the Cuscusu alla Tarapanese, a local Sicilian couscous with saffron, tomatoes, almonds, and fresh shellfish.

Kenya's phone dinged and her eyes were glued to the screen.

"What is it?" Lu asked.

She turned the phone around, and they watched video footage of Deacon Charles being escorted from his home.

"The FBI has been investigating his business for tax fraud, money laundering, among other things, for the past few years, and now that their case is airtight, they've moved in, made the arrest."

In the video, with handcuffs on his wrists, Deacon Charles held his head low, attempting to shield his face from the cameras.

"That's a win for you," said Lu.

"Indeed it is. He won't go to jail for murder, but he'll go to jail nonetheless. That's a win for the church, my family, my father . . ." Kenya raised her glass in the air.

Natalia and Lu raised their glasses in a toast with Kenya.

"I'll have whatever you're having to eat," Lu told Natalia. "I know you've already scoped the menu in great detail."

"I'm having the Cuscusu alla Tarapanese," Natalia announced.

"Good, make it two." Lu brushed her hair from her face.

Natalia noticed that her friend, the newly married woman, was wearing her hair differently since her nuptials. It was much shorter, and a bit sassier.

"Zach and I received a wonderful wedding gift after the wedding. It came to the seaside inn, a set of designer monogrammed towels, and underneath the towels was this black-and-white photo." Lu pulled the photo from her purse.

Natalia grabbed it and peered at the photo of a man tossing a toddler into the air. The child and man both laughed.

"Is this you, and your father?" Natalia asked and then handed the photo to Kenya.

"Yes," said Lu.

'Wow," Kenya exclaimed.

Lu said, "The note read, '*I found this in Dad's stuff. Hope you enjoy. Your sister.*' "

"She signed it, '*your sister?*' "

"Yes."

"That's huge," said Kenya.

"I'm so happy for you, Lu. Maybe she'll come for a visit someday."

"I wouldn't go that far, but it did seem to be a step in the right direction. I think that if I build a relationship with her, my younger sister, Jess will follow."

"I think so, too," Natalia raised her glass in the air.

"Doesn't it seem like the things in our lives are finally coming full circle?" Kenya asked.

"I think you might be right," Lu said.

"I think our next trip should be to the Napa Valley. I think we seriously need to go check out that wonderful piece of property that Papa John left for you. What do you think?" Kenya raised an eyebrow at Lu.

"I agree. Maybe we can stay a few days, or even a few months," said Lu.

"Whoa! Wait a minute. Some of us still have employers and jobs," Kenya reminded her.

"You have flexibility," Lu insisted.

"Maybe." Kenya backed down. "Put it together and we'll see how flexible I am."

"I will," said Lu.

"I'm available. After the baby's born, of course."

"Of course," Kenya agreed.

"Napa Valley it is, then." Lu raised her glass in the air. "To Napa."

Kenya and Natalia said it simultaneously. "To Napa."

After dinner, the trio found themselves exploring the beautiful town of Cantania, In Piazza Università, one of the many squares along the endless street of Via Etnea, they admired the picturesque buildings in the square, and then headed out onto Via Etnea to do a little window-shopping before retiring to their luxury hotel.

She stood in the shower, the water cascading over her head as she rubbed her growing belly. She thought about Nic's words. *I guess we never got over each other.* When he admitted that he still loved Angelina, it was as if he'd punched her in the stomach, leaving her breathless. She cried openly this time. Deeply. The water shielded her tears, and she could no longer tell where the tears ended and the water began. She wanted to get it all out, though, right here, right now, because after tonight she wouldn't cry another tear for Nicolai Oliveri. She had too much to look forward to—a new baby who was kicking the heck out of her ribs, a new life with her married and possibly soon-to-be-married girlfriends, Napa Valley—and finally, but most importantly—the entire dozen of Sicilian cannolo pastries that she'd ordered from room service just before she hopped in the shower. Life was certainly looking up for her, and she was ready for every single bit of it.

Visit our website at
KensingtonBooks.com
to sign up for our newsletters, read
more from your favorite authors, see
books by series, view reading group
guides, and more!

Become a Part of Our
Between the Chapters Book Club
Community and Join the Conversation

Submit your book review for a chance to win exclusive
Between the Chapters swag you can't get anywhere else!
https://www.kensingtonbooks.com/pages/review/